"You don't know me."

"I think I do. I may not know everything, but the Tyler Blackwell I know is a good man with a good heart and way too hard on himself."

Hadley lifted up on tiptoe and kissed him. He didn't think anyone could care about him, but the truth was she was beginning to care quite a bit.

His hands dropped to her waist and he was pulling her closer. Her mind should have been spinning but her focus was razor sharp. All she could think about was how good this felt.

The kiss ended, but their embrace did not. Tyler rested his forehead against hers. "I thought we had rules."

"New rule—no self-loathing allowed."

"You don't understand," he whispered.

"I don't care what I don't understand. It's our new rule."

"You make the rules and break them," he said. "What if I want to break them, too?"

Dear Reader,

As the older sister of two brothers, I know all about the love/hate relationship that can exist between siblings. My brothers could be the best of friends or the worst of enemies on any given day. I am also married to an identical twin and have witnessed the incredible bond that exists between them.

I happily used my insights into brothers and twins while writing my part of Return of the Blackwell Brothers. Brothers fight. Brothers tease and know all the right buttons to push. But when it matters, brothers always have each other's backs. As much as Tyler Blackwell tries to convince the world that he wants nothing to do with his brothers or the family ranch, he's there when they need him and sucked back into everything he loved about Montana when he returns.

None of this would have been possible without the awesomeness of the four other writers in this continuity: Carol Ross, Cari Lynn Webb, Melinda Curtis and Anna J. Stewart. Their creativity and humor inspire me not only in my writing but in life. They are an integral part of my writing family. Luckily, we have nothing but a love/love relationship. Although...some teasing does go on, especially after we've been on the dance floor together given that we are all rhythmically challenged!

Amy Vastine

HEARTWARMING

The Rancher's Fake Fiancée

USA TODAY Bestselling Author

Amy Vastine

H HARLEQUIN® HEARTWARMING™

Recycling programs
for this product may
not exist in your area.

ISBN-13: 978-1-335-63385-9

The Rancher's Fake Fiancée

Copyright © 2018 by Amy Vastine

This edition published by arrangement with Harlequin Books S.A.

For questions and comments about the quality of this book, please contact us at CustomerService@Harlequin.com.

® and TM are trademarks of Harlequin Enterprises Limited or its corporate affiliates. Trademarks indicated with ® are registered in the United States Patent and Trademark Office, the Canadian Intellectual Property Office and in other countries.

Printed in U.S.A.

Amy Vastine has been plotting stories in her head for as long as she can remember. An eternal optimist, she studied social work, hoping to teach others how to find their silver lining. Now she enjoys creating happily-ever-afters for all to read. Amy lives outside Chicago with her high school sweetheart turned husband, three fun-loving children and their sweet but mischievous puppy dog. Visit her at amyvastine.com.

Books by Amy Vastine

Harlequin Heartwarming

Grace Note Records

The Girl He Used to Love
Catch a Fallen Star
Love Songs and Lullabies

Chicago Sisters

The Better Man
The Best Laid Plans
The Hardest Fight

The Weather Girl

"Snow Day Baby" in *A Heartwarming Thanksgiving*

Visit the Author Profile page
at Harlequin.com for more titles.

To my amazing writer friends—Carol, Cari, Melinda and Anna. Your support and friendship are priceless.

CHAPTER ONE

"FOR THE LOVE of all that's good in the world, would you please call your brothers back?"

Tyler Blackwell glanced up at his obviously infuriated employee. Tucking her wavy blond hair behind her ears, Hadley Sullivan scowled. That meant she was serious this time.

Tyler's gaze returned to his computer screen. Regardless of her ire, finishing the presentation for Lodi Organics was a bit higher on the priority list than his bothersome brothers. "Which one?"

Hadley let out an exasperated sigh. "Take your pick. That was Ethan just now, but Ben has bombarded the office with at least a dozen calls this week and Jonathan phoned yesterday while you were at lunch. I know you know this. We put all the messages on your desk."

Tyler had seen the notes and promptly tossed those slips of pink paper in the recycling bin because he was nothing if not ecologically minded.

"The next time they call, tell them I can only be reached on my cell."

"The same cell they've called five hundred times already?" Hadley paused even though it was a rhetorical question. "They've caught on to the fact that you'll decline their call, Tyler. They've resorted to harassing the people in this office who actually answer their phones."

Clicking Save on the Lodi Organics file, Tyler ran a hand through his thick hair. He'd successfully made himself too busy to return a hundred phone calls from his overreacting brothers but also too busy for a much-needed haircut.

"I'll talk to Kellen about hiring a real office manager who will help us screen all of our calls."

Hadley wasn't appeased. She mumbled something about how she'd *love* to talk to Kellen.

Tyler wasn't Hadley's favorite person at 2K Marketing. He wasn't sure why that was. He thought she was competent at her job and often asked her to do things for him because he knew she'd get them done. It seemed strange that she was so bothered by his brothers' constant calls. They weren't really her problem. They were all his.

"They've got to be close to giving up," he said.

"Ethan said it was an emergency."

"That's what they keep telling me." For the last three months. He dropped his chin to his chest. These calls were literally a pain in the neck. He gave it a rub.

First, their grandfather ran away from home. The way Tyler saw it, Big E was a grown man with every right to go where he pleased. That was hardly an emergency.

Jonathan and Ethan came to the rescue and managed to get the guest ranch ready for the summer rush. Obviously, they wouldn't be able to manage it forever. Jonathan had his own ranch to run and Ethan couldn't do it on his own. If that meant they had to get rid of the Blackwell Family Ranch, so be it. Tyler wouldn't shed any tears over the end of it.

"Maybe they haven't been able to get things settled with the water," Hadley offered. She'd been privy to more information than she needed because she didn't have the option of hanging up the phone when they called. "Maybe they need your help with that."

Emergency number two had to do with water rights and bad deals Big E was most likely responsible for orchestrating. Tyler had replied via text that he was way too busy at work to talk about something he had no control over. "Ben's the lawyer, not me. From what I heard, they got it settled."

"Knock, knock." Tyler's business partner pushed open the door. Kellen Kettering clearly had more time on his hands and less stress than Tyler did given his perfectly coiffed hair and easy smile. "Is this a bad time?"

Hadley sighed as if relieved. "You're back."

Kellen gave her a crooked smile and adjusted his black-framed glasses. His salt-and-pepper hair was damp from the morning rainstorm that had swept in. "My flight got in early. I hear I've been missing all the fun around here."

"If by fun you mean work, you are correct," Tyler said, leaning back in his chair.

Kellen had the title of company president while Tyler was the executive creative director. When they started the business five years ago, the two of them worked on every project together. In the last year or so, their accounts had almost tripled. It could have been more, but it seemed the harder Tyler worked, the more Kellen pushed him to slow down.

"Well, I will let you two catch up," Hadley said to Kellen before turning her baby blue gaze on Tyler. "Call your brothers back, Ty. I'm begging."

Kellen picked up the shadowbox of arrowheads Tyler had on display on his bookshelf. Tyler resisted the urge to wrestle them away. They had belonged to his father, one of the few mementos he had from either of his parents.

"I heard you accepted a meeting with Rockwell's Hardware," Kellen said, setting the box down. "I thought we agreed we weren't going to take on any other clients until we cleared a couple projects."

"It's a simple rebrand."

"I'm not sure Eric's ready to take on another rebranding account. He's still trying to get his bearings here."

"I'll do most of the work." If he didn't bother sleeping, he'd get it all done easily. Tyler didn't have any other choice. Eric would most likely never find his bearings.

Kellen sat down across from him. "Tyler, you know I appreciate your drive. It's why I partnered with you. But we can't overextend ourselves. We run the risk of choosing quantity over quality."

Tyler tried to sound reassuring. "I got this. Don't worry."

"You sent me thirty-two emails between the hours of nine at night and six in the morning. I hate to say it, but you've got to slow down."

This was how Tyler worked. People appreciated hard work. If he wanted to get noticed in this competitive world of marketing, he had to rise above the rest. "All of this will be worth it. We're going to be the number one advertising agency in Portland this year."

"Tyler." Kellen rested his elbows on his knees. "Maybe after the Lodi Organics presentation, you should take some time off. Relax. Get away for a couple weeks."

Tyler's brow furrowed. He must not have heard Kellen correctly. "Are you suggesting I take a vacation?"

"I'm not suggesting. More like telling you. You need a break. We all need a break." Kellen sat back and seemed to struggle with the right words. "Let me be straight with you. There's been some grumbling. People are feeling… stressed."

"Like who?" Tyler looked out at the office

cubicles. The eight-person staff all scurried around, refusing to make eye contact.

"Like everyone."

They had planned this. They had gone to Kellen behind his back. He felt his blood pressure rise, which made it difficult to control his volume. "Stressed about what? Having a job?"

THE GLASS WALLS of Tyler's office were far from soundproof. It wasn't surprising that he was taking Kellen's feedback poorly. Hadley had warned Kellen that Tyler was on a mission. A mission to work himself into an early grave. The main problem with that was he was taking the rest of the office with him.

"On a scale of one to ten, how mad is he going to be with us?" Veronica was the web designer and one of the biggest complainers over the last couple of weeks. She fidgeted with her oversize gold hoop earrings.

"Fifty-seven," Lee, one of the project managers, guessed as he made his way over to Hadley's desk. He stroked his goatee. "Look how red his face is."

"Fifty-seven?" Hadley shook her head at the random number choice. "I don't know if it's *that* bad."

She glanced over at the two of them having it out, secretly hoping Tyler was stubborn enough to dig his heels in. Maybe the two of them would realize that Tyler had too much on his plate for a reason. Perhaps they'd admit the real problem was that they had given the brand strategist position to someone so woefully unqualified instead of her.

Hadley could manage a hundred more accounts than Eric. She had deserved that job and hated Tyler for not going to bat for her. She blamed him even more than his partner. Had Tyler called Kellen out on his nepotism and fought for her, Kellen would have backed down and given the job to Hadley.

"Look at how tight his jaw is. That is not a good sign," Lee said.

"Don't worry," Eric assured them. "My uncle will get Ty to chill. I made it clear we could not work under these conditions any longer, right?"

Hadley bit her tongue and tried not to roll her eyes. Eric couldn't work under any conditions. He was so far over his head, it was ridiculous. He probably asked her close to fifty questions a day, trying to get her to do his job as well as hers.

Tyler's glare zeroed in on her. The open lay-out of the converted warehouse left nowhere for people to hide. He pushed open his door and folded his arms across his chest. Even though Hadley may have had her issues him, she couldn't deny that Tyler Blackwell was at-tractive. Broad chest, dark hair, denim-blue eyes and a jawline that could make Holly-wood's A-list leading men jealous.

"Anyone here want to tell me they're un-happy to my face? Are some of you unhappy with…I don't know…having a job? Because last time I checked, without clients there's no work and with no work there's no jobs. Any-one out here who doesn't want a job?"

"Tyler, come on," Kellen said, putting a hand on his shoulder. "Don't worry, everybody. No one is losing their job!"

Tyler shrugged him off. "I hope you enjoy the amount of work you're all going to have while I'm on vacation." He pointed at Hadley. "I need you."

This was her chance. If she could convince Tyler he could trust that the work he'd started would be finished to his standards while he was on his forced getaway, maybe she could make him see she should be the brand strategist instead of Eric.

He dropped into his chair and shuffled through some papers on his desk. His frustration came off him like smoke from a fire. "Did you talk to him about being overworked?"

"Me? No," she asserted. "I think all this business is great. I wish I could do more to help." She had to be cautious about how she proceeded. She needed Tyler's help if she was going to convince Kellen to get rid of his nephew. Kellen always preached about the importance of family, but giving a job to someone who didn't know what he was doing was bad business.

"Well, I need help figuring out how I can pretend to be on vacation while still getting things done."

The main line rang, lighting up the buttons on Tyler's phone. Hadley reached over and picked it up. "2K Marketing, this is Hadley. How may I direct your call?"

"Hi, Hadley. It's Ben, Ben Blackwell. I know you told Ethan that Tyler was on another call, but I am done with this. Tell him he doesn't need to call any of us back."

Hadley couldn't believe Tyler had been right. Rejoice! They had finally given up.

Ben continued, "He needs to get on a plane and get his butt out here or else he will be served a subpoena and forced to appear in court instead."

"Wait, what? Hang on a second." Hadley pushed the hold button. "Your brother is going to take you to court if you don't take this." She held the phone out.

Tyler folded his arms across his chest and rolled his eyes like a petulant child. "He's bluffing. He can't take me to court because I won't answer the phone."

"Please just talk to him. I will help you with anything you need if you answer this call."

He narrowed his eyes and let out a gruff breath. Refusing to take the phone from her, he pressed the button to put the call on speaker. "What part of I am extremely busy are you three not understanding?"

"You need to come home, Ty. I know you don't want to. I know you are so busy out there in Portland and your company will probably fold if you aren't there for one second, but you need to come home."

"Why? What do you need me to do that I can't do from here?"

"We want to sell the ranch, but we need your help. We need you here to make it happen."

Hadley scribbled a note: *Perfect vacation! You should go.* Tyler could go help his family, Hadley could prove she was worthy of the brand strategist job, and when he returned, he would have to convince Kellen to give it to her.

TYLER PICKED THE receiver up. He didn't need Hadley hearing anything else. He definitely didn't need anyone else trying to encourage him to go to Montana.

"Sell it," he said. "Send me whatever you need me to sign. I'll be happy when all my ties to the ranch are cut."

"Can't sell it unless it's a profitable place."

"I thought Ethan got the guest ranch booked through the summer."

"Yeah, with Sarah Ashley's friends. Not real, honest-to-goodness customers. We need your help with marketing. Ethan tried to revamp the website and it's a disaster."

"I wouldn't call it a disaster," Ethan could be heard saying in the background.

"The sooner you get out here, Ty, the sooner we can get this place for a fair price."

"Or maybe you'll realize that this place is worth keeping in the family!" Ethan shouted.

Tyler could picture the glare Ben was most likely giving his twin. "Stop dragging your feet, Ty. Ethan is in over his head. Don't say anything," he obviously said in warning to Ethan. "You know it's true."

Ethan knew everything there was to know about animals, but marketing and brand management had very little to do with animal biology. If Ethan's only plan for getting customers in the door was to beg friends for a favor, the ranch was done for.

"You gave up your job in New York, Ben. Use your free time to help Ethan make things work."

"I have my own ranch to take care of." Ben had come home to solve the water rights dispute with their neighbors, the Thompsons, and somehow ended up giving them everything they wanted. He even married into their family. The Double T Ranch was Ben and Rachel's responsibility now. "Get on a plane and come do your part."

Tyler loosened his tie. His breathing became

unsteady. He cleared his throat. "I can't come back, Ben."

"You mean you won't. You could if you really wanted to."

"I can't. It's not only work. I have other things going on, too."

"Well, Jon and Ethan also have things going on. Both of them are planning weddings. On top of that, Jon has the girls and Ethan has a baby on the way. You, on the other hand, have no one to worry about but yourself."

Something inside Tyler snapped. If there was one thing he couldn't stand, it was being the last Blackwell to accomplish something. In the last three months, his three older brothers had fallen in love and gotten either engaged or married. Tyler's twin, Chance, had been the first to get married years ago when they were only twenty. Jon had married next and divorced a few years later. Of course, Jonathan the overachiever had managed to find someone else before Tyler even met one woman he cared enough about to marry.

"Well, I'm busy...planning a wedding, too."

Hadley giggled, quickly covering her mouth. He shot her a look that took all the humor out of the situation. The best way to get through to his brothers was to speak their language, and apparently love was the only language they spoke recently.

"Really? Whose wedding are you planning exactly?" Ben's tone clearly suggested he wasn't buying it.

Tyler locked eyes with Hadley and put a finger to his lips, hoping she'd stay silent. She tipped her head and her eyes narrowed in curiosity.

"Mine and Hadley's."

CHAPTER TWO

THERE WAS NO way this was happening. Hadley felt her heart stop for a second. What in the world would make Tyler say such an outrageous lie?

"You guys aren't the only ones who can fall in love and get married. I'm in the same boat and probably headed down the aisle before Ethan and Jon. I can't leave now when Hadley and I have so much going on professionally and personally."

Hadley must have been hallucinating. Why in the world would Tyler be telling his brother they were getting married? How was that the best idea he could come up with to get out of going to Montana to help them out?

Tyler's face turned red. "Subpoena me for what? I have nothing to do with anything that's going on out there."

Hadley underlined the word *vacation* on the piece of paper she had shown him a minute ago before he had announced to his family that she was his betrothed. The man needed to go. It was the only way she was going to prove her worth around here.

"Hold on, my fiancée needs me for a second." Tyler put the call on Hold. "Listen, I know this isn't making any sense."

"You mean you didn't just reveal your love for me and propose?"

Tyler sighed and his shoulders slumped. "It's a long story and I just need them to understand that I can't come to Montana right now."

"Why not? Kellen just told you to take a break. I've been begging you to get your brothers to stop calling. You taking a vacation to Montana and helping your brothers sell your family's ranch seems like it solves all of our problems."

"It won't work," Tyler argued. "Even if I went to Falcon Creek for my two-week 'vacation,' there's no way that I could turn things around enough to make a difference." He paused and stared at her for a second. "Not by myself."

Hadley felt her face warm. She didn't like how he was looking at her. Feeding his ego was her only hope. "You're Tyler Blackwell.

You can rebrand companies in your sleep. You can do anything."

Tyler put the phone back to his ear and resumed his call. "Hadley and I will be there in a week."

"No," she interrupted. "I can't go with you."

Tyler ignored her. "We'll do what we can for two weeks."

Two weeks? In Montana? With Tyler Blackwell, pretending to be his fiancée? No. No. And no.

"I'll do some research, find some potential buyers and paint a pretty picture for them. With any luck, someone will take it off our hands before the summer is over."

Hadley shifted in her seat and took a deep breath. This was not the plan. The plan was Tyler goes to Montana by himself. Hadley stays in Portland and manages Tyler's accounts while he's gone. Tyler comes back and gives her the job she deserved in the first place.

As soon as Tyler hung up the phone, she pounced. "Ty, I can't go with you. Who's going to handle everything you've got going on here if we both go? You wanted my help getting things done while you were on vacation. I can't do that if I go on vacation with you."

"I need you to come with me. If both of us work on this, we'll have the place sold in no time. Plus, my brothers can't wait to meet the woman who convinced me to settle down."

The knot in the pit of her stomach got tighter. And then it hit her. He needed her. He needed her to do something for him. "If I go, what do I get in return?"

Tyler blinked. "What do you get in return? What do you want?"

Hadley leaned forward as a sly smile spread across her face. "You know what I want. I want the same thing I wanted a couple months ago, but you let Kellen give it to Eric."

SHE WAS SO darn smart. He'd have to give her that much.

"Looking back, I probably should have gotten a little more information about Eric's qualifications," he said. "Or maybe I should say lack thereof."

"He's Kellen's nephew. That's it. He does not know how to do the job. You know that. I know that. Kellen would know it if he was here day in and day out. You need to tell him. Convince him to give the job to me. If you do that, I'll go to Montana with you and help you sell your ranch."

She wasn't wrong. Hadley was the better choice for brand strategist. Given Eric's difficulty finding his bearings, Kellen might not be so reluctant to reassign him to a more suitable position.

"And you'll pretend to be my fiancée."

"I was thinking a better plan would be telling your brothers you were just kidding about that part."

His spur-of-the-moment lie about getting married was supposed to keep him from going to Montana. He never imagined having to pretend, but if she wanted him to go, Hadley had to come with and there was no way he was letting his brothers know he wasn't as blissfully in love as they were.

"Nope," he said, folding his arms across his chest. "Fake engagement is a go. Either you're in or you're out. And if you're out, Eric keeps his job."

Hadley sank back in her chair, contemplating her options. There were no options. If she wanted the job, she had to go along with this plan.

"If I do this, there will be very strict rules.

I don't know what you expect out of a fake fiancée, but there is no way I will compromise myself or my morals."

"Come on, Hadley. I'm not going to ask you to make out with me in front of my brothers." Clearly, there was no way the thought of kissing him could be unappealing, but he wouldn't ask her to do anything that would make either of them uncomfortable. He didn't need a harassment charge brought against him. This was still a business arrangement.

"As soon as we're done and back in Portland, you will let your family know the wedding is off."

"No problem." Hadley wasn't his type anyways. He'd be lucky if they didn't notice how incompatible they were as soon as they got there. Tyler would have to put on a real show if he wanted to keep them in the dark.

Hadley stood up and smoothed her skirt. She reached a hand across his desk. "Then, we have a deal."

The two of them shook on it and Hadley hustled out of his office. Tyler opened a new window on his computer and began his search for flights to Billings. Like it or not, he was headed back to Falcon Creek.

HADLEY'S HEAD WAS SPINNING. Had she just made a deal with the devil? Or had she made the deal of a lifetime? Two weeks marketing some ranch in Montana to potential buyers and she would have the job she deserved. That had to be a win for her.

She tried not to think about the fact that she had to pretend to be engaged. To Tyler Blackwell.

"Can I ask you a question about the Kingman account?" Eric stood next to her desk with a file folder in his hand. She couldn't imagine what was in the manila folder given that they did everything electronically.

"Sure."

"So, I'm supposed to be doing some market research and put together a report analyzing the market data and trends, right?"

"That's what a brand strategist does." She had answered this question more than once. He seemed to need constant confirmation of his role. She couldn't tell if he kept forgetting or was asking in hopes he'd get a different answer one of these days.

Eric scratched the back of his head. "Do we have any of that from maybe a similar account? I mean, no reason to reinvent the wheel if it already exists, right?"

If he ended one more sentence with the word *right*, Hadley was going to lose her mind. She tried hard not to sound too condescending even though she wanted to let him know his incompetence was the reason she'd be taking his job in a few weeks.

"Kingman is a unique brand that sells men's shaving supplies and gift sets. We don't work with any other companies that sell in that niche market. You'll have to start fresh."

"It sounds like you know a lot about them. That's great!" It was clear the file folder in his hand was empty, a shameless prop to make him look like he was doing something. "Maybe you could help me out with this one. Put together a few things for me and I'll do the analyzing part afterward."

"I wish I could," she said with a frown. "But Tyler just roped me into another project. I'm going to be out of the office for a couple weeks."

"A new project?" Veronica sounded panicked.

"Don't worry," Hadley reassured her. "Tyler and I will be handling this one by ourselves.

We won't be asking you to do anything. Stay focused on the Paint-A-Lot redesign."

Eric wouldn't leave. "You sure you can't get me started on this Kingman thing before you move on to whatever Tyler has you doing? I'll run out and get you some coffee from that place you like on the corner."

Hadley couldn't hold back a sigh. What did it matter? The truth was she would be handling the Kingman account as soon as she got back from Montana and took over Eric's job. *Her* job. "Let me see what I can do."

"Thank you! You are the best. She's the best, right?" Eric scanned the room for someone to agree.

"She'd be better if she'd let us use her Hollywood connections," Lee said from his desk. He'd been giving her a hard time ever since Veronica let it out of the bag that Hadley's older brother was Asher Sullivan, star of TV's popular family drama *When We Were Young*.

"I heard there are already rumors your brother is a shoo-in for an Emmy this year," Eric said before his eyes went wide. "Hey, I bet your brother shaves, right? Maybe he'd want to be the spokesman for Kingman."

He was unbelievable. Did he know anything

about the client? "I'm going to assume you've at least glanced at Kingman's financials, so you know Asher is definitely not in their budget."

"But he's your brother, right? You could talk him into doing it for a steal."

Wrong. Hadley did not mix business with her personal life. Asher was her brother, not a potential spokesman for a client. "I have a ton of work to do, especially if you want me to gather some market data for you."

"That's her way of saying no, Eric," Lee said, clueing him in.

An email popped up from Tyler. Hadley opened it to find a confirmation notice for their flight to Billings, Montana, one week from today.

She bit down on her bottom lip. Hadley didn't get personal when it came to business. Apart from pretending to be her boss's fiancée in order to get the job she deserved.

What could possibly go wrong?

CHAPTER THREE

"DID YOU SERIOUSLY buy one first-class ticket?" Hadley watched as he handed his suitcase over to be weighed.

"I always fly first class," he said, ignoring her obvious reason for asking.

"Are you really the type of man who would let your fiancée sit in the back of the plane while you're pampered in first class?"

The woman from the airline tagging his bag gave Tyler a well-deserved dirty look. Hadley had no issue with shaming him.

Tyler, however, appeared completely unfazed. "You're not my fiancée until we step foot on Blackwell land."

"So there's still time to change my mind?" Hadley lifted her suitcase onto the scale.

Tyler slid his driver's license back into his wallet. "Don't start with me before we even leave Portland."

"You can't marry him," the woman behind

the counter whispered. "You deserve better than that."

"Don't worry. I wouldn't marry him even if he *had* bought me a first-class ticket." Tyler Blackwell was the last man on earth she'd want to end up spending her life with.

He was already headed toward the security checkpoint. Hadley weaved through the crowd of anxious travelers to catch up.

"You're a real charmer, Ty," she said just as her carry-on with its one bad wheel veered left when she wanted it to go right. It crossed paths with an older gentleman walking past her, ramming him in the leg.

Hadley apologized profusely as Tyler took the bag from her and carried it to the security line. "How was that for charming?" he asked as he handed it back.

"If that's all you got for charm, our engagement is doomed."

"I'm fine with that. It only needs to survive the next two weeks. After that, we go back to boss and employee."

"Boss and brand strategist."

"Boss and whatever you want to be called." He got out of the line. "I have precheck. I'll meet you at the gate. Try not to take out any other unsuspecting passengers with that thing," he said, pointing at her bag.

"I'll try." Hadley had to keep her eye on the prize. Two weeks and she would be promoted. It didn't matter if Tyler was so standoffish. She wasn't his real fiancée. They didn't have to sit by each other or walk through the airport side by side. She was fine with the fact that the act began and ended at the ranch.

Once through security, she stopped and bought a coffee. There was no reason to buy one for Tyler since he'd be sipping whatever his heart desired once he boarded the plane. They weren't together until they were on Blackwell land—his words, not hers.

She lugged her defective bag to the gate and took a seat without even bothering to look for Tyler. She stared down at the ring on her finger. A fake diamond ring for a fake wedding. Tyler had bought it a couple of days ago. It was so cheap Hadley wouldn't get it wet for fear it would turn her finger green or something.

How was she going to pull this off? Her phone chimed with a text from her best friend, Maggie, asking for an update on this nightmare adventure. Maggie already thought Hadley was taking a risk by going on this trip without having the promotion secured. She feared that Tyler might not hold up his end of the deal. What if Kellen wouldn't agree with the change?

He's sitting in first class without me, she texted.

Are you kidding me? Maggie wrote back.

Doesn't matter. I'm going to enjoy my alone time while I can, Hadley messaged.

I swear if he doesn't give you a promotion for this, you better quit. You've gone above and beyond! He's a schmuck. Hot but a schmuck.

Hadley smiled. Maggie had developed this weird crush on Tyler after she stopped by one day to take Hadley to lunch. One look at him and she thought she was in lust. Hadley had popped her bubble real fast. Tyler wasn't anyone's Prince Charming.

"Thanks for getting me a coffee." Tyler stood in front of her with his eyebrows raised. "And after you made me feel guilty for only thinking about myself." He held out a new boarding pass. "Here, you'll need this."

He had upgraded her to first class and she suddenly felt like the schmuck. "You didn't have to do that. I was only giving you a hard time earlier."

He sat down in the empty seat next to her and took a deep breath. "I want you to know that I appreciate what you're doing for me. I might not know how to show it all the time, but I want you to know I feel it."

"Thanks," she replied, staring down at her new boarding pass in her lap. Hadley had never flown first class. Her brother had once bragged about how he'd never fly with "the averages" again. Asher always had a way of making her feel small without even trying.

"Hopefully it won't be torture."

"It's only two weeks and we'll be working most of the time. It won't be much different from any other day at the office. The only difference is you'll have to be nice to me the whole time."

Tyler's brows pinched together. "Am I not usually nice to you?"

She hadn't meant to offend. It wasn't like Tyler was a tyrant, he simply wasn't warm. He was all business, all the time. Which was fine with Hadley but one of the reasons everyone in the office liked Kellen better than Tyler. It was also a huge reason the staff asked Kellen to force him to take a break.

"You're very focused. On whatever it is that you're working on. Which is great," she added. "It's the reason 2K is doing so well as a company. But if we are supposed to convince your brothers that we're in love, you're going to have to make an effort to pay me a little attention."

Tyler gave an understanding nod. "I'll work on being extra nice."

"The upgrade was a good start."

"Well, maybe I'll be a fast learner."

He wasn't the only one who would have to learn a thing or two. All she knew about Tyler was that he was the hardest-working person she'd ever met. She didn't know what he liked to do in his free time, the little that he left himself, or what his favorite anything was. She knew practically nothing about the person sitting next to her.

It wasn't like her to be going into something so woefully unprepared. She'd been following Tyler's lead thus far, but his way seemed like a recipe for disaster.

"Speaking of learning, perhaps we should do a little getting to know each other before we face your family. I mean, I know how persistent your brothers can be. What if they have a lot of questions? What's the plan here?"

"We'll be on our own most of the time. I wouldn't worry."

Not worry? He didn't know her very well if he thought she was capable of not worrying. Meeting the family was nerve-racking when she was the real girlfriend. Being the fake one made it a thousand times worse.

Tyler knew two of his brothers had way too much going on in their own lives to worry about his. Ben and Jon weren't going to pry too much. Ethan, on the other hand, could be a problem. He was running the ranch presently, which made him troublesome. But there was one person who might be more of a hard sell than his brothers.

"I think the only person I'm really worried about is Katie, our ranch hand. Growing up, she was like the annoying little sister we didn't ask for. Always in our business. Ratting us out for everything we did. She's the one we might need to be wary of."

Hadley paled. "Wait a minute, I didn't realize we had to outsmart a woman. Not that I haven't been nervous about pulling the wool over your brothers' eyes," she quickly clarified. "But women are more attuned to the intricacies of relationships. They pay attention to things like body language and the details that are shared with them."

She had to be kidding. Katie was female, yes. But honestly, she was more like one of the guys than a woman "attuned to the intricacies of relationships." Annoying? Yes. In touch with her feminine intuition? No.

Tyler chuckled. "Then maybe we should be more worried about Grace, my brother Ethan's pregnant fiancée."

"Pregnant!" Hadley was loud enough to attract the attention of more than a few people sitting near them. "Pregnant?" she repeated in a whisper.

Tyler was confused by her outburst. "What's the matter with being pregnant?"

"Pregnant women are freaks of nature!" Hadley threw her hands up. "They have superpowers you can't imagine. Do you even realize the amount of blood flowing through their bodies, feeding their brain? Not to mention the fact that all of their senses are in overdrive during pregnancy. She might be able to smell our lack of pheromones."

Pheromones? Tyler was quickly reconsidering his lack of a plan. Not because he feared being unable to convince everyone because of Grace's apparent bloodhound sense of smell but because Hadley was hysterical. He had chosen her because she was the smartest, most put together person in the office. He hadn't expected her to lose it over pheromones.

He placed a hand over hers. "Look at me," he said as calmly as he could. Her blue eyes locked onto his. The vulnerability he saw there was definitely new and created this strange sensation in the center of his chest. It was such a foreign feeling, he forgot what he was going to say.

"Are you going to tell me we're going to be fine?" she asked.

That was it.

"We're going to be fine. Grace and Katie will be preoccupied with a hundred other things while we're there. We'll just have to save our best stuff for the few times we're around them, okay?" he said with a wink.

The tension seemed to leave her body as her shoulders relaxed and she gave him a small smile. "You're right. We'll be fine." She thankfully sounded sure. "Good thing you got me that upgrade. We'll have plenty of time to cram."

"Cram?"

The gate agent announced they were ready to board first-class passengers. Hadley stood up. "Get ready to learn everything there is to know about me. I know I can't wait to become a Tyler Blackwell expert."

Tyler swallowed hard. No one was a Tyler Blackwell expert. He never let anyone get that close and he wasn't sure he could start now.

THEY'D BEEN IN the air for over an hour and Hadley was already a lifelong fan of first class.

"Favorite color?" she asked, starting with an easy question to get Tyler to open up.

"Don't have one."

"Come on, everyone has a favorite color."

"Not everyone because I don't. I have no preference."

Of course he was going to be difficult. "Favorite food?" she tried.

Tyler glanced out his window. They were flying high above a white blanket of clouds. "Nothing really stands out as a favorite."

"Favorite movie?"

He stared blankly back at her.

"Book? Television show? Band? Coffee shop? Come on, Tyler."

"What? I'm not a favorites kind of guy."

Hadley took a deep breath to keep her anxiety at bay. She'd told Tyler everything she could think about herself. Perhaps embarrassingly too much about her obsession with Harry Potter during middle school. The important thing was he'd be prepared with plenty of Hadley knowledge.

He seemed determined to leave her completely in the dark about himself, however. She couldn't go into this knowing next to nothing.

"Tell me about your brothers. What are they like?" she asked, hoping he'd be more willing to discuss the other Blackwells.

"Jonathan is my oldest brother, the only one who isn't a twin, but he does ironically have twin girls."

"What's Jon's wife's name?"

"No wife. Jon is divorced. Although, he recently got engaged to his nanny, Lydia." Tyler raised his eyebrows like it was a bit scandalous.

"He left his wife for the nanny?"

"No, no. His ex has been out of the picture since the twins were born." The invitation to talk about someone else was all it took to open up the floodgates. "Jon's the quintessential good guy in the white hat. He's a hardworking cowboy. He was my dad's favorite, probably because they were so alike. You'll never see the guy in anything other than jeans, a plaid shirt and cowboy boots. Total opposite of Ben. Ben is all city boy. I'm sort of shocked he gave up his life in New York to settle back down in Falcon Creek, especially since he got dumped at the altar a few years back. No one likes getting dumped, but it was worse than that. She left him for our grandfather."

"Whoa, wait. What?" Hadley knew about family dysfunction, but that was really messed up.

"Trust me, I think Ben got the better end of the deal. Zoe was nothing but a superficial gold digger. Ben deserved better and I've always thought that maybe Big E proposed to her because he knew Ben would have been miserable if they had ended up together. Ben has always been our grandfather's favorite. The two of them have the same cutthroat mentality."

"What's keeping him in Montana, then?"

"Since he's been home, he somehow managed to fall in love and get married to Rachel, an old friend whose family lives on the ranch next to ours. You'll meet her, too."

Fantastic, another woman in the mix. Hadley needed more information if she was going to trick three men and four women.

"In fact, the latest is that Big E filed for divorce and Zoe is back in Falcon Creek heartbroken," Tyler said with a smile.

"Will I have to meet Zoe, too?"

"Lord, I hope not," Tyler said as the flight attendant offered them a refill on their drinks and a warm cookie. Hadley might never be able to fly economy ever again.

"Jon and Ben will be busy with their own ranches. Ethan will be with us. Ethan is Ben's twin," Tyler continued after devouring his cookie. "Ben will tell you he's five minutes older so that makes Ethan the middle child, which fits his personality. He gets along with everyone and always tries to be the peacekeeper. He was the softy in our brood and our mother's clear favorite. The two of them had the same love of animals. She's probably the reason he became a vet."

For someone who didn't have any favorites, he was awfully aware of how his family played them. "So let me guess, you and your twin brother were the black sheep of the family. No one's favorites?"

Tyler chuckled. "Chance would tell you he's the lone Blackwell black sheep because living in Big Sky Country wasn't for him, but when we were little and our real grandma was still on the ranch, he was by far her favorite. She used to sing and play songs on the piano with him. I'm the only one in the family who didn't have anyone's undivided attention." His gaze drifted back out the window. "I was the invisible one."

Hadley knew exactly how it felt to be the invisible child. How frustrating it was to never quite be enough. She had felt that way her entire life. Being the younger, less successful sister of Asher Sullivan wasn't all it was cracked up to be.

"Maybe we have more in common than I thought," Hadley said, turning her body in his direction.

"You don't want to be like me. No one loves me the most for a reason."

"Oh, come on. You aren't that bad."

His jaw tightened and he took a deep breath through his nose. "Trust me, Hadley. I'm the worst."

CHAPTER FOUR

TYLER STRUGGLED TO ignore Hadley's incessant fidgeting in the passenger seat of his rental car. He had warned her that she should be prepared to be in the middle of nowhere.

"We're almost there. Can you try being still for a minute?" he asked. When she wasn't peppering him with her millions of questions, she was distracting him with her anxious silence. After two hours on the plane and two hours in the car, maybe they had both hit their limit of togetherness.

"Any chance we can stop to use a bathroom?" she asked. That explained her wriggling.

They were only a few miles away from Falcon Creek. Tyler was more than happy to delay their arrival at the ranch. Actually, he wished he could turn around and get back on a plane headed anywhere but here. Being this close to the place he used to call home made his stomach ache with something other than hunger.

"Maybe we should grab some lunch in town. We'll be eating at the ranch the rest of the trip."

Hadley seemingly had no issue with that idea given that her stomach growled loudly. Tyler spotted the sign for Falcon Creek and exited the highway. This place was still a one-stoplight town. It hadn't changed since Tyler was a baby.

The dive bar where Chance played his first real gig was still standing. Pops Brewster sat out front Brewster Ranch Supply playing chess just like he had for as long as Tyler could remember. Maple Bear Bakery was where Big E used to buy Ty and his brothers doughnuts when he was feeling generous, which wasn't often, but that made the treat so much more delicious.

Clearwater Café was probably the best place to stop for a hot meal. Tyler sat in an open booth while Hadley ran to the bathroom. He glanced over the menu and ordered a couple of sodas for the two of them.

"That was the cleanest public bathroom I have ever used," Hadley reported as she slid into the seat across from him. "I think I love this place."

"They also serve your favorite—macaroni and cheese." Tyler could tell anyone who asked Hadley's favorite everything. She had been more than thorough in preparing him today.

She smiled and he noticed the way it lit up her entire face. "You remembered."

"Tyler Blackwell? Is that you? Oh, my goodness, it is."

Tyler had hoped they would go unrecognized, but that was impossible in this small town. He turned his head to find a pink monster headed his way.

"Grandma, is that you? You look so much older than the last time I saw you."

Of all the people he didn't want to run into, Zoe was at the top of the list. She scowled at him as she flipped her long, blond ponytail behind her shoulder.

"You're really going to kick me when I'm down, Ty? That horrible excuse for a human being you call your good-for-nothing grandfather already did quite enough to make me feel like a worthless piece of trash."

An unexpected guilt washed over him. Tyler didn't realize he could feel sorry for Zoe given all she had put his family through, but he did.

"Big E has a way of making everyone feel small. Don't take it personally."

"I'll try to remember that," she replied, her face softening a bit. "What are you doing back here? I thought you were never coming back. And who is this?" Zoe turned all of her attention on Hadley.

"Hadley, meet my ex-stepgrandma, Zoe. Zoe, this is Hadley."

"His fiancée," Hadley clarified.

Tyler internally chastised himself for not being prepared to begin this charade. Remembering to refer to her as his fiancée was important and he'd failed right out of the gate.

"Fiancée?" Zoe's eyes nearly bulged from her head. "I can't believe Rachel didn't tell me."

"We were pretty surprised to hear Ben and Rachel got married so quickly." Hadley reached across the table and grabbed Tyler's hand. "We thought we'd be first down the aisle. Right, honey?"

She was good at this fake relationship stuff. Maybe her brother wasn't the only actor in the family.

"The Blackwell boys all caught the wedding bug at the same time, huh?"

"Guess so." Tyler prayed she wouldn't ask too many more questions or want to see the ring. Zoe was one of those people who might be able to sniff out a fake diamond when she saw one. "Well, it was good to see you again. We'll see you around," he said, hoping she'd take the hint.

"Oh, please don't tell me Day Four is back," a voice full of disdain said behind Zoe. That voice could belong to only one person.

"Is this where all of Big E's exes come for lunch?" Tyler pondered aloud as Myrna Edwards, with her hair as white as the snow-capped Smoky Mountains, approached the table.

"I'm positive three Blackwells is all this town can handle. You should head back to whatever hole you crawled out of, Tyler Alexander Blackwell." She may have been short in stature but her memory was long. Myrna was Big E's second wife, who, thanks to the boys, didn't last very long as Mrs. Elias Blackwell.

"I'm here to help my brothers sell the ranch so you never have to worry about the Blackwells ever again."

One side of her mouth quirked a smile. "Oh,

don't tease me, Day Four. No more Blackwells? That's too much to hope for."

"Just give me a couple weeks. We'll have a big ol' sold sign hanging out front." He glanced across the table at Hadley. Darn, he'd forgotten again. "We, as in me and my fiancée," he quickly added. "Hadley, this is another one of my ex-stepgrandmothers. Myrna, this is Hadley, my fiancée."

"You may call me Myrna," she said to Hadley. "You, Day Four, may only refer to me as Judge Edwards. Don't ever call me your ex-stepgrandmother again. Please stay on your ranch until you sell it. I am tired of seeing Blackwells in my courtroom and my restaurants of choice. Have a nice day."

She walked across the restaurant and sat down at a table by herself. She probably never remarried after Big E. Leave it to Elias to make a woman give up on men completely.

"She hates you guys. Not that she likes anyone that much, but she *hates* you," Zoe said with such awe.

Myrna had good reasons to dislike all five Blackwell brothers. Although in their defense, they were only kids when they ran her off the ranch a short five days after her marriage to

Big E. She had tried to take over as the mother figure too soon after their grandmother left and their parents died. The boys were knee-deep in their grief and unable to welcome anyone into their lives.

"It was great to see you again, Zoe. Have a good one." It was the last hint he was giving her. If she didn't leave them alone, he was going to get rude.

Zoe wasn't oblivious, but she was obnoxious. She grinned and, instead of moving along, sat down next to Hadley. "I'm late for an appointment, but I am so curious about how you and Ty got together. He was always such a little brat when we were younger. Maybe once you settle in, Rachel and I can take you out for some girl time."

"That would be—" Hadley began.

"Unnecessary," Tyler finished for her. "We're only here for two weeks and supposedly have a ton of work to do to get the ranch ready for sale. I hear someone's vision for the place was a bit out of touch with what's marketable."

"Ha! I have great taste and amazing ideas." Zoe pointed a finger at him. Her hot-pink manicure was so her. "You just wait and see how popular the petting zoo is."

"Are you folks ready to order?" the waitress asked, finally coming to the table to rescue them from this unpleasant family reunion.

"I'm not staying," Zoe said, getting to her feet. "I hope Tyler doesn't make you work the whole time you're in town, Hadley. Maybe we'll see each other again."

"Looking forward to it," Hadley replied.

Zoe left and Tyler and Hadley ordered some food. When they were alone, Hadley smoothed her napkin on her lap. "You didn't prepare me for all the ex-stepgrandmothers. How many more are lurking in this town?"

"Big E was married five times. The other ones don't live around here, so you're safe. *We're* safe."

"Until we get to the ranch," she said, raising her water glass.

Tyler felt a tightness in his chest at the thought of stepping foot on Blackwell land. It had been a long time since he'd been there, and Zoe hadn't been wrong—he'd sworn to never return.

With a dry mouth, he lifted his own glass. "Until we get to the ranch."

HADLEY'S NERVES COULD not be more out of control. She had played it cool while meeting Tyler's ex-stepgrandmas, but inside she had been shaking in her boots. Keeping up this ruse for two weeks might be the death of her.

Tyler drove like a little grandma the whole way out of town on their way to the ranch. Maybe he was just as anxious about getting there as she was. He slowed down to a stop and Hadley looked to the left. The metal arch over the entrance read Blackwell Family Ranch.

They were here. Time was up.

"Maybe we should drive around the property, take some pictures and jot down some notes before meeting up with Ethan and Ben," Tyler suggested. "It's been a while since I've been here. I'm not even sure what changes have been made that we'll need to play up when we market it."

Classic Tyler, rolling up his sleeves and thinking about nothing but the job at hand. Perhaps that was the best plan. If they stayed focused on the work, the lie would create less stress.

"Good call." Hadley grabbed her backpack out of the back seat. "I started a list of things we want to focus on, like what wildlife people might see and the different recreational opportunities. We have to play up these mountain views."

Having grown up in Washington State, Hadley was partial to mountains. She couldn't imagine living somewhere without them. The Blackwell Ranch had the gorgeous Rocky Mountains to the west. Location was not going to be an issue in the marketing plan.

Tyler drove in and turned left before they got to the enormous green-roofed lodge. He shared what he remembered about the wildlife from the area.

"We're not far from an elk refuge, and whitetail and mule deer used to graze on the ranch when I lived here."

"People will love that." Hadley jotted down *elk* and *deer* on her list.

"I remember when I was around twelve, my brothers and I were playing a very intense game of capture the flag up in the hills. It was me and Ben versus Ethan and Chance. Ben and I had found the best spot to hide our flag, so we just needed to find theirs. Ben and I were like navy SEALs. Ethan and Chance didn't have a prayer against us. Only when we found their flag, they had an extra teammate we weren't expecting."

"Who? Jon?" Hadley guessed.

"No," he said with that cocky laugh. "Jon would have been easy to get past. There was this huge bull moose that had wandered into our game and decided to graze next to their flag. Ben and I had no idea how to get rid of it. Ben tried scaring it by throwing some rocks at its feet, but that only made it mad. Before I could try my idea, which totally would have worked, the hair on its back raised up."

"I take it that's a bad sign." Hadley loved the way he got that sparkle in his eye when he told stories from his childhood.

"Oh, yeah. I've since learned that there are seven signs a moose is about to attack you, and that is number one. The second sign is it smacks it lips, but instead of smacking its lips, our moose urinated all over Chance and Ethan's flag. It was disgusting and there was no way I was touching that thing after that."

Hadley covered her mouth while she laughed. "Going to the bathroom is a sign a moose is going to attack?"

"It is! I swear. But I thought it was trying to make us mad. I yelled at it and the next thing I know, it came at me like it wanted to kill me, so I took off. Ben shouted at me to climb a tree, which I did, but the moose rammed the tree and almost knocked me out of it. I thought I was going to die that day. I was stuck up in the tree for a good hour before that animal decided it was bored of me. Ben and I made sure to learn everything there was to know about moose after that. We were never going to lose because of some dumb animal again."

She had no doubts about that. Tyler was someone who didn't get caught unprepared very often, and if he did, he made sure to be overprepared the next time.

Hadley giggled as she stared out her window at the green fields. There were a few horses grazing in the distance. She made a note to find out how many horses the ranch owned and to clarify if all the livestock would be part of the sale.

Tyler slammed on the brakes, causing Hadley to nearly knock her head on the dashboard. "What in the world?" she said, pressing a hand to her chest to make sure her heart had restarted.

"Katie," Tyler said with a sigh.

Hadley glanced up and saw why Tyler had

made such a quick stop. A redheaded woman stood in the middle of the dirt path with her hands on her hips and a tan-and-black shepherd dog by her side.

She walked over to Tyler's side of the car. He rolled down the window as she bent down to get a look at them.

"Ty?"

"Hi, Katie."

"I thought you might have been some guests who got lost. Welcome home."

"Thanks. I'm driving Hadley around the property. We thought it would be nice to get a sense of what we have to work with before we talk to Ethan and Ben about the marketing plan."

"The marketing plan...of course." Katie dipped her head a bit lower to see farther in the car. "So, you're Hadley. The woman who somehow managed to pin this guy down. Boy, do we have a lot of questions for you."

Hadley's full stomach ached. The questions would be nonstop now that they were here. She only hoped she could convince Tyler's family they were a real couple. Her promotion depended on it.

She put a hand on Tyler's leg. Thankfully,

he didn't flinch at the contact. "Well, I can't wait to answer all of them. Tyler's my favorite subject these days."

Katie smiled and stood back up. "Well, you two have a nice drive. I'll let your brothers know you're here."

"Great," Tyler said even though Hadley knew he was less than thrilled about their arrival being discovered.

Katie waved at them as Tyler put the car back in Drive and rolled up the window. "We can't spend too much time out here now. It won't be long before the where-are-you phone calls begin," he lamented.

"We could get the reunion over with and then hide."

"I'm not hiding," he snapped.

"Right."

"I'm not. I'm…" His jaw tensed. "Fine. I'm hiding. It's been a long time since I've been here, and there are a lot of things I left behind on purpose."

That was about as vague as he could get. Hadley got the impression that there was always a lot of drama on the ranch, but at the same time, Tyler seemed to have good memories of his family. When he spoke about his brothers, there was always this small smile playing on his lips.

"There are clearly things you do not want to talk about, and I respect that. But we have to work with your brothers to get this place in tip-top shape so you guys can sell for what you want."

"Why did I tell them I was engaged?" he asked himself aloud. It wasn't like Hadley had the answer to that question. She wondered why he felt like that was the best plan, as well. "I didn't want them to think I was the only one incapable of being normal. That's why. I hate being the only one no one loves."

His confession surprised Hadley. At work, he never seemed bothered by who he was or apologetic for what he wanted out of life. Tyler Blackwell usually had confidence to spare.

"Hey, I know a lot of people who aren't in a relationship. That doesn't make you abnormal. If that were true, then I'm abnormal. My best friend, Maggie, is abnormal. Half the people in my book club are abnormal."

Tyler's forehead wrinkled. "You're in a book club?"

"That was the part that stood out to you?"

"I heard you. I get it. There are plenty of single people in the world. I wasn't implying you were abnormal for being unattached. It's more than being single for me. I can't explain it."

"It doesn't matter. You told them we're engaged and now we're here and have to play our parts. Let's go say hello and then get to work."

"You're good at this," Tyler said, side-eyeing her.

"Good at what? Convincing you to man up?"

"That and playing the part of my fiancée. You're a natural, so calm and cool. Your brother should be glad you didn't go into acting. You might have outshined him."

Hadley laughed. She had never outshined Asher at anything. He probably could outwoman her if he put his mind to it. "Asher has nothing to worry about. Trust me, I'm freaking out every time we talk to someone new."

His phone chimed with a text. Hadley saw Ethan's name. "Katie works fast. I guess we should head to the house. We'll try hard not to freak out together," he said, giving her knee a squeeze.

His hand felt nice until she realized how wrong that was. Tyler was her boss. His hands should not make her feel anything—good or bad. His hands needed to be the last thing on her mind. So why couldn't she stop thinking about how warm and gentle his touch was? Or how that warmth seemed to spread throughout her body? Maybe Hadley didn't have as much acting to do as Tyler thought.

CHAPTER FIVE

"MY BABY BROTHER is finally home." Ethan stood on the wraparound porch of the old, white two-story house. Standing there in his jeans and plaid button-down, he reminded Tyler a little too much of their father.

"I don't know about you, but my home is about seven hundred miles that way," Tyler said, pointing west.

Ethan made his way down the steps to meet them, wrapping Tyler up in a hug. "It's so good to see you, Ty."

"Why are you being so nice to me?" The Blackwell boys, in general, didn't hug. They punched each other in the arm or tackled one another to the ground. "I already agreed to help with the marketing plan."

"Ah, the marketing plan." Ethan let go and stepped back. A huge grin spread across his face. "I can't wait to talk about how you plan to bring guests to the ranch. This must be Hadley! I'm Ethan. It's so great to meet you."

Ethan held his arms open and Hadley humored him by accepting his weird greeting. When did his brother become such a hugger?

"It's good to meet you, too," Hadley said, her eyes wide for Tyler to see.

"Okay, let go of my fiancée." Tyler patted his brother on the back. "You have your own."

Ethan released her. "I do have my own and a baby on the way. Can you believe I'm going to be a dad?"

Tyler really couldn't see it. It was easy to imagine Jon as someone's father. He basically stepped in and parented the four of them after their parents died. But Ethan wasn't like Jon. He might have been good with animals, but human babies were another story.

"It's a good thing you have Grace, brother."

"Ouch." Ethan placed a hand over his heart. "I'm going to let that slide because I am so happy you two are here. Grace and I set up one of the new cabins for you. We figured you should get the full experience while you're here."

"Why wouldn't we stay here in the house?"

Ethan rubbed the back of his neck. "I don't

think you'll want to stay here. Not until we do a little post-Zoe remodeling."

Tyler jogged up the steps. What had Zoe done to his family's house? The outside looked the way he remembered. The shutters were the same color green they had been when the boys were little. Tyler had noticed the old tire swing still hung from the elm tree out back when he drove up.

It was obvious what Zoe did as soon as he walked through the door. The once warm and cozy house was unrecognizable. The furniture in the front room didn't look the least bit comfortable. There was no way Big E ever sat down and fell asleep on the couch. Given Zoe's love for the color pink, he was a bit surprised and terribly horrified that she had hung red velvet wallpaper.

"Wait until you see the kitchen. It's like something out of your bubblegum nightmares," Ethan said from behind him as if he could read Tyler's mind.

"How could he let her do this?" Tyler's eyes had to be deceiving him. Nothing was the way it should be. His mother would have hated this. It was as if every bit of Blackwell had been erased from inside.

"You should see our old bedrooms. I get physically ill just thinking about it. Grace and I figure we can remodel in here once we make the ranch profitable."

The new owners would probably tear this house down. It was a wonder Big E could stomach living in it for a second. Gone was the farmhouse table they all used to sit around to eat Mom's homemade dinners. Gone were the comfy sofas the boys used to stretch out on after school. Gone was the oak mantel over the fireplace where their stockings used to hang at Christmastime.

This place was no home.

Tyler's heart ached. As much as he hadn't wanted to come back, he imagined it frozen in time. He hated that this was no longer the house where he grew up.

"Maybe Ethan can show us the cabin where we'll be staying." Hadley gave Tyler a sympathetic smile as if she could tell he was crushed. She took him by the hand. The contact startled him, but he didn't pull away.

"Yeah, we can do that," Ethan replied.

The front door opened and Ben strode in like he owned the pink palace. "Is that Impala outside your rental car, little brother? I thought a big-time advertising executive like yourself could afford to show up in style like I did. They rent Mercedes in Billings, you know."

"Not all of us need a car to make us feel like a man," Tyler replied, snapping out of his private pity party. "Sorry to hear you felt you needed a prop."

Ben gave him a real Blackwell greeting—a punch in the shoulder. "It's nice to see your face instead of talking to you on the phone."

"I'd say the same if I hadn't been forced to look at Ethan's ugly mug since we got here. Let's be honest, all you'll ever be is a better-dressed version of him. Downside to being an identical twin, I guess."

Ethan sidled up next to him and slapped Tyler on the shoulder. "Do you want to put him in a headlock or should I?" he asked Ben.

"Maybe we should do that thing to his underwear that used to make him cry when he was in middle school," Ben proposed.

Tyler shoved Ethan away. "Maybe we should act like grown-ups in front of my fiancée."

Ben raised his eyebrows. "I can't believe she's real."

Tyler introduced Hadley to his brother, who thankfully didn't try to hug the stuffing out of her. Instead, he reached into his pocket and pulled out his money clip. He handed Ethan ten bucks.

"What's that about?" Tyler asked.

"Ben thought you were lying about getting married. He was sure you made it up so you wouldn't have to come home, but I said you weren't that desperate." Ethan waved the ten around. "We bet and now I'm a little richer."

Tyler fought to control his expression. Part of him wanted to come clean. End the charade right then and there. He imagined taking the money from Ethan and handing it back to Ben. But that would be admitting he was exactly who everyone thought he was—the unlovable one.

"That's so funny!" Hadley stepped up and held her hand out in front of Tyler. "Pay up, sweetheart. I said one of them would think you were bluffing. That's what happens when you don't mention to your family that you have an amazing girlfriend *before* you ask her to marry you."

Amazing was right. She was an amazing liar. Tyler was thoroughly impressed. He took out his wallet and handed her a hundred-dollar bill. Both of his brothers' mouths hung open.

"I might not be driving a Mercedes, but at least I play for real money when I make a bet. Let's go check out these cabins," Tyler said, pushing past Ben and making his way to the front door. He wouldn't doubt this plan again.

HADLEY SLIPPED THE hundred-dollar bill into the pocket of her jeans. She had earned that money and there was no way she was giving it back. Meeting Tyler's brothers had proved to be even more stressful than she imagined.

Of course they had questioned the legitimacy of this relationship. It was incredible that anyone believed their made-up love story. The thought that Tyler made time in his life for dating was comical. If his brothers truly knew him, they would have known this was a lie because there was little room in Tyler's life for love.

Ben and Ethan climbed in Ben's car and led the way to the new guest cabins. Hadley relished having a moment to let her guard down.

"From now on, I will never know if you're telling me the truth," Tyler said. "You are that good at lying."

It was a strange thing to feel proud of, but Hadley still blew on her fingernails and buffed them on her shirt. "Thank you very much," she said, assuming he meant that as a compliment.

Tyler's opinion had always mattered. He was her boss and what he thought about her ability to get a job done was imperative to keeping said job. Convincing his family they were in love was her current job, and she was doing everything she could to make it happen.

Tyler cleared his throat. "My family brings out my competitive side. It's never been easy to stand out in this crowd. When I left, it was so nice not to be compared to any other Blackwell. I swore I'd never worry about one-upping any of them again. Yet, the second they ask me to come back, here I am trying to convince them I am just as good, just as rich, just as smart, just as…almost married."

Tyler was all of those things, except for the almost-married part. Somehow that seemed to irk him the most. "It bothers you to lie to them."

"It bothers me that I don't want to see the way they'd look at me if they knew this wasn't real. Like, *poor Tyler. He's all alone.* There's nothing wrong with being alone."

He didn't have to convince her. Hadley was perfectly content with being single. It didn't matter so much that all of her college friends were either getting married or already married. Some of them were even starting to have kids. She was only twenty-six. Far from being a spinster.

"Exactly," she agreed. "There's no shame in building a successful career first. That's my goal. I want to be something other than someone's wife. Is that wrong?"

"Not in my book. And given your performance today, you're definitely on track to be our brand strategist." Tyler cracked a smile.

He somehow managed to be even more attractive when he smiled. His eyes crinkled at the edges and softened just enough to make her think less about being a brand strategist and more about being his fiancée.

She turned her head, focusing her gaze on the scenery rather than the man sitting next to her. Her boss. Not her fiancé.

They pulled up to a one-story log cabin that backed up to the tall pines of the forest. It had an expansive front porch that overlooked the horse pasture. Two buffalo-check flannel pillows sat on a wooden bench, the perfect spot to sit and watch the sunset over the mountains.

"We set you two up here. This one is called

Heavenly Pines. I like to think of it as the honeymoon suite," Ethan said with a wink.

Hadley ignored the flutter in her stomach. This was a game. A means to an end. No honeymoon.

Ben and Ethan helped unload the bags from the car. Hadley wasn't used to having so many strong, handsome gentlemen around to do her bidding. She could get used to the Blackwell Ranch quite quickly if this kept up.

Heavenly Pines was a quaint little cabin. Inside there was a sitting area, a small kitchenette with a microwave and a king-size bed in the bedroom. Two towels were folded on the bed with tiny scented toiletries tucked in the front fold.

"Jon and Lydia invited everyone over for dinner tonight. The twins are excited to see Uncle Tyler and their soon-to-be aunt Hadley," Ethan said, setting her suitcase down in the bedroom.

"Sounds good," Tyler said. He glanced at the bed and she saw the same discomfort that Hadley felt looking at it. "Are we going to talk business now or when we're all together tonight?"

"That depends," Ethan answered, his gaze

jumping back and forth from Tyler to Ben. "We're wondering how set you are about selling the ranch."

Tyler's eyebrows pinched together. "I'm all in. Why wouldn't we sell?"

"Ethan thinks the ranch should stay in the family," Ben interjected. "He's been trying to convince me to do this with him, but I can't. Rachel and I are focused on keeping Double T afloat. Jon has his ranch to run."

"So that leaves you and Chance," Ethan chimed in. "We both know Chance doesn't care what happens to this place. He sure isn't going to help run it—"

"But I might?" Tyler interrupted. "Have you lost your mind? I didn't want to come here in the first place. I'm definitely not going to stay and help you run it. Sorry, man. I don't know what you thought was going to happen, but I am set on selling."

"Seriously, Ty. I saw your face when you walked into the old house," Ethan said.

"That's all you've got?" Ben asked. "Everyone looks sick when they walk in there. Zoe ruined it."

"It was more than Zoe's bad taste."

Hadley knew Ethan was right. She had seen

it, too. Tyler had been devastated by what had been done to the house.

"That house means something to all of us," Ethan continued. "It's where Mom and Dad tucked us in. Where—"

Tyler put his hand up. "Stop. I don't need a walk down memory lane. I don't want to talk about Mom and Dad. I don't want to rehash the things that happened in that house. I want to help you sell this ranch and go back to Portland. Where I live. Where I work."

"Where your fiancée lives and works," Ben added.

Hadley had no place in this discussion. Stuck in the middle of a very private family matter was not where she wanted to be. Tyler's brothers might have thought she influenced whether Tyler stayed, but the truth was she had no say in what was happening here.

"I'm sorry, Hadley," Ethan said. "I know what I'm asking impacts you, too. You two have a life together in Portland, but I'm asking you to consider another possibility."

"It's never happening," Tyler said through gritted teeth. "Drop it."

"Okay..." Ben jumped in. "Ethan and I are going to let you two get settled. We'll see you at Jon's for dinner. We can talk about the marketing plans when all of us are in the same room." Ben guided Ethan toward the door.

Hadley could see the frustration coming off Tyler like steam. His chest rose and fell like he'd been out for a run. She'd seen him upset before at work but not like this. This wasn't simply anger. This was pain.

"I'm sorry," she started.

"Go unpack, Hadley," he snapped.

She didn't argue. She turned on her heel and headed back to the bedroom. He was the boss. This was a job. They weren't a real couple. They never would be.

CHAPTER SIX

SLAM!

Hadley had never been so happy to hear a door shut behind someone as he left. After a half hour of silence, Tyler announced that he was going to finish the drive around the ranch. *Alone.* He'd take some pictures and they could talk about how they want to proceed with things when he got back.

It was a relief to finally be by herself. The tension in the cabin after Tyler's brothers left was so thick, Hadley felt like she was suffocating back in the bedroom while he brooded in the sitting room.

She wasn't sure why Tyler hated it here so much, but whatever the reason, it was clear he had no intentions of staying past the two weeks already on his calendar. She would have to play the part of the supportive fiancée tonight at dinner. Let the brothers know she didn't want to live in Montana either.

Hadley stretched out on the king-size bed and texted Maggie about her day so far. Before she could update her completely, her phone rang. It wasn't Maggie, though. It was Hadley's mom.

She suppressed a groan and answered. "Hi, Mom."

"Hadley?" For some reason, every time her mother called her, she acted surprised that Hadley was the person on the other end of the line. Who else did she think was going to answer?

"It's me."

"Oh, good. It's your mother." She also didn't realize that Hadley always knew it was her calling.

"I know, Mom. How are you?"

"Good, good. Your father and I are driving down to Portland next weekend and thought maybe we could do lunch before we fly out to see your brother. Did you see last night's episode? That was one of my favorites. I'm so glad they're replaying episodes over the summer."

Hadley occasionally watched Asher's show. It wasn't on her DVR, but if she remembered, she would have it on in the background while she was surfing the internet at night. She didn't watch the reruns, though. Her parents, on the other hand, never missed an episode—new or previously aired. They wouldn't want to miss a second of Asher's brilliance.

"It's always great. That's why it's getting all that Emmy buzz."

"Can you imagine if your brother won an Emmy this early in his career? He's been so fortunate and your dad and I are just so proud."

So proud. Always *so* proud when it came to Asher. Even if Hadley could do something worthy of their pride, it wouldn't make them *so* proud like her brother always did.

"If he does, it will only be the first of many," Hadley said, knowing that was what her mom wanted to hear.

"That's what I was thinking! I can't wait to see him. He invited us to be there when they announce the nominees. He also said he's got some good news about a movie. Did I tell you he auditioned for the lead in a movie directed by... Oh, I shouldn't say. I don't want to jinx it for him. Let's just say it rhymes with Hint Leastwood."

Hadley stopped listening. This was so typical. Her mom would call to ask her to lunch and they'd somehow spend the next twenty minutes talking about Asher. It never failed.

"I'm not in Portland," Hadley said once her mom stopped giving her the latest details of Asher's fantastic life.

"What do you mean you're not in Portland?" Her mother actually sounded concerned.

"I'm away on business for the next couple of weeks."

"Since when do you travel for work?"

"Since now. The boss asked me to help him with a special project, so I'm here in Montana."

"Montana! What in the world could you be doing there?"

"We're doing some marketing for a guest ranch out here. It actually belongs to my boss's family. It's pretty important to him, so it's a big deal that I was asked to come help him."

"You're on a ranch? Asher's new movie is a Western. What a coincidence!"

Hadley smacked her forehead. The Amazing Jane Sullivan could turn any conversation into one about Asher in ten seconds flat.

"Well, it was good to catch up." Talking to her mom was almost as torturous as not talking to Tyler. She needed a good excuse to get off the phone. "I guess we'll have to do lunch the next time you visit Asher. I'm gonna have to let you go, Mom. Tell Dad I said hello."

"Oh, okay, sweetheart. I'm going to call your brother and tell him you're at a ranch. He'll get a kick out of you following in his footsteps."

Her mother's mind was a very strange place. Something told Hadley that when she got the promotion at work, instead of being excited for her, they would somehow make it about Asher.

Maybe Tyler wasn't the only one who was tired of trying to compete with family when winning was never an option.

HADLEY SEEMED DISTRACTED. She played with a lock of her hair as she stared out the window of the car. The dress she'd picked out was probably too fancy for dinner at Jon's, but she had insisted that looking out of place would only help him in the end. A city-girl fiancée would never survive on a ranch. Ethan would have to leave him alone about moving back.

She was so good at this. Bringing her along was the best decision he made even though things had been awkward this afternoon. Tonight might be as bad. Tyler hadn't been to Jon's ranch in years and the last time he saw Jon's twins, they were babies. He had no idea what to expect from his brothers. He could be walking Hadley into a lion's den.

"You look beautiful, by the way. I should have said that before we left," he said, breaking the silence.

She turned her head in his direction and suddenly that word didn't do her justice. Her blond hair had a soft curl in it. It framed her face so perfectly. Her lips were painted pink and the highlighter on her cheeks shimmered in the early-evening sun. She took his breath away.

"Thanks." She smiled and averted her eyes.

"Only a few more hours of major pretending. Tomorrow, we should be on our own and we can be our normal selves. I'd like to work on the website, get the new one up and running."

Talking business was easier than thinking about how good she looked and how comfortable he had begun to feel around her. Maybe his feelings were getting muddied because of the lies they had to tell.

Hadley crossed her legs and smoothed out the wrinkles in the skirt of her dress. "We'll survive dinner and your family. I figure anytime one of them asks me something about you that I don't know, I'll say, 'Oh, you know

Tyler.' And if they really think about it, they'll know the answer."

He chuckled at her reasoning. "Too bad I can't use that when they ask me something about you. Although, you did fill my head with quite a bit of Hadley history. If they need to know which fictional character you would marry instead of me, I know it's Ron Weasley."

"Don't you dare. That was when I was thirteen. I don't know why I even told you about that." Her cheeks turned red.

Stunning. It was the new word that kept running through his mind. He gripped the steering wheel a little tighter and forced all the adjectives he could use to describe Hadley out of his mind as he pulled through the gates to the JB Ranch.

"Welcome!" A smiling brunette answered the door and ushered them inside. Jon's black-and-white border collie was there to greet the new guests, as well.

"You must be Lydia," Tyler guessed.

"And you must be Tyler and Hadley. It's so good to meet you. Please come on in. The rest of the gang is in the living room."

Hadley handed her the bottle of wine they had bought in town beforehand. "It's nice to know there's someone else here who hasn't known the Blackwells forever."

Lydia beamed, her blue eyes shining almost as bright as Hadley's. "Oh, that's exactly how I feel!"

The two of them hugged like they were longtime friends. Women had a way of bonding over the strangest things. Tyler didn't get it, but he did appreciate the smell of some good home cooking.

"Is that chili I smell?" he asked, stepping farther in the house.

"It's an old family recipe. We're going to have chili with all the fixings and my famous jalapeño corn bread. I hope you're hungry."

"He didn't sweat all day out in the fields like the rest of us, but maybe all his traveling helped him work up an appetite." Jon, tall and lean like their father had been, folded his arms across his chest. "Welcome home, Ty."

Home. That's what everyone wanted to call Falcon Creek, but it hadn't been Tyler's home for a long time.

"It's good to see you, old man," Tyler said, knowing it would bug his eldest brother. Five years wasn't that big of an age gap, yet Jon had always seemed so much older than the rest of them. Maybe it was because he had been fifteen when their parents died—right on the cusp of being grown. Without them around, Jon had to become a man earlier than most.

"Hadley and Tyler brought some wine," Lydia announced. "Wasn't that thoughtful?"

"Hadley Sullivan, meet my brother, Jonathan. Don't let his serious face fool you. He's actually very… Wait, his serious face is the real deal. Jon is always very serious. I don't think he knows how to smile."

One side of Jon's mouth inched upward. A half of a smile was progress. "It's nice to meet you, Hadley. I'm sorry you settled for this guy. I'm sure you could have done much better."

"Oh, he's not that bad. He has excellent taste in just about everything—food, wine, movies—"

"And women," Tyler added. He wrapped his arm around her waist and pulled her against his side. Hadley stiffened but kept a smile on her face. "We both love Portland and our jobs. We're completely simpatico."

"Simpatico?" Jon raised an eyebrow.

"That's so great," Lydia said. "There's nothing better than marrying someone who can also be your friend. Someone who gets you."

She put her arms around Jon. "I know I feel very fortunate to have found that."

Jon grinned bigger than Tyler had ever seen before and pressed his lips to hers. "I'm the lucky one."

"I just realized we have another thing in common," Lydia said to Hadley. "We both fell for our boss. I don't know about you, but that made things real awkward at first."

"Awkward is the perfect way to describe it," Hadley replied.

"Well, Lydia doesn't work for me anymore. We're partners now." Jon took her hand and kissed the back of it like he thought he was Prince Charming. "Why don't we find a cork-screw and join the party. The girls are champing at the bit to see Uncle Ty and Aunt Hadley."

Tyler could feel Hadley tense. She tucked some hair behind her ear and fidgeted with her earring. He prayed she'd be able to pull this off. They were in so deep. No going back now without humiliating himself. None of his brothers would ever let him live this down.

"Come on, Trout," Jon said to the dog as he led the group back to the rest of the family.

"One more time!" Abby shouted as she held

on to Ethan's hands and climbed up his legs before flipping herself over.

"It's my turn," Genevieve insisted. "Daddy, Abby keeps taking my turn."

"Abby, you can't monopolize Uncle Ethan," Jon scolded.

The sweet girl titled her head to the side. "What's mononolize?"

"It means you have to give your sister a turn," Jon explained.

"Hey, Gen, I bet Uncle Tyler would love to flip one of you around," Ben said from the couch. He had an arm wrapped around Rachel's shoulders while her sweet baby girl sat on her lap. On the other side of Rachel sat Grace and her baby bump. Tyler watched as both women gave Hadley a good once-over.

"Can you help me flip?" Gen stood in front of Tyler and stared up at him with her big blue eyes.

Tyler wasn't used to being around kids. He certainly didn't know how to help them flip. "I'm not sure I know how to do that."

"It's easy," Gen said with confidence. "Hold my hands. And then hold me tight so I can flip." She put her bare feet on his jean-clad shins and scaled him like a tiny ninja. She flipped over and beamed up at him. "I did it!"

Abby ran over. "My turn with Uncle Tyler. You can flip with Uncle Ethan."

"No! I get to play with Uncle Tyler and you get Uncle Ethan."

It was an all-out battle and the prize was Tyler's attention. Ethan's face fell. He went from the favorite uncle to chopped liver in two seconds flat.

"How about the two of you go wash up for dinner and give your uncle Tyler a chance to talk to the adults for a couple minutes," Jon said. The girls groaned but with a little more coaxing went to clean up.

"Don't worry, Ethan," Ben said. "Once they get to know Tyler, you'll be their favorite again."

His comment stung even though he was probably right. No one ever chose him when there were so many Blackwells to pick from.

HADLEY WRESTLED WITH her nerves as they stood in Jon's family room. Hadley Sullivan, Brand Strategist for 2K Marketing. It had such a wonderful ring to it. She kept repeating her new title over and over in her head. She was here to get that job. All she had to do was convince Tyler's family they were in love.

The word *love* made her stomach turn. Tyler had placed his hand on the small of her back as they made their way to where the rest of the family was waiting. It had sent a tingle up her spine.

"I think once they get to know him, they'll fall head over heels and it won't have anything to do with the flips he helped them do," Hadley said in her fake fiancée's defense.

"I like her already," Rachel said, getting up off the couch and handing the baby to Ben. "She's protective, which is good. The Blackwell boys are always at each other's throats. It's been a long time, Ty." She gave him a hug and held out her hand. "Rachel Blackwell. It's nice to meet you, Hadley."

Hadley had felt more confident about winning over Lydia than she did Rachel and Grace, but maybe they wouldn't be as tough on her as she feared. Grace jumped up and introduced herself, as well. She was the same age as Tyler and Chance and knew them well. Hopefully not too well that she'd catch on to the lie.

"You look so nice. Didn't Tyler tell you we

were just hanging out on the ranch?" Grace asked.

Dressing up had been Hadley's idea, but seeing the other ladies in their shorts and T-shirts made her long for some comfy clothes. Hadley was used to blending in, not standing out. Her floral shift dress and high heels made it impossible to fade into the background. But that was the point. Tyler didn't want to be in Montana and Hadley was there to help him drive that point home.

"Guess I was trying to make a good first impression. Plus, I have no idea what you wear on a ranch. The most casual I get back in Portland is when I'm at yoga."

"Another city girl," Jon said. "Lydia was a little bit of a fish out of water when she got here, too. Remember those boots?"

Lydia scowled at him playfully. "I liked those boots. But this place and way of life does have a way of growing on you real quick."

"Can you imagine if everyone moved back to Falcon Creek? Wouldn't you boys love that?" Grace asked, pushing her glasses up her nose.

"I sure would," Ethan piped up. "I wouldn't even mind sharing the best uncle title with you,

Tyler." He was trying too hard and they were already prepared for his oversell of Montana.

Tyler gently placed his hand on the back of Hadley's neck. The tingling returned. "Hadley and I love Mount Hood and Portland's eccentricities. We'd never survive in Falcon Creek. Would we, honey?"

"I can't imagine," Hadley said. "Don't get me wrong, this is a beautiful place to visit and family is so important, but I need my Black Rock Coffee and Voodoo Doughnuts in the morning."

"Doughnuts?" Both girls came running and squealing.

"Are we having doughnuts?" Genevieve asked as she slid to a stop in the middle of the room.

"The next time you guys come to Portland to visit me and Hadley, we'll take you to Voodoo Doughnuts. You can get one with Froot Loops on it."

"Cereal on a doughnut?" Abby asked with wide-eyed disbelief.

"My favorite one has bacon on top," Hadley confessed. That was the honest truth. Maple bacon doughnuts were her favorite indulgence.

"Bacon on a doughnut?" Gen couldn't believe it.

"I thought everyone in Portland was vegan. Last time we were there, I saw a sign advertising gluten-free vegan pizza as if people were in the market for that. I still wonder what it could possibly taste like," Jon said with his arms folded over his chest.

"It's actually pretty good." Hadley had shared one with Maggie before. Maggie was the quintessential Portlander. If there was a Portlandia cliché, she fit it.

"Maybe we need to eat some chili and corn bread to purge the thought of gluten-free vegan pizza from Jon's wheat-and-meat-loving brain," Lydia suggested.

"Corn bread is actually gluten-free," Ethan pointed out.

Jon rolled his eyes and invited everyone into the kitchen. Hadley started to follow the family when Tyler moved his hand to her cheek and leaned in to press a soft kiss to her lips.

"You two are so cute," Grace said with a sigh before following Ethan out of the room.

"You're so awesome at this," he whispered.

Hadley couldn't think straight. Her insides were mush. Kissing was not part of the deal.

She had made that clear before she had accepted his insane proposal. Of course, that was back when she thought kissing him would make her uncomfortable. Right now, she wanted to wrap her arms around his neck and kiss him a little harder.

One stupid kiss and she was ready to renegotiate the terms of their deal. Hadley needed to pull it together or she could lose everything—the job and herself in the process.

CHAPTER SEVEN

"No kissing. That was the rule." Hadley had managed to wait until they were in the car to confront him.

"Why are you bringing that up now?"

"You kissed me," Hadley reminded him. It was a little offensive that he acted like it was forgettable. "Before dinner. That wasn't part of the deal."

"Come on," Tyler said with a groan as they drove back to the Blackwell Ranch. "It wasn't like I made out with you in front of everyone. I gave you an innocent little kiss. Grace is fully convinced that we're a couple. Heck, I think the whole family believes it to be true."

Oh, everyone was convinced tonight. Even Hadley started to believe that they had feelings for one another, and that was nonsense. Tyler Blackwell loved nothing but his work. He even had a love/hate relationship with his own brothers. Falling for someone like him was asking for nothing but trouble.

"I am not comfortable with being that comfortable with each other. You are still my boss. This isn't a partnership like Jon and Lydia. This is a business arrangement and we need to make sure it stays that way."

"What else could it be?" Tyler's gaze slid to her for a second. "Did you think... You didn't think I was... Please tell me you weren't confused about my intentions."

Hadley's face burned from the embarrassment. She turned her head so he couldn't see it. "No. I wasn't confused. I know what this is. I just think that we don't want to muddy the waters moving forward so neither one of us gets confused."

"I'm not falling in love with you, Hadley."

She knew that shouldn't hurt her feelings, yet there was a little twinge of rejection in her chest. "I have no plans to fall in love with you either," she scoffed. "It's actually inconceivable to me."

"Good." He paused. "I mean, *inconceivable*? I feel like that's a strong word choice. *Misguided* or maybe *wishful thinking...*"

She glared at him for a second. Was he serious? What were they arguing about here?

"Forget it," he said. "It's good. I feel the same as you do. I'm not going to ever be confused. I kissed you because it was part of the act, but if that made you uncomfortable, I won't do it again. Kissing is off the table."

"It's totally off the table. It's not even in the room. It's not in the house. It's out of town."

Tyler laughed. "Boy, tell me how you really feel about it."

Hadley had too many feelings about this arrangement. None of them were particularly positive either. "I feel nervous. I feel like my future rides on how well I play your fiancée and that's really scary."

"We made a deal. You want a promotion and I want to get through this visit without my brothers finding out I lied. I don't understand why you're worried. There's no reason we both shouldn't get what we want."

Hadley fingered the hem of her dress. The fact that she had to do this to get the job also made her angry. They were in this mess only because he didn't want to admit to his brothers that he was single. He had issues. Another reason to dismiss any chance of their being in anything more than a fake relationship.

"Well, I shouldn't have to kiss you to get a promotion."

Tyler pulled up in front of Heavenly Pines. He put the car in Park and turned his body in her direction. His eyes were the kind of blue that made a woman stop and stare.

"I respect you, Hadley. I shouldn't have kissed you. The promotion is not dependent on you doing whatever I say. I don't want you to feel like you can't say what you're really feeling, at least, to me. I'm asking you to help me get the ranch sold and to help me save face with my family. That's it."

She wanted to believe what he said. He sounded sincere. The look in his eyes screamed he meant what he said. Yet, the uneasy feeling in her gut said there was no guarantee.

"I know you're putting your trust in me. I want to trust you, too."

"I won't kiss you again. I promise."

Hadley swallowed hard and nodded her head. All she could focus on was his lips as they told her they would never touch her again, even though they had felt so good against hers earlier tonight.

Maybe she could trust him, but could she trust herself? One minute she was telling him he better never kiss her again and the next minute she was thinking about how good it would be to try once more. How did this get so complicated?

Hadley Sullivan, Brand Strategist for 2K Marketing. This needed to be her battle cry. She had a goal and it had nothing to do with Tyler's lips or his hands touching her. Her goal was to work for him and Kellen in the position she deserved.

With her resolve back, she got out of the car and took notice of the millions of stars shining bright in the Montana sky. She paused on the porch to take it all in. What happened tonight was like one of those stars, a tiny point in an enormous sky. There was so much more ahead. She wouldn't lose sight again.

"Are you coming?" Tyler asked from the door.

"I'm going to enjoy the view for a few minutes," she replied, resting her elbows on the railing. Hadley needed to clear her head and figure out how to make sure nothing derailed her from getting what she wanted.

HADLEY WAS SO STRANGE. Tyler had thought he'd known her when he asked her to come with him, but she was way more complicated. Sometimes, usually in the most stressful situations, she was beyond calm. Other times, he seemed to rattle her with little effort.

He tossed his rental car keys on the coffee table in the sitting room. Tonight had been a win. No one suspected he was lying. Hadley had helped him successfully convince everyone that Portland was the only place he wanted to call home. And…he'd kissed her.

In truth, the kiss was a bit more impulsive than he had let on. Hadley had this way of drawing him in that was catching him off guard time and time again. It was extremely unexpected given the fact that before they got to Montana, he'd never thought of her as anything more than an employee.

Not that he thought of her any other way now.

Tyler shook his head, hoping to shake all thoughts of kissing Hadley from it permanently. He couldn't let it happen again. She certainly didn't want that. He went back to the bedroom and unbuttoned his shirt. He slipped out of it and was just about to put it on the bed when he noticed one of the dresses Hadley had been considering for dinner laid out on the other side of the king-size bed they were in no way going to share.

He needed to be a gentleman and offer her the bedroom. He went into the closet in search of some extra blankets. Snatching a pillow off the bed, he headed for the couch, hoping it had a pull-out hiding under those cushions.

Hadley walked in and froze. "I didn't realize you…" she said, quickly averting her eyes. "I'll go back out on the porch until you put on a shirt."

She was out the door before he could say anything. This was the kind of rattled he didn't expect from her. He threw on a T-shirt and grabbed two bottles of water from the fridge.

Hadley sat on the bench, hugging one of the pillows. He handed her a water bottle. "We're going to have to get used to sharing a living space. I plan to sleep on the couch, by the way. The bedroom is all yours."

"You don't have to do that. This is your family's place. You should have a bed."

Tyler took a seat next to her. The moon was almost full and cast a soft light across the horse pasture. "I told you I was working on being nice to you while we're here. Please take the bed so I can feel as if I accomplished that goal."

"How about we take turns? First week, I get the bed. Second week, it's yours."

She was hard to please or maybe just unwilling to let him have his way. He realized that was one of the things he liked most about her at work. She challenged him. Challenged the way he thought about things, made him question his ideas before they moved forward on a project. It made him better.

"Sounds fair," he conceded. They spent the next few minutes in silence. It wasn't as uncomfortable as Tyler might have thought.

"I bet the sunsets are gorgeous from this spot," Hadley mused.

"We'll have to make time to watch one before we head home."

Hadley blew out a long breath. "I can't wait to go home."

"We just got here and you're ready to leave?"

"Aren't you?" She quirked an eyebrow.

"Of course I am. I never wanted to come here in the first place. You were the one who said it solved all the problems. I'm still waiting for one to get solved."

"I think we need to solve one big problem," she said, crossing her legs. "We've got to be able to trust each other if this is going to work."

He trusted her. He must. To bring her into this and to let her see this side of his life, there had to be trust. Tyler let her words sink in for a second. Maybe she wasn't talking about him trusting her.

"Do you not trust me?" He recognized that he could demand a lot out of the people who worked for him, but he was always a man of his word. At least, he tried to be. He didn't like how her potential distrust felt.

"I want to."

That was clearly not a yes.

"Is this still about the kiss?" He threw his hands up. "I can assure you that I'll be hands-off from now on. We're going to be too busy working to have to put on a show."

Hadley shook her head and hugged the buffalo-checked pillow closer. "That's not it. It's more about the job. I'm here for one reason, and that's to get the promotion. But there's part of me that's afraid there's no guarantee."

"I said I would talk to Kellen. It won't be hard to convince him given Eric's performance so far."

"And what if he is hard to convince? What if he doesn't want to give me the job, then what?"

Kellen wouldn't fight him on this. Eric was his nephew, but he was also terrible at the job. They wouldn't have to fire him. He could become office manager, something a little more appropriate for his skill set.

"I'll promote you no matter what Kellen says about Eric. We can have two brand strategists if that's what he wants."

"I want to believe that…"

What did she want him to say? Did he need to sign his name in blood? Since when was his word not good enough? She wasn't going to let this go until he proved to her that the job was hers.

"How about I call Kellen tomorrow and let him know that when we get back, you'll be taking over the job? Will that ease your mind?"

Hadley got up and walked to the porch railing. She spun around and leaned back against it. "That would help tremendously."

"We have a busy day ahead of us," Tyler said, getting to his feet. "I'm going to get some sleep now that we got all these trust issues resolved."

"Good idea." Hadley walked past him and

into the cabin. The flowery scent of her perfume was left in her wake. It was a bit intoxicating.

Falling for him was inconceivable, she'd said. He'd promised never to touch her or kiss her again. She'd made it clear that being here was only about her promotion. There was no reason he should be thinking about how good she smelled.

He was the unlovable Blackwell. That wasn't changing anytime soon.

CHAPTER EIGHT

"Kiss me," Hadley whispered.

"I can't. I promised." Where his self-control was coming from, Tyler didn't know.

Hadley ran a finger down his nose and pressed it to his lips. "You've never broken a promise before?"

He'd broken a few, but not one like this. Kissing was off the table. It wasn't even supposed to be in the house. However, that look in her eyes was saying he had the green light.

"I don't want you to get the wrong idea," he said, wondering what the right idea truly was at this point.

"Kiss me, Tyler."

How could he resist?

A pounding on the door disrupted Tyler's well-earned sleep and dangerous dream. He rolled over and fell off the couch. He'd forgotten he wasn't in a bed. The knocking persisted.

He shook off the fog of sleep. No one could

know that he'd slept on the couch. He gathered up his blanket and pillow.

"Just a minute!"

Tyler tossed his bedding into the bedroom and shook Hadley awake. "Someone's here. We have to get up."

Hadley bolted upright. Confusion was quickly replaced by panic. "What time is it?"

Tyler had no idea. He scanned the room for a clock. His phone was still charging out in the other room. An alarm clock on the far nightstand read eight thirty.

"Way too early," he grumbled. "Stay back here."

He checked the sitting room for any signs he'd slept out there before opening the door. Katie smiled on the front porch.

"Good morning, sunshine!" She grinned, proving she was nothing but redheaded trouble.

"What are you doing here this early in the morning?"

"Early? I've been working for over an hour and it's about time I got some help. We have fencing that needs fixing on the north side of the horse pasture."

"And what does that have to do with me?"

Katie tipped her hat back. "You're here to help, right?"

"Not to fix fences. I'm here to fix the website and build a Facebook page. You must have me confused with Ethan. He can help you and Lochlan with the manual labor." Tyler began to shut the door. Katie stuck her hand out to stop him.

"Listen, my dad is in Arizona visiting an old friend and finally getting some R & R. I'm in charge around here and Ethan is already up and helping. I thought your fiancée was here to handle the internet stuff. You, on the other hand, are a Blackwell. We need your muscle."

"That's pretty sexist for a female ranch hand," Hadley said from behind him. She was wrapped up in a robe and had her hair pulled into a ponytail. Thoughts of her asking for a kiss crept back into Tyler's consciousness. "What if I want to help with the fence?"

"Truthfully, I would be happy with either one of you. If you want to join me, you're welcome to come."

"Will I get to see the horses if I come?" Hadley asked.

"I'll show you all of our horses if you help me out," Katie promised.

Tyler was annoyed by Katie and impressed by Hadley. "Give us a few minutes to get ready," he said, shutting the door in Katie's smiling face.

"You don't have to fix the fence. I can do it," he said, following Hadley back to the bedroom. "Spending the morning with Katie wasn't exactly how I imagined my first full day back, but I'm a little worried that with her dad gone, she's got too much on her plate. If she's asking for help, she must really need it."

"Look at you putting someone else's needs before your own. I like this side of you." She pulled some jeans out of the dresser and yanked a shirt out of the closet. "But, you *need* to make a phone call, so I will help Katie with the fence."

Hadley wasn't about to let him forget about talking to Kellen. He had to admire her determination. "I'll call Kellen first thing."

"Perfect. I'm going to get ready so I can mend a fence," she said, grinning from ear to ear and disappearing into the bathroom.

Tyler sat on the edge of the bed and ran his hands down his face. Why was he dreaming about Hadley? Everything had been settled last night. The two of them were on the same page.

Mutual trust had been established. Why would his subconscious try to ruin everything?

Throwing himself into work would help keep his focus where it should be. He had pictures to take, a website to build and a phone call to make. Hopefully, Kellen would be on board with Hadley's promotion.

He moved back out to the sitting room and grabbed his phone off the side table. Resisting the urge to check all his emails, he dialed Kellen.

"Tyler, you're supposed to be on vacation." Kellen sounded like he'd been woken up. It was almost eight there, why wasn't he on his way to the office? There was so much to do and Tyler trusted him to take care of all of it.

"I am on vacation."

"Why are you calling me? People on vacation do not call their business partners."

He wanted to point out that when one partner was on vacation, the other one should perhaps work a little harder. Lucky for Hadley, Tyler remembered his true reason for calling. He couldn't risk getting Kellen angry if he wanted him to agree to the job changes.

"I forgot to mention to you before I left that I feel Hadley should take over as brand strategist when I return. Eric is a great kid, but he'd be better suited for a less challenging position, one that suits his skill set."

Kellen was quiet on the other end. Tyler feared he'd hung up until he spoke. "Eric needs some time to adjust. He's learning and he likes what he's doing. I'm not going to fire him."

"I didn't say fire. I implied reassign."

"You want me to demote him before we give him a chance to shine." Kellen was overprotective of his sister's son. That made him a good uncle but a terrible businessman.

"We can't afford to keep him where he's at. There will be repercussions if we drag this out much longer. Plus, Hadley would need no time to acclimate to the job. She'd be ready to go day one."

"What we can't afford is to pay Hadley to be brand strategist. She's great, but I made a commitment to Eric. I'll work with him. Get him up to par before your return."

"Kellen." Tyler needed be more persuasive, but Hadley came out of the bedroom in her tight jeans and T-shirt knotted at her hip. Her hair was pulled into two braids that hung over her shoulders.

"Am I dressed right for the job?" she asked

before noticing he was on the phone. She smacked a hand over her mouth.

"Was that Hadley?" Kellen asked. As far as everyone in the office was concerned, Tyler was on vacation visiting family and Hadley had taken over one of his California projects while he was gone. No one at 2K knew they were together.

"Hadley? Of course not. Why would Hadley be in Montana with me? That was my ranch hand. I have to go fix a fence so the cattle don't get loose in the mountains."

"Sorry, I guess I had Hadley on the brain," Kellen said. "I'll let you get back to your vacation."

"I'll talk to you later." Tyler couldn't argue about the job in front of Hadley. If she knew Kellen had shot down the idea, she'd reconsider helping him out.

"Was that Kellen?" The expectant look on Hadley's face tightened the knot in his shoulders.

"It was. We're all set. When we get back, you'll have a promotion."

Hadley threw her fists in the air. "Yes! Thank you, Ty. I appreciate you talking to him today. I promise to do everything I can to keep your secret."

She was so happy. It made him feel amazing and terrible at the same time. He hadn't planned to lie. It just came out like the lie about being engaged. This one would hopefully be untrue only until the next time he talked to Kellen and argued his point a little longer.

"You better get out there. Katie's probably champing at the bit to get to work."

HADLEY WAS THRILLED. Everything had worked out in her favor. All she had to do was smile and play Tyler's wife-to-be. Without the doubt that Tyler wouldn't come through with the job, she could stay focused on the present instead of the future.

"I have to admit, I was a little surprised you offered to get your hands dirty," Katie said as they drove her pickup truck to the broken section of the fence.

"I figured I might as well enjoy the whole experience while I'm here. I also love horses. I've been waiting to meet them."

Katie's brow furrowed. "Really? Ethan told me he got the impression you were a city girl through and through."

That was the impression she had wanted to give. Hadley was a little surprised that Ethan had already shared that with Katie.

"I am, but a city girl can love horses. Can't she?"

Katie mulled that over for a second. "I don't see why not."

Fixing the fence wasn't as labor intensive as Hadley had imagined. Katie did most of the work while Hadley basically held things in place. The two women loaded the tools back into the truck. There wasn't a cloud in the sky today and things were heating up. Hadley wiped the sweat from her brow.

"It's supposed to be in the mideighties today. You need a hat or you're going to be red as a strawberry later tonight," Katie said, flicking the front of her cowboy hat.

"I didn't bring a hat like that. Portland girls wear beanies."

"Beanies?"

"You know, a knit hat. A beanie."

Katie's freckled nose scrunched up like she'd smelled something bad. "Yeah, we don't wear those unless it's snowing. Even then, we wear one of these," she said, pointing to her cowboy hat.

"I'll have to go into town and get me one of those. It will be a fun souvenir to take home."

"I wonder what Tyler did with all of his hats. That boy used to live in cowboy hats." Katie made her way around the driver's side of the truck and hopped in.

Hadley climbed in the other side. Katie was full of interesting information. "Really? I can't picture him like that. He's so suit and tie."

"Tyler used to be all cowboy. Before his parents died, he used to tell everyone he was going to run this place. Of course, most people assumed it would be Jon."

"Jon was their dad's favorite, so that makes sense."

Katie started the truck up but didn't put it into Drive. She rolled down her window. "Is that what Tyler told you?"

"Of course he did. He thinks all his brothers were someone's favorite. Except for him. He was no one's favorite apparently."

Shaking her head, Katie laughed. "The Blackwell boys compete over everything. Even who loves who the most, I guess."

"They are a unique crew. Must have been fun growing up with them. Tyler said he thinks of you like a little sister."

"Annoying little sister, I bet."

Hadley held her hands up in defense. "I didn't say that."

"I know Tyler well enough."

"The stories you could tell." Hadley didn't know why she was so curious. Maybe it was because he had been unwilling to share much about himself after she unloaded everything there was to know about herself.

"Oh, I could tell you things that would entertain you for hours, but get me in a world of trouble with Tyler."

"Tell me one thing. Something you don't think I know about him." Which was pretty much anything. Something told Hadley the Tyler she did know wasn't the same one Katie grew up with.

"Tyler was famous for taking off and being gone for hours. He used to roam this ranch from one end to the other. When he was a teenager, I can remember Big E calling my dad more than once and asking him to go looking for him. Ty would take a horse out on his own and disappear all day. It drove his grandpa and his brothers nuts."

Tyler was a wanderer? That was not the Tyler that Hadley knew. Her Tyler was in the office all the time. In fact, he probably went in on the weekends. Enjoying the great outdoors didn't seem like his thing at all. It was part of the reason she offered to help Katie this morning. Tyler had seemed less than pleased with the idea of working outside.

"It's hard to imagine him like that. He's very controlled and a bit of a workaholic," Hadley shared.

"Ben was the one I figured would love working in a corner office overlooking a big city and wearing fancy suits. No one would have guessed Ben would show up here, fall in love with the girl next door and settle down in Falcon Creek. When Tyler left, he said he'd never be back, but I thought for sure he'd miss this land. He's the one I imagined running this place."

That was *definitely* not the Tyler that Hadley knew. Her boss wanted nothing more than to finish his business here and go back to Portland.

Katie pulled the truck up to the horse barn, where the guests came to meet up for the various riding activities the ranch had planned every day. Ethan led a horse out of the barn.

"Looks like I'm stuck with Ethan, though. Ready to meet the horses?" Katie asked.

Hadley couldn't wait. She loved horses as a kid. Her mom had let her take riding lessons for a couple of years before she went to high school and all of her after-school time had been filled with sports and Future Business Leaders of America club meetings.

"Good morning!" Ethan greeted them. "Where's Ty?"

"Most likely redesigning the website," Hadley said. "He's very determined to get things done so we can focus on planning our wedding."

Ethan adjusted the baseball hat on his head. "Grace and I keep saying we need to do that, too. It's not easy when we have so many other things on our plate. I don't think we even talked weddings last night at dinner. Have you two picked a date?"

"I'd like to get married next spring. It's my favorite time of the year."

"Big wedding or small?" Katie asked.

Hadley had no reason not to dream big since this was all a fantasy anyways. "Oh, I want a big wedding with all our family and friends. I want to be a princess for an entire day. Big dress, lots of flowers, a party to remember. Tyler said I can have anything I want. He's been so supportive of all my crazy ideas."

"Tyler would want the biggest and the best. He'd want to make sure he outshined the rest of us," Ethan said, opening the gate to the paddock. "We've got our adult group going out for a ride in a few minutes. They get a little cattle clinic, as well. You want to join?"

Hadley couldn't say yes fast enough. She wasn't so sure about the cattle working, but she was all about going horseback riding. "I used to ride when I was younger. I loved it."

"You did?" Ethan seemed as surprised as Katie had. "Miss City Girl used to ride?"

"Well, not to wrangle cattle. I used to do English riding. Very civilized."

"That makes more sense," he said with a nod. "We're going to make a Western rider out of you over the next couple weeks. You know, we do a rodeo with the guests on Saturdays. We let them show off what they've learned. Maybe we can get you into an event."

"That sounds like fun." Something to look forward to. Maybe being here wouldn't be so bad.

"This lady needs a hat and some sunscreen

before she heads out otherwise she's going to be so sunburned, she won't be able to do anything the rest of her visit," Katie said. "Here, take my hat and I'll grab another one later."

"Thanks," Hadley replied, taking the hat and trying it on. "Do I fit in now?"

Ethan was quick to answer. "It's like you were born to wear a cowboy hat. I don't know, Hadley. I think we might convince you to stay after all."

Shoot. That wasn't the plan. Was she enjoying this too much? "Don't get your hopes up, Ethan. I can probably convince Tyler to visit more often, but moving back here is never going to happen."

"Never say never," he said with a wink. "I learned that the hard way."

CHAPTER NINE

TYLER WASN'T A professional photographer, but he was quite impressed with the photos he had taken so far. Maybe he had missed his calling or maybe this landscape was simply too gorgeous not to shine on camera.

He leaned against his car and rested his foot on the bumper. Taking a deep breath, he found himself transported back in time to when he used to roam the ranch in search of adventure. Back then, all he had needed was the fresh air, the quiet rumblings of nature and the sun on his face. Back then, he had imagined himself growing old on this ranch.

That feeling lasted until it became abundantly clear Big E didn't have any plans to trust Tyler with anything having to do with the ranch. Sometimes he wondered if Big E lumped him together with his twin, who was never interested in a rancher's lifestyle. In the end, Tyler decided he simply wasn't good enough, smart enough or important enough for his grandfather.

In the distance, a group of people on horseback came up over the ridge. Tyler took a few pictures of them and waited for them to get closer to take a few more.

"Now, if you look up ahead, you'll see something very rare. Over there by that car is one of the infamous Blackwell brothers. These guys don't come out much, so this is a real treat." Conner Hannah was their newly hired wrangler. Ethan had been searching for someone with the gift of gab and Conner seemed to fit the bill perfectly. They had gone to high school together. Conner was Ethan's and Ben's age.

"Tyler!" Hadley waved from the back of the pack.

He zoomed in on her through the lens of his camera. She had on a cowboy hat and threw her head back laughing when her horse sped up to a trot for a second. Before he realized what he was doing, Tyler had snapped several pictures of her.

He dropped the camera down and rubbed the spot in the center of his chest that suddenly was aching. Hadley worked for him. He was her boss. That was all he could ever be. Should ever be.

He walked over to the group as they approached. "You folks having a good time?"

Everyone agreed that it was a blast. Hadley looked like a kid in a candy store. It made him smile to see her so happy.

"Come here and meet Dewey, Ty. He's such a good horse." She turned to the rider on the chestnut trail horse next to her. "Pete, this is my fiancé. Tyler, this is Pete Sunnywell. Pete's here with his family this week but was thinking about having his company retreat here next summer. I told him we would love to talk to him about setting something up."

Tyler gave Dewey a pat on the neck even though he wanted to hug his fake fiancée. Hadley managed to create business opportunities for the ranch while getting her horseback riding in.

"We could absolutely set something up. We'll sit down with you sometime this week to talk it over."

Conner circled around to the back of the group. "We've got to keep moving, boss."

"I'm going to hang on to this pretty lady and

her horse. We'll get Dewey back to the horse barn safe and sound, I promise."

"No problem. It was good to meet you, Hadley. Anytime you want a mini cattle clinic, let me know. I'd be happy to take you out."

A strange sensation began to build in Tyler's chest. "If anyone is going to teach her how to wrangle cattle, it's me."

Conner tipped his hat. "Gotcha, boss."

Hadley dismounted the horse and waved goodbye to her new group of friends. She had a way of fitting in no matter what the situation. Tyler envied that.

"Sorry for taking off on you after Katie and I finished fixing the fence. Ethan talked me into going on this ride and I couldn't say no."

"It's fine. Glad you're having fun." He meant it, which was odd for him to say. Usually he cared only about getting the job done. *Fun* wasn't in his vocabulary. "I like your hat," he said, flicking the brim so it fell over her eyes.

She pushed it back. Her smile was dazzling. "It's Katie's. She let me borrow it so I didn't fry in the sun. You forgot to tell me to pack some hats."

Tyler adjusted his own baseball cap. "I didn't

think about it. I was lucky I thought to pack one for myself."

"Katie said you used to live in ten-gallon Stetsons."

Tyler felt the corners of his mouth curl up at the memory of the impressive hat collection he had when he was younger. "I don't know about ten-gallon, but I had a pretty sweet black cattleman's hat."

"Katie also said you used to get lost, roaming around the ranch in your cowboy hat."

His lips fell into a straight line. He didn't want to think about what else Katie might have said about him. "I'm sure Katie had lots to say, but let's talk about the ranch."

Hadley paused and tilted her head to the side for a second. "Okay, let's talk about the ranch." Before Tyler could say anything she began, "Did you know that there's an archery area on the south side and sand volleyball court? I know that there are enough cattle here to still consider this a working ranch, but Ethan has this idea to add more hands-on experiences for guests, which would make it potentially twice as profitable for you guys. And I have this idea, it might seem a little crazy, but hear me out—"

Tyler put his hands on her shoulders. "Whoa, slow down."

Their eyes locked and Tyler felt frozen in place. She licked her lips and his mind wandered where he had forbid it to go. Kissing her was off the table. He had to take a step back so he didn't do something foolish like pull her against him.

"Sorry," she said, tugging on one of her braids. "I didn't mean to get overexcited, but your brother has some really great ideas that could make this place successful."

"Successful for whoever comes in and buys it from us so we can all go back to our real lives," Tyler added.

Hadley's face fell. "Right. Of course."

"I got pictures of everything on the property. I need you to help me figure out how we want to put everything together. I also need you to rough out a few marketing brochures for us to send out to potential buyers."

"Tyler Blackwell—all business, all the time," she said. "I told your family I might know you better than they do now."

Tyler wasn't sure how to take that since she sounded disappointed. How could the Tyler his family knew be better than the one he was now?

Hadley's thoughts were all over the place, making focusing on the task at hand more difficult. She felt like there was something she needed to tell Tyler, but she couldn't remember what it was for the life of her.

"Which one of these do you like better?" Tyler asked, turning his laptop screen toward her. "This one or this one?"

She got off the couch and moved over to the desk he had claimed as his workspace. "I like the first one better."

"Me, too." He added it to the webpage he was working on.

Hadley raised her arms above her head and stretched. She'd forgotten how riding a horse made her use muscles she usually didn't. "I'm almost done with the cabin descriptions. I'm not sure how to make the Evergreen sound distinctive. It's basically the same as Sunrise Ridge."

"It's closer to the main lodge for people who don't want a long walk to dinner."

Mentioning dinner made Hadley's stomach growl. She was starving. She'd left first thing in the morning to help Katie and came back to the cabin to work on the website with Tyler after horseback riding. No breakfast, no lunch. It was almost one o'clock. She needed food.

"Speaking of food… What do you say we go check out what's to eat in the lodge?"

"I really want to get this page done. But you can go if you want."

She put her hands on his shoulders and gave them a little rub. His muscles were so tight. "Don't make me eat lunch by myself. Even you take a lunch break when we're at the office. I've seen you eating at your desk."

"Working lunches are not a lunch break. If we want to get this website up and running, we have to keep working."

"I promise not to ask you to take another break if you go with me now. We can grab some stuff to bring back here for dinner so we can have a working dinner," she offered in compromise.

He gave a heavy sigh. "Fine."

She talked him into walking to the lodge instead of driving, so they could stretch their legs. They passed the horseshoe pits. A family was playing kids versus parents. The youngest boy was up and his brother was cheering him on as he tossed the horseshoe at the stake.

He managed to throw a ringer and the boys high-fived.

"Nice toss!" Hadley shouted as they walked by.

The boy beamed. "Thank you!"

Tyler smirked.

"What?" she asked, tugging on his arm.

He stared at her hands wrapped around his forearm. She quickly let go. "You make friends wherever you go," he noted.

"No reason not to."

Being nice to people encouraged them to be nice back. It was something her father had taught her since she was little. Her dad was the kind of guy who made nice with everyone, from the mailman to the attendant at the gas station. At restaurants, he treated the busboy as kindly as the manager who came over to see how their dinner tasted. It didn't matter how important someone's job was, everyone was treated with the same respect.

"Wouldn't it be fun to put in a playground for the kids in this space here? Maybe sell ice cream and some snacks from a food truck." She pointed to the spot that was absolutely perfect for that setup.

Tyler shoved his hands in his pockets. "Maybe."

"When I was doing some research on guest ranches, I found one that had an outdoor cooking spot, too. That would be so much fun. We've already got the picnic benches behind the lodge. Set up a fire pit back there and get someone to cook some eggs to order and some bacon or sausage. People would love it. And pay for the cowboy experience."

"You're just full of ideas. Ethan's going to think you want to run the place instead of sell it, which is the opposite of what I want."

All the wind was taken from her sails. There was so much potential in this place and she couldn't stop herself from seeing it and wanting to build on it. But Tyler was right, those ideas were better sold to whoever would buy this place. Getting Ethan excited about the future was pointless when the ranch wouldn't be the Blackwells' anymore.

"Right. I'll save it for the prospective buyers. Help them see what they could do to expand."

"Thank you. The less Ethan thinks about what he can do with this place, the better. His focus needs to be on being Falcon Creek's veterinarian. The guest ranch will be someone else's problem soon enough."

Hadley felt sorry for Ethan. She could see how someone might feel connected to this place. Letting it go was going to be hard. Not for someone like Tyler, but it seemed the Blackwell brothers were all very different from one another.

They entered the lodge and found the dining room almost empty. Everyone must have hit the buffet early. A morning full of outdoor activities could work up some mighty appetites. Hadley knew she was ready to eat all of whatever was left.

"Tyler! Hadley!" Grace waved from one of the long banquet tables. She had two plates of food in front of her. Hadley wondered for a minute if Ethan was here, as well. "Come sit with me. I hate eating alone."

No Ethan. In her defense, Grace was eating for two. Hadley and Tyler took seats across from her. The dining room had a rustic charm to it. The tables were covered in white table-cloths and guests could either order off the menu of foods served family style or go through the buffet.

"Finally getting some lunch?" Grace asked.

Hadley put her hand on Tyler's back, trying to appear more like a happily engaged couple. "I had to drag this guy away from his computer or we were going to starve."

"I'll have to remember to check in and invite you to eat with me in case he tries that again. I love coming here for lunch. All-you-can-eat buffets are a pregnant woman's dream come true."

Grace was easy to talk to. She seemed like someone Hadley would be friends with if they lived in the same town. She'd be the perfect sister-in-law if they were both really marrying Blackwells. But Hadley wasn't a real member of that special club.

TYLER THOUGHT HADLEY was hungry but all she wanted to do was chitchat with Grace. He had a million things to do, like find a moment to call Kellen back without Hadley around.

"I'm going to go grab some food. Do you want to come with me, dear?" he asked Hadley.

Reminding her there was food seemed to do the trick. She was quick to end their conversation about the deer Hadley had seen on her horseback ride this morning. Today's buffet theme was Southwestern. They filled their plates with cheesy quesadillas and refried beans and Spanish rice. Hadley grabbed one of the fish tacos. Tyler couldn't pass up the chips and guacamole.

"You two weren't kidding about being hungry," Grace said with a laugh when they returned.

"I forgot to get some sour cream," Hadley said, getting back up.

"She's really sweet," Grace said after swallowing down some water. "She seems like a good match for you."

"Glad you approve." It was funny that anyone would think that when it was so clear to him that they were completely incompatible.

"She balances you out. You need some light to your dark."

"I'm not dark."

"You make fun of Jon for being the serious brother. Have you ever looked in the mirror?"

"I'll never be all smiles and hugs like Ethan."

There was a dreamy look in her eye. "Your brother is one of a kind. I'm very lucky."

Tyler ignored the prickly sensation of envy that ran over his skin. Grace was truly in love. He had to remind himself that Ethan deserved it. "When are you two going to tie the knot?"

"We're thinking maybe a Christmas wedding after the baby is born. What about you and Hadley? Have you made any plans yet?"

Tyler and Hadley hadn't had time to come up with fake wedding plans. He didn't think people set wedding dates right after they got engaged. He'd keep it vague and let Hadley know later what he said so she could stick to the same story.

"We haven't gotten that far. We'll probably do something like Ben and Rachel. Maybe not elope but definitely low-key. Hadley's pretty private given she's got a famous brother. She wouldn't want a lot of attention."

"Famous brother?"

"Her brother is Asher Sullivan, the actor."

"Asher Sullivan from *When We Were Young*?"

"That's him. Don't tell her I told you."

Grace waved him off. "Your secret is safe with me. It sounds like Jon and Lydia will be the first wedding. They were thinking this fall. Of course, I'll be as big as a barn by then." She picked up a chip and seemed to think twice about eating it. After a second or two, she opted to eat it anyways. "This baby better be twenty pounds when it comes out because

I have gained so much and I refuse to believe that it's due to my addiction to sweets."

"You sure it's not twins? I hear they run in my family."

Grace chuckled. "There's only one in there. We've checked. And double-checked."

Hadley returned with her dish of sour cream and two enchiladas. Tyler stopped and stared.

"What? They looked delicious. I couldn't say no."

"You are my favorite new person. I think we were destined to be sisters," Grace said.

The guilt born from his lies spoiled Tyler's appetite. He hated to get anyone in his family too attached to Hadley when she wasn't going to be around past the two weeks they were here. They were all going to be so bummed to lose her given how easily she had been accepted.

Everyone would mourn her loss except for him. At least that was what he told himself. Hadley had no place in his personal life.

Guilt wasn't the only thing making him not want to eat. There was another emotion creeping into his gut. Tyler set down his fork. Why would he feel disappointed? It wasn't like any of this could possibly be real.

CHAPTER TEN

"YES, WE'D LOVE to set up a meeting. We could tour the property, talk about our current assets. Would someone be able to come out next week?"

Tyler had been on the phone all morning trying to work a couple of leads he had regarding potential buyers for the ranch. It was Friday, day five on the ranch, and they were done updating the website and Facebook page. The rest of their time and efforts needed to be spent on booking guests and wooing buyers.

He glanced back at Hadley, who was on the couch with a piece of red licorice hanging from her mouth. She had almost eaten the entire bag they bought during their late-night run to Brewster's after Hadley had threatened to move into the lodge if they didn't stock the kitchenette with some basic staples. Tyler wasn't sure when licorice became part of a routine diet, but what Hadley wanted, she got.

"We'll see you then," Tyler said, scribbling down the date and time. He hung up and spun in his chair. "Representatives from the Mendes family are coming out on Wednesday to tour the property and hear our sales pitch."

Hadley pulled the licorice out of her mouth. "These are the people from Colorado Springs?"

"The extremely wealthy people from Colorado Springs who already own and run a dude ranch out there. They have a son who wants his own ranch, though, and they think this might be perfect for him."

"I'll dig deeper into their ranch and see how we match up in terms of facilities and livestock," Hadley said, taking a bite of the licorice and going back to her laptop. She was good at using her initiative and knowing what to do. He really liked that about her.

She had her feet up on the coffee table in front of her. Dressed in shorts and a worn-out UW T-shirt, her bare legs seemed to go on forever. Tyler liked that about her, too.

He spun back around because those were not the kind of thoughts he should be having. She was his employee. Not his fiancée. Not even his girlfriend. She was his brand strategist. He internally chastised himself. He still hadn't called Kellen to plead his case for her being promoted.

"I'm going to find Ethan. I'll be back in a few."

Hadley set her laptop down. "I'll come with you. I could use some fresh air."

"No," he said and stopped abruptly. "Sorry. I mean, I need you to get started on gathering that information. When I get back, we'll take a break. We can steal a couple horses and I'll show you all my secret spots on the property. How's that sound?"

She seemed to need a minute to adjust to his mood swing. "That sounds great," she finally replied, picking her laptop back up.

Tyler headed out and dialed Kellen. It took three rings before he picked up.

"Three days? That's as long as you could hold out for?"

"I'm calling to simply reiterate that I feel very passionate about Hadley... Wait, that came out wrong." Had it? Tyler wondered if he was beginning to lose his mind. "I meant I feel very passionately about promoting Hadley."

"I've been working closely with Eric and we're making real progress. You should see what he sent me for the Kingman account. He did really thorough research. I'll send you a copy of it so you can see he's coming around. Don't count him out yet."

Leave it to Eric to figure things out right when Tyler needed him to fail. "What if she didn't take a pay raise? What if we just gave her the title?"

"Why is this so important to you? I don't understand."

There was no way he could tell the truth. This was why lying was such a bad idea. It never ended with one lie. They always multiplied until no one could remember what the truth was anymore.

"I'm afraid we're going to lose her if we don't. She's an asset to the company and if she ever got an offer from someone else, I think she'd be gone in a heartbeat."

"Hadley's loyal, Ty. I'll talk to her when she gets back from this trip you sent her on. I'll find out what she wants and how we can keep her happy."

Tyler already knew what she wanted and how to keep her happy. He certainly didn't need Kellen to do it. It was like he thought he had a better rapport with her than he did.

Kellen always insinuated the employees liked him better. Tyler's insecurities were triggered.

"I already know what she wants. She asked me for that job months ago. I listened to you and let you hire Eric instead. I was wrong. I should have fought for her to get that position."

Kellen let out an exasperated sigh. "Look at what he did on the Kingman account and tell me he's not qualified to do the job. If you see what he put together and still think we should give the job to Hadley instead, I'll consider it in title only. We can't afford to pay her more."

Would that be good enough? Hadley hadn't asked for a raise, but surely she assumed the money would come with the title. Tyler didn't have any other options at this point. He would find fault with Eric's research report if it killed him. Tyler ended his call with Kellen and realized he had walked all the way to the barn.

"Look who has finally emerged from his cabin in the woods," Ethan said as Tyler approached the petting zoo.

His brother patted one of the baby goats on the head. The kid was desperate for some food and when it realized Ethan had none, it moved on to a little boy with a cup filled with feed pellets. A sheep and the llama also took note of the boy's cup. He was surrounded. Joy turned to fear in an instant. He threw the cup on the ground and cried for his mom, who was quick to swoop in with a reassuring smile. He was fine. The animals wouldn't hurt him.

It made Tyler remember his own mother introducing him to the animals on the ranch when he was small. She always emphasized that if he treated the animals with kindness, they would respond without fear. Fear was what made animals attack. Watching the animals grow up on the ranch was one of the few things that he remembered fondly.

"Did you come to cuddle with the llama?" Ethan asked.

"I came to tell you I have a potential buyer coming on Wednesday to look at the facilities. We need to make any ongoing repairs a priority the next couple days. I understand that there'll always be something to fix, but the more we get finished, the better."

Ethan looked crestfallen. "A buyer? Already?"

"That's why you guys asked me to come out here, wasn't it?"

"I thought the focus would be to book new

guests. A profitable ranch is a more appealing sell."

"We're concentrating on that, too. Hadley already connected with a guest wanting to do a corporate retreat here next summer. We're doing everything we can."

"She's really good at this kind of stuff. Grace told me Hadley had some fun ideas for some Kids' Club programs. I think she likes this place more than she's letting on."

Tyler knew where he was going with this. Hadley was never going to be part of the family, therefore it didn't matter if she loved this place or not. Tyler was not staying. Period.

"I'm going to do my best to sell this place before I leave. Hadley and I can't wait to get home."

"You sure you and Hadley are on the same page about that?" Ethan challenged.

"Of course we are." Tyler didn't appreciate his tone. "We're on the same page about everything."

Ethan lifted his chin. "If you say so, little brother."

Tyler didn't have time to fight with him about the strength of his fake relationship. If there was one thing he knew for sure, it was that Hadley and Tyler were the only ones crystal clear about how things were going to play out.

"So DID YOU have a favorite horse when you lived here?" Hadley asked as they walked through the horse barn to the tack room.

"You know how I feel about favorites."

Oh, she hadn't forgotten. Everyone had favorites except for Tyler. The man was so stubborn.

"Well, was there one that you liked to ride more than the others?"

He stopped in front of one of the stalls and tapped on the nameplate. "I did help name Butterscotch. She was always such a sweet horse. I'd say we should take her out today, but she's got a foal to care for."

"Oh, I met the baby horse that first full day we were here. It was so adorable."

"Foal," Tyler corrected her. "They're called foals. No one calls them baby horses."

"Not true. I call them baby horses, so someone does."

Tyler laughed through his nose and shook his head. At least she entertained him from time to time. It was no easy feat either, so she felt quite proud of herself when it happened.

Conner, the ubertalkative wrangler she had met the other day, helped get two trail horses saddled up. He offered her a hand in getting up on Geronimo. The chocolate Rocky Mountain horse had a flaxen mane and a sweet disposition.

"I see you got yourself a hat," Conner said once she was situated in the saddle.

Last night during their snacking spree, Tyler bought Hadley her very first straw cowboy hat. It had a sparkly rhinestone heart and chain embellishment to play up her city-style but still managed to make her feel like a real cowgirl.

"My fiancé knows how to spoil me."

"Well, it looks good on you."

"Everything looks good on her. That's one of the many reason why I'm marrying her," Tyler said after he mounted his horse. "Thanks for the help, but I've got it from here." Conner stepped away and wished them a good ride. Hadley made a kissing noise and gave Geronimo a squeeze with her legs to get him moving. He followed Tyler's horse, Goliath, down the trail.

"You play the jealous boyfriend real well.

Does that come naturally or do you have to think about it?" she said, goading him.

"I wasn't acting like a jealous boyfriend."

"You do every time Conner looks at me. You even snapped at him a couple days ago when he offered to give me a private cattle clinic. And you love to point out that we're attached like he might be trying to get in between us."

"I have no idea what you're talking about," Tyler insisted. She couldn't see his face as he was in front of her, but she could imagine the guilty look that had to be there.

She encouraged Geronimo to catch up and walk beside Goliath instead of behind. "So, where are we headed this fine afternoon?"

Tyler wouldn't look at her. "There are a few secret spots I'd like to show you that people like Conner have no idea even exist on this ranch."

"I promise that I am a one-fake-relationship-at-a-time kind of girl. You do not need to worry about me running off with the horse wrangler anytime soon."

He gave her a sideways glance. "Good to know. Not that I'd care what you did with Conner if you wanted to do something with Conner. I just think it's ridiculous that the guy flirts with a woman who is engaged to someone else."

"We aren't really engaged."

"I know that, but he doesn't. What if he hit on a married guest?"

"He's harmless. He paid me a compliment. He was being nice, not flirtatious."

"We'll have to agree to disagree on that one."

Could Tyler truly be jealous? There was no way. Hadley was overthinking it. He most likely thought about it only from a business perspective. It wasn't as if they had a real emotional connection.

Hadley needed to focus on something else, which wasn't hard given the sweeping mountain vistas along the trail. Acres of prairie grass and wildflowers covered the landscape ahead of them. She could understand why Montana was referred to as the Last Best Place by the people who lived here.

Tyler led them off trail and up into the foothills of the Rocky Mountains. He pulled on Goliath's reins and brought them both to a stop by a small turquoise-blue pond.

Hadley dismounted. "This isn't on the map of the property."

"Too small for anyone to care about, but this is where I would come and skip rocks when I was little. I felt like because of its size, I had the best chance of getting one to skip all the way across."

"Did you ever do it?"

"Nah." Tyler tipped his hat up. "I read somewhere that the world record was eighty-eight skips across a lake. I never made it more than six. And even on this small pond, it wasn't far enough."

"Let's see if you can do it now that you're older," Hadley said, tugging him down off his horse.

They walked down to the water's edge and searched for the perfect skipping stones. The sound of the occasional frog croaking and chirping mixed with the buzzing of bees and dragonflies. Hadley noticed a red-tailed hawk soaring up above them. This place was so different from Portland's quirkiness.

"You want one that's flat. Flat ones go the farthest," Tyler said, crouched down, picking up rocks and tossing them aside when he deemed them unworthy.

"How about this one?" Hadley held up a

smooth, flat stone that fit perfectly in the center of her palm.

"That's about as perfect as you're going to find," he said, seeming pleased.

Hadley slipped the stone into her pocket for safekeeping. She didn't want to lose it while she continued her search. After gathering half a dozen stones each, Tyler gave her a quick lesson on how to skip rocks.

"You want to hold it like this," he explained. "Put your thumb and your middle finger on either side and wrap your index finger around the edge."

Hadley did her best to copy him even though her hands weren't as big as his, making it a bit more difficult.

"Now, the whole idea is to throw the rock at a twenty-degree angle and make it hit the water without breaking the surface."

"Well, Professor Blackwell, I didn't realize there was so much science and math required in this class. I thought we were trying to have fun," Hadley teased.

Tyler turned away from her. "If you don't want to learn, I won't teach. We'll see who skips the rocks the farthest."

She grabbed him and spun him around. "Teach me."

He stared at her for a beat longer than she expected. Whenever she touched him, he froze. She couldn't read him, though. Did he hate it when she did that? All she knew was that the physical contact made her feel like someone set fireworks off in her belly. She let go and they both snapped out of it.

"Make sure to bend your wrist all the way back and flick the rock against the surface. I'll show you." Tyler wound up like a baseball pitcher and threw his first stone sidearm. It skipped six times before sinking into the water. He was still a good distance from the other side of the pond.

"Six hops. Very impressive," she said, knowing he wasn't happy it didn't make it across by the look of disappointment on his face. "My turn."

Hadley tried to hold the stone the way Tyler had shown her. She wound up and let it go. It hit the surface hard and bounced up high and then right back down into the water. She cringed at her complete fail.

Tyler came up behind her and put a hand around her throwing wrist. "You're throwing it down too close to yourself. Try making a wide angle and throw it farther away."

He guided her through the motion, which would have been helpful if she could focus on his instructions instead of his touch. Those earlier fireworks were now in the grand finale phase, hundreds of rockets exploding at the same time.

"Okay, give it another try," he encouraged.

Hadley took her second rock and gave it a flick. This time, she managed three skips before it sank to the bottom.

"Better." Tyler was being generous. "Just remember to follow through with your arm after you release. Like this." He threw his second one and it skipped across the pond almost to the other side.

"Nine!" Hadley clapped. "You almost got over there."

They took turns tossing the rocks they had left. Hadley managed to get four skips and about halfway across the pond. Tyler skipped two more near the edge of the opposite side. Hadley pulled the perfect rock from her pocket.

"We should switch. You take this one. You said it was almost perfect. I feel like it's destined to be the one you get across." She kissed it for good luck and handed it to him. "Take it."

Tyler switched stones with her and watched as she threw hers, managing only two skips. He stared down at the rock she had given him and rubbed his thumb over the side she had kissed. He glanced over at her.

"Here goes nothing."

He wound up and let it go. Ten skips across the water. Ten rippling circles left in its wake. The stone came to stop in the grass along the edge of the other side. Both Tyler and Hadley threw their arms in the air and screamed.

Without thinking, she wrapped her arms around him in congratulations. For the first time, he didn't seem to mind the contact, returning the embrace. She pressed the side of her face against his solid chest. He smelled like expensive cologne even though he was dressed like a down-to-earth cowboy. Both suited him just fine.

"Looks like you might be my lucky charm."

Hadley stared out over that turquoise water that had gone back to being as smooth as glass. It was like a mirror, reflecting the trees and mountains around it. It immediately became her favorite pond in the world.

She lifted her head and looked up at him. Tyler's chiseled jaw had a day's worth of stubble, making his jawline even more pronounced. He was so handsome. He was also more fun to be around than she'd expected. There was a sweet guy hiding under all that intense work ethic.

His hand cradled her cheek and her insides turned to mush. She had been adamant about the no-kissing rule, but this was different. This wasn't for show or to convince someone else they were in love. This was…real.

Kiss me, she begged with her eyes. For a second, she was sure he would, but Tyler took a step back and broke their embrace.

He cleared his throat and made toward the horses. "We should finish our ride, so we can get back to work."

All business, all the time. Hadley was foolish for thinking he'd be anything else.

CHAPTER ELEVEN

KISS ME. THAT was what Tyler could have sworn her eyes were asking him to do back there by the pond, but he must have misread the situation. She was happy for him, not in love with him.

He didn't understand why he let himself get so mixed up when they were together, especially when they were alone. With no one else around, they didn't have to pretend to have feelings for one another, but somehow, that was when he was the most confused about how they felt.

"Where to next, boss?"

That was more like it. Boss and employee. Clear lines. No confusion.

"We're going to head down to where Falcon Creek crosses the property and then we'll follow it back up and around to the main lodge."

It had been years since Tyler roamed these

parts of the ranch. It was bittersweet being back, knowing this would be the final time.

"Tell me the wildest thing you and your brothers ever did out here on the ranch," Hadley asked, breaking the silence.

"Wildest?"

"I'm sure you five boys have a million stories, but what's the one you'd all agree was the wildest?"

"That's harder to answer than you think." Tyler and his brothers were pretty wild growing up. There was always some mischief to get into on a ranch like this. "I'm sure Judge Edwards would say it was when we managed to run her off the ranch in five days. Each day was pretty off the charts."

"Judge Edwards?"

"Our very first ex-stepgrandma. You met her at the Clearwater Café on our first day."

"Ah," Hadley said with a giggle. "The lady who hates you."

"That's her. We tortured her until she couldn't take any more. We all did something horrible to her. I was responsible for leaving a cow pie next to her side of the bed that she just happened to step in when she got up on the morning of day four."

"Hence your nickname."

Tyler nodded. "We have done a lot of things, but what we did to Myrna was probably the worst. The only other real screwy thing we did involved some BB guns and a bet that no one could hit someone's bare butt from a hundred feet away."

"Oh, no. That doesn't sound like a smart bet."

"Ethan will attest to the fact that Chance could be a military sharpshooter."

Hadley winced. "Poor Ethan. I imagine you also got in a lot of trouble in this creek."

Falcon Creek ran across the ranch east to west, separating the grazing pasture from the neighboring property. The banks were lined with elm trees. Late in the summer when the creek was slow-moving, Tyler and his brothers used to try to cross it by jumping from rock to rock before the accident. In the spring, when all the melting snow flowed down from the mountains, a little bit of rain could make it more like a raging river.

Tyler felt a sharp pang in his chest. He knew all too well how the creek could turn into a monster.

"Maybe when we were really little. The creek wasn't a place we liked hanging out."

"It's beautiful out here," Hadley said from behind him.

Beautiful wasn't the word he would use. Not unless beauty evoked pain. The remnants of the bridge still remained down on the southeast corner of the property. He hadn't gone there since the accident. He used to avoid it at all costs. If this was the last time he was ever going to be here, he wanted to see it.

"I love the sound of the water. It's too bad they didn't build some guest cabins out this way to take advantage of this view."

To the Blackwells, the creek was basically a grave site. There was no chance Big E would let anyone back here. It was too close to where the accident had happened.

He could see the road up ahead and his throat tightened. He used to roam the ranch so often but never here. He would climb the mountains before he'd get close to the spot where his parents lost their lives.

His heart pounded in his chest as he dismounted Goliath and tied him to the pasture fence. On the other side of the road was the Double T Ranch, where Ben now lived.

Carefully, Tyler approached the spot where his parents had met their maker. He stopped dead in his tracks as soon as he noticed the patch of bluebells that had grown around what was left of the bridge's abutment. His mother had loved bluebells.

"What's the story behind this bridge? Let me guess, you and your brothers blew it up. Am I right?"

Tyler pressed his fingers against the corners of his eyes to stop the stupid tears from flowing. He struggled to clear his throat. "This is where my parents died."

HADLEY FELT HER heart stop. There was no hope that she could even begin to remove the foot in her mouth. Mortified, she took off her hat and tried to apologize. "I'm so sorry, Tyler. I didn't mean to make light."

"You didn't know," he said, turning his back.

"That doesn't make it any better. I would do anything to take that question back." She felt like such a heel. He didn't talk much about his parents. He'd never mentioned how they died, only that they had.

Tyler crouched down and lightly touched the wildflowers growing around what was left of the bridge on this side of the creek. He pulled his hat off his head and pressed it to his chest. Hadley hung back, giving him some privacy. She wondered how long it had been since he had been here.

As much as her parents frustrated her with their obvious favoring of Asher, she couldn't imagine not having them in her life. In fact, she felt terribly guilty for the times she had taken them for granted.

"People used to ask my mom if she ever wished she had a girl, as if having five boys was some sort of disappointment," Tyler said, standing upright but still facing away from Hadley. "She'd look them in the eye and say being our mom was the best thing that ever happened to her. She had the privilege of teaching five amazing boys to become five incredible men, which meant someday she'd be the proud mother of five spectacular daughters-in-law."

"It sounds like she had no regrets."

He turned enough for Hadley to see his tear-streaked face. "She didn't get to see us grow into men, though. And if she was here, she'd only have four spectacular daughters-in-law. I would have failed her."

Hadley moved closer. "Don't say that. You haven't failed, Tyler. You just haven't found the woman you want to marry yet."

Tyler wiped his face and shook his head. "I was never good enough. My brothers all stood out in their own way. Jon's the best rancher. Ben's the smartest. Ethan has the most compassion. Chance is musically talented. They all fell in love with someone and managed to convince that person to fall in love with them. I disappointed my parents in life and in death."

It broke her heart to hear him talk like that. She'd never seen him or anyone be that vulnerable before. Hadley threw caution to the wind and stepped in front of him. Tossing her hat on the ground, she grabbed his face in her hands.

"Katie says your love of this land is like no one else's. You run one of the most successful marketing companies in all of the Pacific Northwest. I don't know how smart Ben is, but you are smarter than anyone I know in this world. You also came here to help your family even though it's obvious this place holds a lot of painful memories."

Tyler put his hands over hers. "You don't know me."

"I think I do. I may not know everything,

but the Tyler Blackwell I'm getting to know is a good man with a good heart and way too hard on himself."

She lifted up on her tiptoes and kissed him. It didn't matter what she had told him or what kind of messed-up situation they were in. He didn't think anyone could care about him, but the truth was she was beginning to care quite a bit.

His hands dropped to her waist, and if she had caught him off guard, he wasn't backing away. In fact, he was pulling her closer. Her head should have been spinning but her focus was razor sharp. All she could think about was how good this felt.

The kiss ended, but their embrace did not. Tyler rested his forehead against hers. "I thought we had rules."

"New rule—no self-loathing allowed."

"You don't understand," he said in a whisper.

"I don't care what I don't understand. It's our new rule."

"You make the rules and break them. What if I want to break them, too?" A tiny smile played on his lips. Those lips were darn good at kissing. He might not make music or love animals but Tyler could kiss.

"This new rule can't be renegotiated."

"But the kissing one can be?"

She didn't know what to say. The kissing was a good idea a minute ago, but was it a good idea moving forward?

"Maybe."

"Maybe?" Tyler's hands dropped from her hips and he bent over to pick up her hat, placing it on her head. "Okay, we need to get these horses back before we find ourselves in a heap of trouble."

She wasn't sure what kind of trouble he was referring to—the trouble with Ethan for taking the horses out or the trouble they'd get in if they started kissing again.

They took the road north toward the barn and got the horses some water. Tyler helped Conner untack them. Hadley went out front and waited for her fake fiancé to finish up.

What was she doing? What had she done? When this was all over could she return to Portland and go back to the way things were? Unlikely. Could she see herself in a relationship with Tyler? Maybe.

The thought of it made her smile. That had

to be a good sign. She touched her lips and closed her eyes, letting her mind wander back to that moment by the bridge.

"Hadley!"

Her eyes opened to find Ethan jogging over. "Hey, Ethan."

"Did you just get back from your ride?"

"We did. It was…perfect."

"So, Grace and I were thinking it might be nice if we had dinner together tonight. Grace was going to make chow mein. Tyler still loves Chinese food, right?"

Hadley had no idea how he felt about Chinese, but if Ethan said he loved it then he must. "Of course he does! We order it in at least once a week in Portland. There's this great place in the Pearl District we like to get it from."

Ethan nodded. "And does he still like listening to jazz? I found a bunch of Big E's old records in storage. I thought maybe Tyler would like to go through them and take some home with him."

She knew his favorite kind of music like she knew the square root of 422. If Ethan said he loved jazz, he had to still love it. Why would his musical taste change?

"He would love that. Best thing about Portland is the music scene. We go to shows all the time."

"I had a feeling you would say that," Ethan said. Only he wasn't smiling anymore. He actually seemed angry. "Can you help me out with something in the main house? It'll only take a minute."

"Sure. Let me tell Tyler where I'm going."

"Carl," Ethan called to one of the ranch hands. "Can you tell my brother that I'm stealing his fiancée for a minute?"

The young guy nodded and Ethan led the way to the house.

"What do you need help with?" Hadley asked as she tried to keep up with his long strides.

"Grace and I had a couple questions about the people coming to look at the property next week."

It seemed strange that he needed her help with that when it made more sense to ask Tyler. Maybe he was hoping he could sway her into convincing Tyler not to sell. Little did he know that was impossible.

Grace sat in the front room when they walked in. She looked uncomfortable on the ultramodern couch. She popped a peppermint in her mouth and smiled. Ethan closed the door behind them.

"Seems Tyler would love to join us for Chinese tonight," Ethan told Grace.

"Would he?"

"He'd also love to look through Big E's jazz records. Maybe take some home. They go to shows all the time."

Grace tilted her head, a look of concern on her face. "Jazz concerts?"

Hadley's stomach rolled. Something was off. Way off. She nervously fidgeted with her hands. "You didn't ask me up here to talk about the prospective buyers, did you?"

"We're worried about you, Hadley," Ethan said, taking a seat next to Grace.

"Worried about me?" She felt like she was going to throw up. The temperature in the room must have gone up a hundred degrees since they walked in. Hadley could feel the sweat beading on her forehead.

"I love my brother, but he's up to something. What's he got on you?"

"Got on me? What's that supposed to mean?"

Ethan leaned forward, his elbows on his knees. "He must have something on you to get you to come here and pretend to be engaged to him."

Hadley felt the walls close in. The air in the room was so thick she couldn't breathe. She had to play it cool or everything would be ruined.

She tried laughing but it sounded more like a wounded animal. "What in the world are you talking about? Tyler and I are very happily engaged. Is this some sort of test? A little initiation game or something?"

"When Tyler was thirteen, we ate chicken chow mein for dinner and later that night he got violently ill. The kind of ill that makes you never want to eat the things that you barfed up because it will always remind you of being horribly, horribly sick."

Tyler didn't like Chinese. Tyler did not order Chinese takeout every week.

"Tyler isn't a huge music buff. He listens to some rock and roll and probably owns all of Chance's records, but Stepgrandma Number Three used to play jazz in the house when we were in high school and it used to make Tyler want to jump out of his bedroom window. He once told me that if he died and he heard jazz, he'd know he hadn't made it to heaven."

No jazz concerts in Portland for Tyler either.

If he found out she had blown it, her promotion was history before it even became a reality.

"Listen, I can explain," she tried. Maybe they would believe she had lied about what he ate and listened to because she didn't want them to know that she didn't know the man she was marrying well enough.

Grace interrupted, "You told Ethan that you wanted a huge wedding and to be a princess for the day. You said Tyler was completely on board and wanted to give you whatever you wanted. Tyler told me that you were a no-frills kind of girl and the two of you would probably do something similar to Ben and Rachel. It's obvious that the two of you have never made plans to get married."

Hadley wished the floor would open up and swallow her. Anything would be better than standing in the ugliest sitting room of all time, listening to how terribly she had lied to her fake fiancé's family.

"We aren't judging you," Grace continued. "We're positive it wasn't your idea to pretend to be engaged. Tyler is obviously the master-mind of this plan. What we want to do is sim-ply get your help."

There was no escaping the truth. She was

going to lose her promotion because she opened her big mouth and said too much. Tears welled in her eyes. She forgot to tell Tyler what she told Ethan and ruined everything. She sat on the chair across from them and buried her face in her hands.

"Please don't tell him you know. Please let him leave here believing that you all believe."

"We don't want him to know that we know," Ethan said, getting up and sitting next to her. He wrapped an arm around her shoulders.

Hadley dropped her hands. "What?"

"We don't want Tyler to know we know. We want him to think he's still fooling all of us," Ethan explained.

"Right now, Ethan and I are the only ones who know. Ben, Jon, Rachel, Lydia, even Katie. Everyone else has no idea what we know."

"We want to work together to make things right."

"Thank you." Hadley felt the weight lift off her chest. "I promise I'll do whatever you want if you keep this between us. Your brother just wanted to fit in. Everyone was getting married and he thought if he said he was, he wouldn't have to come home. But that didn't work and he didn't want to have to admit that he lied because you guys would never let him live it down—"

"Hadley, we get it," Ethan assured her. "All we need to know is does he have anything on you? What do you get out of pretending to be part of this lie?"

It was so embarrassing to admit the truth. It made her feel like a bad person to be doing all this for a step up at work. She had lied to his entire family. They had welcomed her into their homes and hearts and she had deceived them.

"He agreed to follow through on a promotion that I swear I completely deserved a couple months ago if I helped him save face with his family and get the ranch sold."

"Is the promotion dependent on selling the ranch?" Ethan asked.

"Well, he didn't think we'd get it sold while we were here, but he asked me to help him with the marketing so it would sell eventually."

"But if it doesn't sell while you're here, you'll still get your promotion?"

Tyler hadn't made the promotion contingent on a sale during these two weeks. All he said was she had to help him, which she was. "I think so."

Ethan sat back and let out a sigh of relief. "Then there's still hope."

"Hope for what?"

"Hope that I have enough time to convince my brother to help me run this ranch."

"Your brother is very set on selling," Hadley reminded him.

"I know he thinks he is, but the Tyler I know wanted to work this land until he was old and gray."

That was similar to what Katie had said to Hadley the other day. However, Hadley also knew the ranch caused him so much heartache. "The Tyler I know now wants to run the most successful advertising agency in Portland."

Ethan stood up and began to pace across the sitting room. "Maybe that's true, but I have to try. Maybe we can make a deal."

A deal? Hadley had already made a deal with one Blackwell and that wasn't going so well. "What kind of deal?"

"What if we helped each other out? We'll keep your secret and help you keep the rest of the family in the dark, if you help us stop

Tyler from selling the ranch to the buyer he has coming next week."

"You want me to what? Sabotage the sale?"

"That could work," Grace said, popping another peppermint. "Stopping a sale while at the same time making this place more appealing could sway Tyler our way."

"It's going to take a lot more than sabotaging one sale to get Tyler to change his mind," Hadley warned.

Ethan sat down by Grace, a grin spread wide across his face. "Tyler is more attached to this place than he lets on."

All the relief Hadley had felt when they told her they weren't going to expose the lie disappeared with the revelation that she would need to not only continue to tell that lie, but somehow lie to Tyler, as well.

"We all win if we do this. You help us, we get the time to work on Tyler. We keep your secret, you get your promotion," Grace said.

"Do we have a deal?" Ethan asked.

Obviously, Ethan knew Tyler better than she did, but Tyler seemed very adamant about selling the ranch. If she helped Ethan persuade the Mendes family not to buy, would it really stop Tyler from trying to find another buyer and another if that one fell through?

The answer didn't matter. All Hadley had to do was survive another week and a half. She and Tyler would go home to Portland, she'd be promoted at work and he would tell his brothers they had broken off the engagement. The whole ruse would be over and whatever happened with the ranch would have nothing to do with her.

Lying was not her favorite thing to do, but lying seemed like the safest way to get what she wanted.

"Deal."

CHAPTER TWELVE

"How did you and Hadley meet?" Conner asked as Tyler lifted Goliath's saddle, girth and saddle pad off and set them on the saddle rack.

"What we need to talk about is your obsession with my fiancée."

Conner dared to look appalled. "I'm not obsessed with your fiancée. I'm trying to make conversation."

"And of all the things we could talk about, you want to talk about Hadley."

"Listen, boss man, I would be a fool to mess with you and your fiancée. It's obvious she's crazy about you. We can work in silence if that's better for you."

"Perfect." Tyler didn't need Conner talking his ear off about Hadley.

Not that not talking about her made it any easier to not think about her. *Obsessed* was a good word to describe the way Tyler felt at the moment. That kiss had thrown him for a loop.

There he was, mourning his parents, and Hadley swooped in and did what she always does. She challenged him to look at things from a different perspective, to get out of his head and to step outside his comfort zone.

Tyler was so far out of his comfort zone, he was afraid he might not be able to find his way back. It was disconcerting and exhilarating at the same time. They needed to talk about what they were doing. There was too much at stake for them to pretend what happened didn't happen.

He finished cleaning Goliath up and led him out to the grazing pasture. Rules were rules for a reason. He needed to know why Hadley was so willing to break that one. She had made it crystal clear that there were boundaries not to be crossed. Had her feelings changed?

"Please tell me you kidnapped my fiancée to help tear down the wallpaper in here," he said as he came through the front door.

Grace, Ethan and Hadley were sitting awkwardly in the living room. Maybe it was the ultramodern furniture or maybe it was something else. His eyes met Hadley's and he could sense her anxiety. Not the emotion he was hoping to see there.

"We're not, but that's a great idea," Ethan said, rising to his feet.

Tyler took off his hat and combed his fingers through his hair. "Hadley doesn't have time to help you redecorate. We're busy selling the whole ranch, not making small home improvements."

"We were talking about weddings actually," Ethan said. Hadley shifted uncomfortably on the armless chair. He said a quick prayer that she hadn't improvised some wedding plans after Tyler had already told Grace they wanted something small with no frills.

He swallowed hard. "What about them?"

"Grace and I were thinking about having ours here at the ranch over Christmas. We thought it would be a good excuse to get the whole family together for the holidays. We were just checking with Hadley to make sure that didn't interfere with your holiday or wedding plans."

Tyler glanced at Hadley, who still seemed nervous. Had she made a commitment to come back over Christmas? Had she said they were thinking about getting married then?

"What do you think about that, hon?" he

asked, hoping she hadn't had a chance to say anything yet.

She shrugged and her gaze shifted between Ethan and Grace. Couldn't she give him some clue as to what they had been talking about?

"We'll have to talk about it. Obviously, we want to support you two. I'm superhappy for you guys, and we can't wait to meet your little one."

Ethan turned into Mr. Hugs-a-Lot and wrapped his arms around his brother. "I appreciate that, Ty. Family is so important. I want my son or daughter to know all of his or her uncles. You've got a good shot at being the sole favorite since I'll be the awesome dad."

Tyler gave him a strong pat on the back, hoping that was enough embracing for the day. "I really have to get back to work. My fiancée had me playing hooky for too long."

"We were also talking about doing dinner together tonight," Grace said as Ethan finally let go. She had a hand on her baby bump. "I'm not as good as Lydia at cooking, but I'm not terrible. Plus, Hadley said you two would help. We could do it here if that would be more convenient for you. You wouldn't have to leave the ranch."

Hadley stared down at her hands in her lap. He'd never wished so hard for the power to read minds before. Was she full of regret? Was his family overwhelming her? Did she hate cooking?

"Great," he said. "If you let us get back at it, we'll see you two around six thirty? Hadley?"

She seemed glued to her seat. He was ready to scoop her up and carry her to the cabin if she didn't snap out of it soon. He watched her take a deep breath and get to her feet.

The expression on her face suddenly transformed from concerned to carefree. Her smile wasn't genuine, though. This was her game face.

"I'll come by a little earlier to help get dinner started."

"You're the best," Grace said.

Hadley grabbed Tyler by the hand and led him out. Whatever was holding her back a minute ago was completely gone. She was once again selling their engagement like a champ.

"Are you okay?" he asked once they were far enough away from the house.

"I'm fine. Are you okay?"

"Honestly, I'm not sure." He needed to know

more about what she was thinking. "We should talk about what happened."

"Nothing happened. Ethan and Grace were wondering if we wanted to have dinner. They want to talk about their wedding plans. That's it."

She was acting strange again. "I'm talking about what happened by the bridge. I'm talking about the fact that you kissed me."

Hadley let go of his hand and picked up the pace. Tyler nearly had to jog to keep up with her. "I can't talk about that right now. Can we focus on that after we get through this dinner tonight? I can only handle so much and my brain is ready to explode right now."

He was a little taken aback by that response. Of all the things on their plate, talking about the kiss seemed like the most critical. That could mean only one thing—she wanted to take it back.

Of course she did. He was a fool for thinking for a second that they were capable of being more.

IF HADLEY THOUGHT she had made a deal with the devil by agreeing to come to the ranch in exchange for a promotion, she had no idea what to call her second deal. Agreeing with Ethan and Grace to save the promotion and buy the two of them time to steal her boss away to come work with them was too much. She felt like a double agent in a war and she wasn't sure if she was working for the good side or not.

Grace had looked as anxious as Hadley felt back there. Hadley was sorry she hadn't warned the couple how hard it was to keep up a lie this big.

Discouraging one buyer was not that big of a deal. The first was usually not the last. There would be plenty of people looking to add the Blackwell Ranch to their list of assets. If Tyler wanted to sell at the end of all this, he would manage it.

She could do this. She had to do this. There was no other way out of this giant mess she had gotten herself in.

Tyler wanted to talk about the kiss. The kiss that, at the time, seemed like the right call. He needed the reassurance that he wasn't a terrible person, that he wasn't less than his brothers. Plus, she had wanted to. That was before his brother decided to lure her into lying to him.

"What did you find out about the Mendes

ranch?" he asked, having slipped back into work mode the moment they returned to the cabin.

"It's bigger than this one. It's a bit more refined, as well. They must cater to a wealthier clientele than we do."

"A designer dude ranch?"

"I imagine it's a getaway for someone who wants to experience the great outdoors but not truly rough it. The cabins are luxurious rather than rustic. There's no buffalo-check decor, everything is high-end. They claim gourmet dining options and weddings seem to be a big focus."

"Weddings, of course," he muttered.

"Speaking of weddings, we should probably get on the same page about ours. Have you mentioned any plans to anyone yet?" she asked, knowing the answer.

"I forgot to tell you I talked to Grace about it briefly the other day. I told her we were thinking small and no-frills. Maybe even a courthouse wedding."

He really didn't know her at all if he thought that was what she would want. A no-frills wedding was no wedding. She wanted exactly what she had told Ethan—a big, beautiful event with all the bells and whistles. Maybe it was self-indulgent, but she didn't care.

"I'll be sure to mention that tonight so they don't get suspicious."

"Why would they get suspicious?"

Hadley tensed. As far as Tyler knew, everyone believed they were engaged. She hadn't meant to cast any doubt on it. "They won't. I'm being cautious, that's all."

Tyler raked a hand through his hair. He was blessed with good hair, thick and a little wavy. She'd imagined running her own fingers through it.

"What?" he questioned, alerting her to the fact that she was staring and hopefully not drooling. She swiped at the corner of her mouth just to be sure.

"Nothing. I spaced out for a second." How could she think about him like that when there was no chance they could ever be together now that she had agreed to lie to him for the next week and a half? If he ever found out, he wouldn't forgive her and would most likely fire her.

"Figure out how we can play up what this ranch has to offer. Give everything a polish. We can't compete exactly, but we want them to be able to imagine how they could dress this place up to meet their needs."

Hadley nodded. The real challenge was going to be convincing Tyler she would do that yet do the exact opposite instead. Without his noticing. She internally rolled her eyes because that was sure to be impossible. Ethan's plan was a terrible one. Tyler didn't want to move back here. Thwarting his plans to sell would only serve to make Tyler more miserable and even less likely to stay.

"I'll put together some talking points," she said, opening her laptop. She opened her email to find one from Kellen and three from Eric.

The first one from Eric was an over-the-top thank-you for helping him out with the Kingman account. The second one was a request to "look over and offer some input" into his analysis of the data she had gathered for him. She shook her head. It was a good thing the job was hers once she got back to Portland. Otherwise, there was no way she'd do the work for him. Handling it now meant less work later. The third one was the attachment he forgot to add to the last email. He was hopeless.

She clicked on the email from Kellen. It was

an odd request to schedule a meeting with him upon her return.

"Why would Kellen want to meet with me to discuss career goals when I get back?"

Tyler swung around in his chair, a fretful expression on his face. "What did he say?"

"He said let's get together and talk about your short- and long-term goals at 2K." Hadn't Tyler made that clear when they talked the other day?

"It's probably just to go over the transition to brand strategist. Knowing him, he wants to hear it from you that this is what you want and the right move for your long-term goals with the company. I wouldn't worry about it."

A weird sense of dread came over her. "He wants to give me the promotion, though, right?"

Tyler turned his back to her. "Yeah. Of course, he does."

She replied that she was looking forward to talking to him about her future at 2K. She considered thanking him for the opportunity. It couldn't be easy to tell his nephew he was out of a job. Family was important to Kellen, but Eric was the perfect example of why it was bad business to mix your personal and professional life. She opted to keep her response short and sweet. She'd see him soon.

Kellen wasn't the person she needed to thank anyways. Tyler was the one willing to take a chance on her. He was the one who trusted her with not only the new job but with this very personal job of selling his family's ranch.

She felt like such a heel. He believed in her. He thought she could do this job, but she was going to purposely fail. She could try to convince herself it was to help him save face with his family, but the truth was, it was to save her own behind.

CHAPTER THIRTEEN

"I WONDER WHAT these cabinets cost to put in," Hadley pondered aloud. "They must be custom because they don't make pink cabinets on the regular. At least, I hope they don't."

Grace chuckled as she chopped the onions to add to the ground beef. They were making spaghetti and meatballs. "What about the refrigerator? That had to cost a fortune. Where do you even buy a pink refrigerator?"

"I have no idea," Hadley said, running her hand along the smooth, white quartz countertop. The counters were gorgeous. They should keep those and gut the rest of the kitchen.

"Can I ask you something?"

"I guess," Hadley answered warily. The two brothers had gone over to the guest lodge to scavenge some French bread to have with the meal. It gave the ladies a few minutes to speak freely. She took a sip of wine, hoping it would relax her.

"I know the engagement is fake, but you have to feel the sparks between the two of you, don't you?"

Hadley nearly choked on her drink. "What?"

"Oh, please. Tell me you don't feel a tiny bit attracted to Tyler. I have eyes. You might be a good liar, but you aren't that good."

"I'm not lying," Hadley asserted. "He's attractive, but we are not... We couldn't feel like that about each other."

"Couldn't or are afraid to?"

That wasn't something Hadley was willing to debate. How she felt about Tyler after they kissed this afternoon was much too complicated. "I know I have incredible sister-in-law potential, but your wishful thinking is not going to make me and Tyler fall in love. Lying to him isn't exactly the best way to begin a relationship."

"I hate that we're making you lie, but Ethan believes the ranch can and will be successful. He'd hate to see it belong to some other family when it does. He has so many good memories of growing up here."

"But doesn't he also have some painful ones?" Hadley thought of Tyler breaking down by the bridge. There were some dark memories none of the Blackwell boys could escape.

Grace bit down on her bottom lip. She had to know more than Hadley did. "Loss is a big part of their history with this place. But Ethan has tried to embrace the good times rather than dwell on bad."

"Tyler is fixated on the bad. He can remember some of the fun times he had growing up, but the memories always turn sour when he gets lost in them for too long. He doesn't like talking about his parents and he almost never mentions his grandfather."

"That doesn't surprise me," Grace said, placing the meatballs in the hot pan. "Big E doesn't have the softest heart. He wanted the boys to be tough, which might be why most of them took off as soon as they were old enough to be on their own. It's not a coincidence that they're practically all back while Big E is MIA. He's a big reason they've been estranged for so long."

"I know Ethan believes he can change Tyler's mind, but I'm not sure it's going to be as easy as he wants it to be. Tyler's running from more than just a prickly grandpa."

"That may be true, but maybe it's time someone pushes him to face whatever it is that makes him want to run. Ethan can do that for him if he'd just let him."

Grace was an optimist. Maybe love did that to a person. Made them believe anything was possible. Hadley got busy making the salad while Grace watched over the meatballs she said were her mom's special recipe. Alice Gardner was supposedly an excellent cook.

Ethan and Tyler returned with not only a loaf of bread but a strawberry and cream cake on a glittery cake stand. It was beautiful and missing one slice.

"Who dug into the cake already?" Grace asked when Ethan set it on the island.

"Some lucky guest who ordered it before we stole it from the kitchen," Ethan said, swiping a finger-full of whipped cream from the side of it.

Grace held up the wooden spoon in her hand in warning. "Don't go sticking your dirty fingers in our dessert."

"You know you want to do it, too. Just do it. No one here is going to judge."

Tyler raised his hand. "I'll judge."

Grace smacked Ethan's hand as he tried to swipe some more. "Please make yourself useful and help me with the sauce."

Hadley made eye contact with Tyler, who smiled at his brother's antics. Ethan was the light to Tyler's dark. Maybe he could help his younger brother find some peace. Hadley knew it wasn't her place to do it.

"When is dinner going to be ready?" Tyler asked.

"A few more minutes," Grace said, pulling open the silverware drawer and taking out four forks and four knives. "You could set the table and by the time you're finished, dinner will be served."

"What self-respecting cabinetmaker allowed these solid wood cabinets to be painted pink?" Tyler opened the one that housed the plates.

"We were just wondering the same thing," Hadley said. "What about that pink-feathered light? I feel it's safe to say that is one of a kind. There cannot be another kitchen table in the world with that monstrosity hanging above it."

"Big E should have his man card revoked for letting Zoe do this to the house. A man has to draw a line at some point," Ethan said, grabbing the silverware off the island.

"A man has to draw the line, huh?" Grace challenged him. "So if I wanted a pink kitchen, you'd tell me no? Even though I am carrying your child and working three jobs to help make ends meet?"

"Oh, Gracie." He stole a quick kiss. "I'd tell you heck no. But then I'd let you do whatever you wanted because you are obviously smarter and wiser than I will ever be."

"Good answer." Grace beamed up at him. "And I promise all that wisdom will never allow me to ask for a pink kitchen."

"That's why I can't wait to marry you." Ethan gave her another kiss on the cheek.

Hadley smiled at how adorable the two of them were together. She caught Tyler staring at her and guilt washed away all the happy feels. She shouldn't have kissed him today. Not when they couldn't be anything more than what they were.

"So typical," Tyler said. "You know that it's in the Blackwell DNA that when you fall in love with a woman, she gets what she wants. Dad used to say he never denied Mom anything because a happy wife meant a happy life."

"Something tells me your father's happiness mattered to her just as much as hers mattered to him," Grace said. "Did she really get *ev-*

erything she wanted? They never had to compromise?"

"That's the way I remember it," Tyler replied.

"Mom never asked for things like a pink kitchen," Ethan argued. "I think she would have lost that fight."

Tyler glanced in Hadley's direction once again. "Mom had excellent taste. A trait we also inherited."

Hadley smiled. She could see that being very true. "I did say the other night that you have the best taste in food, wine, movies—"

"And women," Tyler said, finishing the sentence the same way he did at Jon's.

The butterflies in Hadley's stomach were all released at the same time and her face warmed even though he couldn't have meant her. He was trying to trick Ethan and Grace. Hadley knew better. At least, she hoped she did.

"Careful, you two," Grace warned. She smirked at Hadley. "Those sparks could start a real fire."

TYLER WISHED HE could erase the memory of kissing Hadley from his mind, but the thought was relentless, popping up every time he looked at her.

She sat across from him at the dining room table and laughed at something Ethan said. Was it silly to be jealous of his brother for making her laugh? Absolutely. Did he still feel envious? Yep.

"Ever since you said you were thinking about getting married here, I can't stop thinking about how you could market this place as Montana's premier wedding destination," Hadley said to Ethan. "You could have people rent the whole ranch for an entire weekend. Their guests could have access to some of the activities, but we could also upsell some add-ons to make even more money."

Ethan's mouth hung open for a second. "That's brilliant."

"Is that what the Mendes ranch does?" Tyler asked.

"Seems like it from what I've researched. They market it as a mountain destination wedding package."

The woman was very good at her job. He wasn't sure why she was getting Ethan so excited about it, though. This was the kind of stuff they needed to sell to the buyers next week, not to his brother, who sadly still thought there was a chance the ranch would keep the family name.

"I also noticed those barns by the creek during our ride this afternoon. What are those for?"

"When this was only a working ranch like Jon's, we needed them for housing animals. Big E sold some of the cattle to build the lodge. Right now, I don't have a use for them."

"What if you could transform them into a full-service spa? When I was talking to one of the guests a couple days ago, he said his wife enjoys the outdoor adventure activities but would love a little pampering, too. It could tie in with the wedding theme, as well. The brides and bridesmaids could use the facilities before the big day."

"I love it," Grace said. "Why didn't we think of that?"

Another great idea to share with Mr. Mendes. Hadley was worth every penny Kellen didn't want to pay her to be a brand strategist. She was expertly rebranding the Blackwell Guest Ranch over a bowl of spaghetti and charming the pants off Ethan and Grace in the process.

"I don't know, but I'm glad she did," Ethan

answered, toasting her with his glass of wine. "I'm still waiting for my brother to come up with something equally amazing. Do you always let her do the heavy lifting?"

"I point her in a direction and she runs with it. We make a good team."

Hadley's blue eyes lifted to his. Her hair was up in a ponytail tonight, exposing her slender neck. His gaze drifted down to her collarbone. He imagined how soft her skin was there and how it would feel against his lips.

"Imagine what the four of us could do here," Ethan said. "With your ideas and my willingness to work hard, we could put this place on the map."

His brother was bound and determined to deny the inevitable. "We could also sell it for top dollar and move on with our lives. Won't you be relieved to focus on being the town's vet instead of breaking your back here?"

"I won't have to break my back if you help me. I remember when you used to tell me I was going to work for you someday."

"And you used to tell me I was an idiot."

"Prove me wrong," Ethan challenged.

The only thing that would make Tyler an idiot was thinking for a second he could come back here for good. After experiencing the pain of visiting the bridge today, he knew he'd never stay and put himself through that again.

He pounded his fist on the black lacquered table. "I'm not staying. Stop fantasizing. It's not happening."

"Is it Big E? Are you worried he's going to come back?"

"I don't care what our grandfather does. Big E hasn't ever cared about me, so why would I waste my time worrying about what he plans to do with what's left of his life?"

Ethan placed his elbows on the table. "Why do you always act like no one cared about you? You know that's not true."

Did he know that? It certainly wasn't how he felt. "I used to take off and no one even bothered to look for me. I can remember more times than not that I'd run away because one of you was being a jerk, and when I'd come home, Mom, Dad, Big E, all of them would act like they hadn't even noticed I was gone."

Ethan shook his head. "That's not true."

"It's completely true. I think I would know better than you. It was my life."

"Tyler, Mom and Dad loved you. They loved all of us."

"We both know that if Mom and Dad had cared about me, they would still be alive."

"What?"

He hadn't meant to let that slip. He pushed away from the table and stood up. Grabbing his plate, he started for the kitchen. "Thank you for dinner, Grace, but I need to get back to work selling this ranch so I never have to visit this place again."

He rinsed his plate and opened the pink dishwasher that was unfortunately full of clean dishes. He slammed the door shut.

"Don't leave angry," Hadley said from behind him. Tyler refused to turn around and look at her. He hated that she had to see this side of him. "Come have some dessert. I'm sure we can all agree not to spend any more time tonight talking about selling or keeping the ranch."

He wiped his hands on the dish towel hanging from the oven door. "I'm leaving. You can stay if you want."

"Tyler…"

He spun around and leaned against the counter. She was kidding herself if she thought he could stay and eat cake. Hadley moved closer.

"Stop." He held up the palm of his hand.

"Don't come over here and tell me that I'm better than I am and look at me like you want to break rules again." He lowered his voice. "You won't even talk about the fact that you kissed me today, so don't act like you're here to comfort me, like you care."

She stopped on the other side of the island. "I'm sorry. Not talking about it doesn't have anything to do with how I feel about you."

"How do you feel?" As soon as the words left his mouth, he wanted to take them back. "Never mind. I don't want to know. I want to go back to the cabin and answer all the emails waiting for me."

He started for the door, but Hadley stepped in his path.

"You know that I feel completely confused," she whispered. "How else would I feel?"

"I don't know because you wouldn't talk to me. You're the one who broke the rules. You're the one who kissed *me*. And it wasn't to fool my family or part of this ruse."

Hadley's head dropped. "I know."

Tyler waited for more, but she didn't continue. He was the idiot. She didn't have feelings for him. She also wasn't as confused as she claimed. She was regretful. He'd been vulnerable earlier and she had felt bad for him.

"I'm leaving. Come with me or stay and eat cake with my brother. I don't care." He stepped around her and headed for the door.

"Tyler." Ethan followed him out. "I'm sorry for arguing with you. I didn't want to make you mad."

"I'm not mad. You don't realize that what I said at dinner is how I have felt my whole life. It's not a big deal anymore."

"I can't change the way you remember Mom and Dad, but I'm asking you to think about the future, not the past. I love you. You're my little brother and there's no one I'd rather do this with than you."

If Ben offered to run the Blackwell Ranch, Ethan would be ecstatic. This wasn't about wanting Tyler specifically, this was about needing one of them to vote to keep the ranch.

There was no point in arguing, though. No one wanted to tell Tyler to his face that he wasn't all that important. "I'll see you in the morning."

"I'm coming," Hadley said, standing in the doorway with Grace behind her. "Thank you for dinner."

They walked back to the cabin in silence. Tyler was tired. It had been an emotionally draining day. The whole week had been more than he was ready to handle. Dusk was approaching as the sun had just over an hour before it sank behind the Rockies. The clouds would soon be glowing a vibrant orange.

It was still light enough to see someone sitting on the bench on their front porch. The confusion on Hadley's face was understandable. It may have looked like Ethan had somehow changed clothes and magically beat them back to the cabin, but Tyler knew it was Ben in his fancy running outfit.

"Why are you sitting out here like a creeper?" Tyler asked, finished with anyone named Blackwell for the day.

"Good evening to you, too," Ben said, rising to his feet.

There was nothing good about this evening and it seemed to be getting worse. Hadley wasn't the only one with regrets. Tyler wished he had never come back.

"Did Ethan call you and tell you to run over here?"

Ben seemed genuinely surprised by the

question. "I haven't talked to him all day. Why? What's going on?"

"Nothing," Tyler said with a shake of his head. "What are you doing here, then?"

"We need to talk."

CHAPTER FOURTEEN

"Talk," Tyler said, wanting this over with so he could go in the cabin and drown himself in work. He needed the distraction from the misery his current situation brought him. Hadley unlocked the cabin door.

"I have a lead on a buyer, but we're going to have to move fast. This guy wants a quick-and-easy sale."

Finally, some good news. It was also about time Ben did his part. So far, all he had done was give the water rights to Rachel's family and make the ranch less desirable for a buyer.

Hadley stopped short. "We have a lead as well, so we wouldn't be able to do anything until both buyers have seen the property."

"Good, maybe knowing there's some competition will drive the price up," Ben said.

Hadley played devil's advocate. "It could also scare them off."

Tyler didn't understand her pessimism. There

was no negative to this news. "Who do I need to talk to?"

"Rachel found this guy in Bozeman. He's only interested in it as a working ranch. He doesn't want anything to do with petting zoos and guests wanting horseback riding tours. I'm not sure how you're going to sell this place as that after all the stuff Zoe did here, but I figure if anyone can do it, it's you."

"Send me his contact information and I'll call him tomorrow. Maybe I can get someone to sign some papers before I fly home."

Hadley interrupted his happy thoughts. "But what about all the work Ethan and Grace have put into this place? If it goes back to a working ranch, they'd be wasting their time and money expanding the facilities."

Tyler's brow furrowed. He didn't care what the buyer would do with the ranch once he paid them for it. "We won't have any say in how the new owner uses the land. I didn't understand why you were getting Ethan all excited about these new ideas at dinner. He isn't going to be the one making them happen. He should save his money and time and focus on his real future."

"I think what she's trying to say is that you

need to take Ethan's feelings into consideration," Ben said. "Which is why I was waiting here to talk to you about this rather than running up to the main house to find you."

"Ethan is a big boy. He'll be fine. It's not like he doesn't have another life waiting for him. He can run the vet clinic, marry Grace and be happy. Why does he care so much about this stupid ranch?"

"It doesn't matter why, it only matters that he does." Ben started for the porch steps. "Trust me, I am all for selling this place. I need the money so I can invest it back into the Double T, but Ethan has dreams he isn't exactly ready to give up on. Just don't shove anything down his throat. Make some calls and follow up on my lead. Good night, you two."

Of course Ben was more worried about Ethan's feelings than anyone else's. Tyler's desire to get the heck out of here wasn't anyone's priority but his own.

"Since you're so in love with the guest ranch idea, you can focus on that. I'll handle prepping the selling points for the other buyer," he said, brushing past Hadley and heading inside.

"I'm done working for the day. It's Friday night. I'm off the clock." She plopped down on the couch and picked up the remote to turn on the television. She put her feet up on the coffee table, crossing her legs at her ankles.

Tyler could only stare at her in utter disbelief. This wasn't the kind of job that she could work Monday through Friday from nine to five. They were here to work until the ranch was sold, and they were so close to making that happen.

"I can't believe my mom didn't call me to remind me to watch tonight's rerun of *When We Were Young*," she said, apparently unaware of how frustrating this behavior was making him.

He stepped in front of the television, blocking her view.

"You make a better door than a window," she complained.

"What are you doing?"

"I'm trying to watch my brother's show because I love my brother. Even though we don't always see eye to eye on everything, I support him and his dreams."

Tyler doubled over in laughter. "Are you serious? You want me to feel guilty? I don't love Ethan because I want to sell the ranch? Ben and Jon want to sell the ranch. Do they not love Ethan either? Or maybe if I side with Ethan, I won't love Ben and Jon? Does Ethan not love me because I want to sell and he's not supporting my dream of going home and getting back to my life?"

"I'm not talking to you about this. Can you please move, so I can watch the show?"

"Why are you suddenly acting like a spoiled child?"

Hadley set down the remote and snatched her laptop off the side table. "I'm taking my cues from you, remember?" She got to her feet.

With dramatic flair, she marched back to the bedroom and slammed the door behind her. Tyler took a couple of deep breaths. Flying off the handle with her wasn't going to get him anywhere.

He paced back and forth in an attempt to ease the tension from his body. Usually, he appreciated it when she challenged him but not today. Not about this. Right now, he was the boss and she was the employee.

"You are here to help me sell the ranch. You are not here to tell me how to manage my relationships with my brothers. Please try to remember that."

The door opened and Hadley came out with a defiant grimace on her face. She made a beeline for the minifridge and pulled out a water bottle. Grabbing the bag of chocolate candy off the counter, she stalked back into the room, slamming the door one more time.

Tyler was on his own tonight. His employee was clearly on strike.

HADLEY WAS ANGRY. Not only at Tyler but at herself, at this situation, at all the lies she was forced to keep up. She texted Ethan about Ben coming up with another buyer. She was a double agent after all.

Her hope was that Ethan and Grace would surrender. Even though the Blackwell Guest Ranch could have been a huge success given enough time, Tyler's determination to sell it would win in the end. Ethan was better off cutting his losses and moving on with plan B in his life.

Hadley wondered if she should do the same. Maybe the best thing to do was to come clean about everything. Tell Tyler his brother knew they weren't really together and resign from 2K Marketing. Finding another job wouldn't be impossible, but sorting out these newly blurred lines between her and Tyler could be. Maybe a fresh start was what she needed.

She opened the email from Kellen again. Even though he had given her job to Eric, she knew he believed she was good at what she did. She could be on a plane by tomorrow afternoon. Back at work on Monday. Maybe if she did the rest of the brand analysis on the Kingman account for Eric, she could show Kellen she was worthy of the position regardless of what happened with Tyler.

It was worth a shot. She pulled up the research she did on shaving companies and got to work.

The more she read about shaving, the more she thought about how Tyler needed to shave. He had been rocking that five o'clock shadow all day. Tomorrow, it would be scruffy but soft to the touch no doubt. Hadley wondered if he had ever gone to an upscale barber shop and had someone shave him. She loved a clean-shaven man. The smell of an expensive aftershave, the silky softness of his skin right after a shave.

Hadley covered her face with her hands. She was losing control. Tyler was invading every aspect of her life. He was seeping into every thought and feeling. He couldn't be hers. Not when things were so messy.

Thanks for the heads-up, Ethan texted back. Don't give up on me. I'm not giving up on Tyler yet.

How could he hang on to hope? Tyler was so stubborn. So dead set against saving this place. Ethan must know something she didn't. What if Tyler was meant to be here? She felt bad for thinking she could ditch out on both brothers. She'd keep helping Ethan. Maybe in the end, it would help Tyler, too.

She shut down her laptop and sank deeper into the bed. Exhausted, she closed her eyes, praying she didn't dream about Tyler's face.

Hadley drifted asleep. In the morning she was awakened by a muffled voice coming from the other room. "Why are you sleeping out here?" a female voice said.

"We had a fight," Tyler replied.

"Oh, no. What are you fighting about?"

"I don't really want to talk about it, Rachel."

Hadley sat up in bed. What was Ben's wife doing there?

"We were hoping Ben's news would cheer you both up. Did you try apologizing?"

"Who said it was my fault?"

"Really?" another voice chimed in.

"Was it your fault?" Rachel asked.

"Am I being cross-examined, Counselor?"

"Definitely was his fault," the other person said.

"What do you two want? I was sleeping and I'd like to get back to it," Tyler grumbled.

"We want to invite your fiancée to our girls' day out. Lydia and Grace are going to join us. I tried to talk Katie into coming, but she said getting her hair and nails done was a waste of time and money given her job on the ranch. I couldn't really argue with her."

"Hadley and I have work to do today. Thanks but no thanks," Tyler said.

Girls' day out? Work? No way was he making that call for her. Hadley searched for her robe.

"It's Saturday. Doesn't the woman get a day off?" the other voice said. "Or does marrying the boss mean she has to work seven days a week?"

"Aren't you banned from Blackwell land? I'm pretty sure Big E put that in the divorce papers. No ex-stepgrandmas allowed on the property after the divorce is final."

Zoe. Zoe and Rachel were here to rescue

her and she was not going to be left behind with Mr. Grumpy Pants. Hadley pulled open the door and stepped out into the sitting room.

"Good morning, ladies."

Zoe looked more like she had just come home from the salon rather than heading that way. Rachel was a bit more down-to-earth. Hadley liked Rachel as much as she liked Lydia and Grace. All the Blackwell and soon-to-be Blackwell women were exceptional. Being a true member of their clan would have been nice. Hadley would have to settle for enjoying her temporary membership while it lasted.

"We're going into town and getting our hair and nails done before a girls-only lunch and we would really like you to come with us," Rachel explained.

"But your stick-in-the-mud fiancé is trying to tell us you would rather work," Zoe said, glowering in Tyler's direction.

"I'd love to go to town with you guys."

Tyler was about to say something, but Zoe stopped him. "I'm pretty sure you don't want to sleep on the couch a second night. Do you?"

Tyler snatched up his pillow and blanket. "No, I'm sleeping on the bed tonight, for sure."

He carried all his things into the bedroom, glaring at Hadley as he passed her.

Guess her shift on the couch began tonight.

CHAPTER FIFTEEN

"WHERE ARE MY favorite mini-Blackwells?" Emma, one of the owners of the Jem Salon, was busy towel-drying Lydia's hair before her cut and style. Hadley could see the whole salon reflected in the mirror in front of the station where she had been led.

Rachel and Zoe were seated in the luxurious massage chairs in the back corner, soaking their feet before their pedicures. Grace was at the manicure station with June, the other owner of the Jem. Lydia was to Hadley's right.

"Oh, Gen and Abby would have come, but Jon offered them a daddy-daughter day complete with a trip into town for ice cream and I think I heard something about a slip-and-slide. They couldn't say no to that."

"So sweet." Emma placed a hand over her heart.

"I bet Poppy can't wait to be big enough to run around with her big cousins," June said.

Rachel looked up from her magazine. "She adores those girls. As soon as she figures out how to walk on those chubby little feet of hers, she'll be following them everywhere."

"I'm not sure if I should hope for this little Blackwell to be a boy or a girl. It might be nice to get a little boy in the mix, but another girl would be fun, too," Grace chimed in.

Grace's sister, Sarah Ashley, looked up from her phone. She sat on the coffee-colored leather couch in the waiting area, next in line for a manicure. "I want it to be a girl. The Gardners know how to spoil girls. Boys are dirty and smelly."

Lydia laughed. "You have met Gen and Abby, right? Dirty and smelly are their middle names."

Hadley stayed quiet, listening to the ladies talk about their family. The family they all thought she was soon to be a part of since they all believed she was engaged to Tyler. Except for Grace, who knew the truth.

Grace gave her pregnant belly a rub with her free hand. "I want a healthy baby. I don't care if it's a boy or a girl. Their personality doesn't depend on their gender."

"What about you, Hadley?" Her stylist

looked expectantly at her through the mirror as she combed through her damp hair. "Are you and Tyler thinking about having kids soon?"

"Nicole! Let the poor girl get married first," June scolded.

"*If* she gets married," Zoe said from the back corner.

Hadley's whole body tensed. Her gaze connected with Grace in the mirror, but it was clear she had nothing to do with Zoe knowing anything. Rachel elbowed Zoe hard.

"Ow! What? He slept on the couch last night. I was fishing for some dirt."

"Rude," Rachel scolded.

"I'm sorry you guys had a fight last night." Lydia was so sweet and sympathetic.

Hadley was so relieved that Zoe was still in the dark, she had to hold back a smile. If one more person found out the truth, Hadley would have no choice but to get on the first plane back to Portland and plead her case to Kellen for her promotion.

"You know Tyler." Wait, Lydia didn't know him at all. "I mean, you know the Blackwell men. They're all a little stubborn, right?"

Everyone in the room agreed with her at the same time, making them all laugh.

Rachel handed her tech the bottle of nail polish she had chosen for her toes. "The other day, Ben told me stubbornness was a sign of perseverance and I should be grateful that he doesn't give up easily."

Grace swore she could top that. "Ethan has been hounding me to take it easy now that I'm almost in my third trimester. I promised I wouldn't push it, but that wasn't good enough for him. Yesterday, he admitted to screwing all the lids on the jars in the refrigerator as tight as he could so I would have to ask him to open them for me."

"Why did he rat himself out?" Sarah Ashley asked. "Did he get tired of having to open the pickle jar for you?"

"Actually, I never had to ask him once, but he could not get into the mayo when he was making himself a late-night snack and had to confess."

The whole spa erupted in laughter again.

"Jon would rather be miserable than admit when he's made a mistake. One time, he offered to help me make salsa. Only he grabbed the serrano peppers I'd bought instead of the jalapeño ones. It was so spicy I refused to eat it and I sure wasn't going to let the girls dig in. He swore it was fine and said he'd eat the whole thing himself to prove it. Five scoops in, his face was fire-truck red and he was sweating so much that even the girls told him he had to stop."

Hadley could completely relate. Tyler was exactly like his brothers. She could see him doing all of those things, but her biggest problem with Tyler was that he wanted her to talk about her feelings, but he wouldn't talk about his own. He wanted her to do all the risk-taking, and with all the lies she was juggling, she didn't have it in her to risk anything else.

"So what did Tyler do to get him sent to the couch last night?" Zoe wasn't giving up on getting that dirt.

"You don't have to answer that," Grace said, knowing it might be difficult for her to answer. She appreciated the help.

"Everyone else shared," Zoe whined.

"You didn't," Rachel pointed out.

"Do I need to tell you that Elias is more stubborn than all of them combined? I don't think I do."

Hadley had to give them something. "Tyler wanted to work all night and I told him I was off the clock. I went to bed and he was mad.

We're still struggling with how to separate our business from our personal lives."

It was as close to the truth as she could get. She was having difficulty keeping those two things separate. He wasn't wrong when he accused her of kissing him and then shutting him out. She was full of mixed messages yesterday. Only, she wouldn't have shut him out if she hadn't agreed to help Ethan and Grace.

"Knowing Tyler, he probably doesn't like it when he can't be the boss all the time," Rachel guessed.

Maybe what Hadley had to accept was Tyler was the boss, period. She thought she understood that, but something had changed over the last couple of days. One, she had kissed him. Two, she was double-crossing him.

She wished she could tell these ladies what really was going on so they could help her sort out her own emotions. She was having feelings for him. If she didn't care about him, this would be so much easier.

"All engaged men should have to take a class where they are taught that the key to a successful marriage is to admit that your wife is always right," Emma said, releasing a lock of Lydia's hair from the clip she was using to hold it up.

"Tyler will come around," Grace said. "I can tell how much he respects Hadley's thoughts and feelings. He struggles with giving himself a break more than anything. No one is harder on themselves than that man."

Grace was right. Tyler's perception of himself was so different from what it really was. For some reason, he thought no one cared.

Nicole made sure she had trimmed the same amount from both sides of Hadley's head. "Sounds like he has the potential to turn things around. Don't worry too much. All couples fight."

"Amen," June said as she finished filing Grace's nails. "No relationship is perfect. What matters is that you care enough to make up after the fight."

"I bet a gorgeous makeover will help encourage him to make up real fast," Lydia said.

Hadley smiled even though she feared it wouldn't be so easy to find a way for the two of them to make amends.

TYLER JUMPED AT the sound of someone knocking on his door. He had been so focused on preparing for the meeting with Ben's buyer, the disruption was startling.

He opened the door to find Jon and the twins. "Uncle Tyler!" Abby shouted, hugging him around the leg.

Gen latched onto the other one. "Hi, Uncle Ty."

"Hello! To what do I owe the pleasure of this visit?" He kept his voice light but glared at Jon.

"We're crashing the ladies' lunch. We decided you should come with us."

Tyler didn't have time to take a lunch break. Didn't anyone understand that about him? "Thanks for the invite, but the ladies wanted to have a lunch with no boys."

"We're not boys," Gen said, letting him go.

Abby still hung on for dear life. Tyler struggled to keep his balance. "You are not boys. That's why your dad should definitely take you guys to lunch with the ladies, but why I should stay here."

Jon shook his head. "You're coming."

"You should have texted or called. I could have saved you the wasted trip over here."

"You never answer your phone or your texts. At least when it's one of your brothers calling. I figured a personal invitation was harder to refuse, as well." Jon smiled down at Abby, who was possibly never letting go of his leg.

Gen held his hand. "Come on, Uncle Tyler. You can sit by me at the restaurant if you don't want to be by the ladies."

She was too cute. Jon was the worst for using these angels as weapons against him. "I need to put on some real clothes. Can I have my leg back, Abby?"

The little girl flashed him the biggest smile. "Okay, but don't take too long. I'm starving!"

He begrudgingly changed out of his basketball shorts and T-shirt. Hadley wasn't going to be happy to see him. She couldn't wait to escape spending the day with him, accepting Rachel and Zoe's invitation without a second thought.

"What's your favorite food?" Gen asked when they got in the car.

What was it with favorites? Was this really the only conversation people started these days?

"I don't really have a favorite food."

"Mine is chicken nuggets," Abby informed him.

"Mine is Lydia's pancakes," Gen said. "What's yours, Daddy?"

"I like Lydia's pancakes, too. And her mashed potatoes. And her chicken noodle soup."

Tyler rolled his eyes behind his sunglasses. "Sounds like your favorite thing is anything Lydia cooks."

The girls giggled. "You can only pick one favorite," Abby said.

"Not true. You both are my favorite daughter. I can't pick just one of you."

The girls high-fived each other. "We're the best."

"Yes, you are."

Tyler glanced out the window as they made their way into town. It was like he had never left. The buildings all seemed the same. Familiar-looking people strolled along the sidewalks. He remembered sneaking into the movie theater with Chance and Clint Bateman to see the remake of *Texas Chainsaw Massacre* when they were fifteen and how good the saltwater taffy had been from the candy shop that sadly was now an insurance agent's office.

"You two would have loved the candy store that used to be on this corner," he said, pointing to the building. "They used to sell three-foot-long licorice ropes. Remember that, Jon?"

"I remember you and Chance thinking you

were Indiana Jones with those things and whipping each other."

Tyler let out a chuckle. That was a memory he would never forget. The Blackwell twins, either set of them, had a way of turning anything into a weapon.

"What's Indiana Jones?" Gen asked.

"It's by Wisconsin," Abby answered.

"It's a movie," Jon said. "One you can watch when you are much older."

"Can we have licorice ropes?" Gen asked, more interested in the candy than the movie.

"I want chocolate," Abby chimed in.

Jon glanced sideways at Tyler. "Thanks a lot for mentioning candy before lunch."

Tyler laughed again as the girls begged for all their favorite candies from the back seat. Jon had his hands full, that was for sure.

Jon parallel parked in front of The Hungry Hog Deli. The sign hanging above the door was a hand-painted pink hog with a napkin tied around its neck getting ready to take a bite out of a sandwich. This place was new since Tyler had been in Falcon Creek last. It might have boasted sandwiches big enough to satisfy giant pigs, but it didn't look large enough to accommodate all of the Blackwells.

"They have a back room with more tables," Jon said as if he'd read his brother's mind. "Let's see who else is here."

The sound of laughter coming from the back room hinted they all were. Tyler's palms started to sweat. He rubbed them on his khaki shorts. There was no reason to be anxious. This was his family. What could go wrong?

"Surprise!" the twins shouted as they ran in.

The back room was a square space with exposed brick walls. Pictures of all kinds of pigs hung from them. They had three rows of picnic tables covered in red-and-white-checked tablecloths. Ben and Ethan had beat them there and were already seated. Ben had brought Poppy, who was in a high chair at the far end of the middle table.

The six ladies were spread out across all three tables. Ethan, Grace and Sarah Ashley were seated at the first table and accepted hugs from Gen and Abby first. Ben, Rachel, Poppy and Zoe were in the middle. Tyler had no idea how Ben managed to stomach Rachel's friendship with Zoe. He was a better man than Tyler.

Lydia and Hadley were seated at the third table. When Tyler finally turned his attention their way, his breath was stolen. Hadley had cut her hair. It used to hang several inches past her shoulders, but now it just brushed the top of them. It had been curled into big, bouncy curls and her makeup had been done in a way that somehow made her blue eyes bluer. Her lips were the same color pink as her fingernails.

She was absolutely the most stunning woman in the room. The twins each claimed a spot on either side of Lydia.

"Your hair looks so pretty!" Gen said, touching Lydia's curls.

Abby grabbed Lydia's hand for a closer look at her manicure. "Can you make my nails this long?"

"I can make your nails this color," Lydia offered in compromise.

"Well, Emma is a miracle worker," Jon said, bending down to kiss his bride-to-be before taking the spot across Abby and next to Hadley. "She somehow managed to make you even more beautiful than you were when you left this morning. I didn't think that was possible."

He was smooth. Tyler would give him that much.

"You look pretty, too, Aunt Hadley," Abby said.

"Thank you."

"So pretty," Gen added.

Tyler sat down on the other side of Hadley, unsure of how to proceed. Did he greet her the same way Jon greeted Lydia? Or was he off the hook because everyone believed they had had a fight and he slept on the couch last night? Since Zoe thought that was the story, he was sure all the women knew that much.

As frustrated with her as he had been last night and this morning, seeing her sitting among his family and looking so beautiful made him consider a kiss on the cheek. Yet, something told him kissing her was a risk he shouldn't take after all that had happened.

"So *pretty* was what I was going to say. You stole my adjective, Gen," he said instead.

"That's the best you can do, Ty?" Zoe asked.

Tyler shot daggers at her with his eyes. She looked exactly the same as she did when she woke him up this morning. "Who invited you again?"

"Not me," Ben mumbled. Rachel shot him a look and he quickly apologized for the slip.

Hadley tucked her hair behind her ears. "It's shorter than I thought she'd cut it. But maybe it will be longer when I straighten it." She ran her fingers through the curls like she was trying to undo them.

To keep up appearances, he put his arm around her. "I like it. Do you like it?"

She seemed surprised to hear him say that. "You like it? It's not too short?"

"No, it's perfect. Did you lighten it?" He reached up and touched it. It was like holding strands of silk. "It looks so blond."

"Nope. I didn't mess with the color."

He smiled and regretted not giving her that kiss. She was a natural beauty who didn't need much to knock it out of the park. "You look gorgeous," he said with complete sincerity.

"I'm sorry for fighting with you last night," she blurted out in front of everyone. The whole room fell silent.

He wasn't sure how to respond with his entire family and then some waiting for his reaction. He decided to say what was real and from the heart. "I'm sorry, too. I hate fighting with you."

Before he could do anything else, she gave him a chaste kiss on the cheek. The other ladies sighed and clapped. The twins giggled. To them, kissing boys was still gross. Were Hadley's words and actions real or for show? He couldn't be sure. She was so good at playing this game. He couldn't trust her or his feelings.

He cupped her cheek and brushed his thumb along her cheekbone. Her eyes were saying things they shouldn't again. He resisted kissing her lips and went in for the hug instead.

"Who's hungry?" Ben asked and everyone made it clear that they were.

Tyler and Hadley let go and faced forward. Jon kicked Tyler's foot under the table to get his attention. Jon smiled like he was proud of him.

If he only knew.

Of all his brothers, Tyler wished he could tell Jon the truth. He wouldn't judge the way the twins would. He would also give him some honest advice. Hadley asked Lydia to share her thoughts on what was good to eat here. As she listened intently, she put her hand on his knee. The confusion set back in.

No one could see their contact under the table. This couldn't have been part of the show for the family. It was only for him. Since Tyler couldn't actually talk to Jon, no matter how much he wanted to, he was going to have to wing this with Hadley. The two of them had to talk about what was happening between them when they got back to the cabin. This time, he knew he'd have to answer some questions if he wanted some answers in return.

CHAPTER SIXTEEN

ANTICIPATION WAS WREAKING havoc with Tyler's stomach. Lunch seemed to stretch on for hours. "Let's play the alphabet game," Abby suggested.

"How do you play?" Hadley asked.

"We take turns saying a word that starts with a letter. I say a word that starts with *A*," Gen said.

"Then Lydia says a word that starts with *B*," said Abby. "Then I have to do a word with *C*. Then Daddy says a word that starts with *D*. Then you—"

Jon interrupted. "I'm pretty sure they've got it, honey."

"We have definitely got it," Hadley said with a firm nod. "I know the alphabet, so I should be good at this game."

Tyler chuckled behind his glass of pop. It was sweet of her to play along.

"What are you laughing about over there?"

Hadley poked him with her elbow. "You better start thinking of a word that begins with *E*. You wouldn't want to get out in the first round."

"Easy." He threw his arm around the back of her chair. "See what I did there? *Easy* begins with the letter *E*."

Jon tossed a balled-up napkin over Hadley that hit Tyler square on his head. "Adults have a three-second time limit. Don't get too overconfident. You'd be surprised how hard it is once we get going."

The girls started them off. The first round was a piece of cake, everybody at their table saying a word as soon as it was their turn. Round two was a bit more challenging.

"Fries," Gen said.

"Giraffe," Lydia quickly returned.

Abby took a second, mouthing all the letters of the alphabet starting with *A* until she got to *G*. "*H*. Hadley!"

"Ice," Jon said after a beat.

Hadley panicked for a second before spitting out. "Jon."

Her pause threw off Tyler's concentration. He completely forgot what letter they were on.

"Three, two—" Jon counted down.

"K." The letter finally came to him. "Kangaroo."

"Just made it, Mr. This-Is-So-Easy," Hadley teased.

"Love," Gen said with a giggle.

"Me!" Lydia pointed to herself.

"I do love you." Jon reached across the table and gave her hand a squeeze. Such a simple but meaningful gesture tugged at Tyler's heartstrings.

Hadley leaned in Tyler's direction ever so slightly, so he let his hand rest on her shoulder and pulled her closer. They were supposed to be just as happily engaged. He was certain that was the reason Hadley had moved his way.

"Pillow," Hadley said as her head rested against him.

He smiled. He didn't mind being her pillow.

"Three…two…" Lydia said. Tyler noticed they were all staring at him.

It was his turn but he hadn't been paying attention. He missed what Abby and Jon had said. Hadley had said *pillow* as part of her turn, after *P* came *Q*.

"Three! You're out," Jon said.

"Quick, quiet, quintuplets, quarterback,

quack," Tyler rattled off. "*Q*. I know a million words that start with *Q*."

"But you didn't say any of them in three seconds, so you are out."

"Let's give him one more chance, Daddy," Gen pleaded. She was a keeper, that one.

"Yeah, everyone gets one redo, Daddy," Abby said, claiming her spot in his heart, as well.

"You guys really want to give him one more try?" Jon asked.

Both girls nodded.

"Milkshakes and cookies for dessert. My treat," Tyler said, showing his appreciation.

The twins cheered. Jon reminded them to say thank you. He was a good father.

"Better pay attention this time," Hadley said. Her hair smelled like coconut shampoo and the root of his distraction. "You only get one second chance."

"I learn from my mistakes. I promise."

She glanced up at him and smiled. "Good to know."

"Thanks for driving us back," Hadley said to Ethan and Grace as they parked in front of the cabin. Tyler almost hopped out of the car the second it came to a complete stop. He wanted to get Hadley alone in the worst way.

Ethan had his arm stretched across the front seat. He glanced back at them, an easy smile spread across his face. "Don't worry about it."

"I hope you had a good time today," Grace said.

"I did," Hadley assured her. "It was really nice to be part of the family. You are lucky to have such a fabulous group of ladies in your life."

"*We* are lucky. They're in your life, too."

Tyler noticed Hadley's smile falter for a second, but she managed to put it back on. He could only imagine what she was thinking. She'd told him she was confused last night. Today could not have made that any better for her.

"Well, that was fun, huh?" he asked as they climbed the porch steps.

"It was. I'm glad to hear you saw it that way, too."

"I'm as surprised as you." Truth be told, it was fun—something he didn't think he'd ever say about spending time with his family. "You're the one who really shocked me, though. I assumed you wouldn't want to go this morning because it meant being 'on' all day. And I know you were still mad at me."

Hadley dropped her purse on the couch. Tyler had papers spread all over the coffee table. His laptop was still open on the desk. Work was his refuge during this trip, but it was time to face what was going on between them.

"It is weird to be a part of something so great but know in the back of your mind that it can't be yours in the long run. Still, I'm glad I went. I'm glad to know these people in your family."

The long run wasn't something Tyler often thought about in relation to anything other than work. He was good at setting professional goals for himself. He checked them off the imaginary list in his head. However, when it came to personal relationships, he tended to avoid making plans. Plans led to expectations. Expectations led to disappointments. Disappointments led to a broken heart and that wasn't something Tyler wanted to experience. When he weighed the cost versus benefit, opening up simply wasn't worth the risk.

Something about Hadley made him want to reconsider. He couldn't remember the last time someone made him feel like this. He wasn't sure there had ever been anyone like her.

"Last night, you said that you feel confused. Can we talk about that?"

There was a knock at the door, causing frustration to flow through every cell in his body. Tyler assumed it was Ethan. Maybe they'd forgotten something in the car.

"What?" he snapped, irritated by the interruption.

Katie didn't even flinch. Dressed in dirty jeans and a plaid button-down, she gave the attitude right back to him. "You're always such a ray of sunshine, Ty."

"We're kind of in the middle of something. What do you need?"

Katie straightened the welcome mat by kicking it flush against the cabin. "Well, I was informed you have some special guests coming in a couple days and we're supposed to make this place look like a diamond in the rough. I figured you might like to help me accomplish that, but if you're busy, I guess I can take care of it by myself. It won't all get done, but at least you won't be bothered right now."

There was always work to be done on the ranch. That was something Big E had drilled into the boys' heads from the moment they could understand words. For Tyler to get rid of this place, more work had to be put in. As much as he wanted to talk about what was going on between him and Hadley, the ranch needed to be ready for its showing on Monday.

"Where do we start?"

"I could use some help getting the haying equipment in working order. We should probably get our first cut in this weekend. We also have some irrigation issues you could lend me a hand with."

Tyler looked over his shoulder at Hadley, who had sat down on the couch. She dropped her head and pushed herself back on her feet, resigned this talk wasn't happening until the chores were done.

"I'll go get changed. More hands on deck means the work gets done faster," Hadley said, heading to the bedroom.

"I like her," Katie said.

So did Tyler.

"WHEN DID BIG E buy a drum mower?" Tyler asked, walking around the bright red-and-yellow piece of farming machinery.

Hadley had no idea what a drum mower was,

but from the sound of awe in Tyler's voice, it must have been special.

"About a year ago," Katie said. "Got it secondhand from a guy outside Billings. It's pretty nice. No hydraulics needed on the tractor, runs with modest horsepower, fast, cuts through anything. This one spits out the cut hay spread out and fluffed, saves an additional trip through the field with a tedder. Shortens drying time by up to a day."

"Nice." Tyler sounded impressed.

Katie might as well have been speaking a different language. None of that made any sense to Hadley. She wasn't sure how she was supposed to help. She only knew that if she offered, maybe they'd get done faster and she could find out how Tyler really felt.

Tyler and Katie got to work oiling and prepping the machinery. Hadley's job was to hold tools for them and to hand tools to them when asked. It reminded her of when she would hang out in the garage with her dad, watching him change the oil on his old Chevy. Her dad never paid anyone to do that kind of stuff. He was of the mentality that if he could do it himself, he should.

Hadley used to hand him a wrench or a rag

when he needed it. She probably should have paid closer attention to what he was doing so she could do it herself, but she cared more about being his special helper than learning about car maintenance. It was one of the few times she got her dad's full attention. Asher liked driving cars, not working on them.

She'd kill for a little bit of Tyler's attention right now. He was busy getting the raker ready while Katie prepped the baler. It was more complicated to make hay than Hadley thought.

For someone who didn't want anything to do with this life, Tyler was smiling while he did the work. "I remember this one time when Ben drove the baler over a dead skunk without noticing. The whole hay barn reeked to high heaven. Big E sent all five of us out there with the threat of no dinner until we found the bale with the dead animal in it. We weren't in there five minutes and Chance poked at this one hay bale and a very alive snake slithered out. Chance screamed like a girl and ran for his life."

"Oh, please. If you think that boy was afraid of a snake, you're kidding yourself. I'm sure it was his way of getting out of the search so he could find my sister and make out."

"I don't know. You didn't hear the scream," Tyler said with a laugh. "If that was acting, my brother missed his calling."

From what Tyler had told Hadley earlier, Chance had been married to Katie's older sister, Maura. The two of them had a little girl named Rosie, but Maura died a couple of years ago from cancer. Tyler hadn't seen Chance since his wife's passing but was the one brother he kept up with via phone and text.

Tyler took a quick water break and came over to stand by Hadley. "Are you having fun now?" he asked.

He had a light sheen of sweat on his forehead and smelled like grease. He had also shaved this morning and Hadley couldn't help but wonder how soft his cheek would feel under her lips.

"Not as much as I did this morning, but it's not the worst."

"Katie and I have to be better company than Zoe."

"Be nice to your ex-stepgrandma. She's not that bad. If Rachel is friends with her, she must have some redeemable qualities."

"Or Rachel is just really nice," Katie interjected.

"I don't know how you survived all those years with her here. I'm surprised you didn't defect and go work for someone else."

"My dad wasn't going to leave your grandfather high and dry. And where Lochlan Montgomery goes, I go." Katie wiped her hands off on one of the rags and then slapped them together. "Break time is over. We need to go fix some irrigation pipes."

Out in the field, Katie had Hadley hold one of the pipes to the sprinkler system in place while she and Tyler fixed whatever was broken. The sun was high in the bright blue sky. Billowy white clouds hung high above the Rockies today. It was a picturesque view from this spot. Hadley allowed herself to take it all in.

Her phone rang in her pocket. She couldn't put down the pipe or let go. Katie came over and pulled it out of her back pocket for her.

"It's your mom," she said, and before Hadley could tell her to let it go to voice mail, she answered it. "Hello, Hadley's mom...No, ma'am, this is not Hadley, but this is her phone. My name is Katie. Your daughter is helping me and her handsome fiancé do a little work on the ranch today."

Hadley's heart stopped the second the word

fiancé came out of Katie's mouth. After everything she had been through to keep up this lie, even after it had been discovered by Ethan and Grace, Hadley was about to be outed by her mother.

"Yes, ma'am, her fiancé, Tyler. Tyler Blackwell." Confusion was written all over Katie's face. Tyler came over and snatched the phone away.

"Hi, Mrs. Sullivan. This is Tyler. Can Hadley call you right back? I promise she is alive and well. Say hi, Hadley." He held the phone up to her.

"Hi, Mom. I'll call you back in a few minutes."

Panic swirled through her body. How was she going to explain this to her mom? How were they going to smooth things over with Katie?

Tyler hung up and put the phone back in Hadley's pocket. "Let's get this sprinkler back in action, shall we?"

His attempt at breezing right past the issue didn't go as well as he wanted. Katie's gaze jumped back and forth between them.

"Oh. My. Gosh."

This was it. It was over. There would be

no way to convince Katie to keep the secret. Hadley wasn't sure if she should be relieved or disappointed. The lies were going to stop right now.

"Katie, I can explain," Tyler started.

"You didn't even ask her father's permission before you asked her to marry you? Did no one teach you there are rules about this kind of stuff?" She turned to Hadley. "You haven't even told your parents you're engaged yet?"

Hadley was speechless. Katie had handed them their cover story.

"We were waiting to do it in person. Thanks a lot for ruining the big surprise," Tyler said, running with it.

Katie's mouth fell open and she covered it with her hand. "Oh, my gosh, I am so sorry, Hadley. I didn't know. I'm sure that was something you had all planned out and I just ruined it."

"It's okay. I did have a plan, but it's fine. Don't beat yourself up about it."

Tyler wiped his forehead with the back of his hand and gave Hadley a thumbs-up. They dodged that bullet. Of course, now she had to figure out what to tell her mother.

Twenty minutes later, they headed back to

the horse barn. Katie apologized for the hundredth time. Hadley was both relieved and disappointed. Part of her was ready to be done.

"I'm going to run up to the cabin and call my mom. I'll see you in a bit?" she asked Tyler.

"We've got a few more things to take care of, but I'll be done in time to take you to dinner."

It was obvious that he was in his element today. He was an excellent marketing executive, but there was something about working with his hands that seemed to bring him to life.

Hadley flipped her phone around and around in her hand. She couldn't put off calling her mom much longer. The woman was probably going nuts trying to figure out why Hadley had kept something this big from her. She had two options: come completely clean with her mom and explain the situation she had gotten herself in or lie.

The thought of one more lie made her stomach turn and all the muscles in her back tighten. At the same time, telling the truth would lead to some major judgment. She had wanted to tell them about the promotion, but if she had to explain how she got it, there'd be little chance of earning their respect and pride.

Hadley didn't like her options, but she had to tell the truth. No more lies no matter what the repercussions. She was about to call when her phone rang. It wasn't her mom. Asher's face smiled at her on the screen. Her brother never called her. It could mean only one thing. She must have given her mother a heart attack.

CHAPTER SEVENTEEN

"HI, ASH."

"Did you really do what I think you just did?"

She had been kidding about giving her mom a heart attack, but Asher sounded a tad too serious. "Is Mom okay? I need to call her back."

"Do you know what happens on Thursday?"

"Thursday?" What did that have to do with her mom's thinking she was engaged?

Asher's sigh was definitely meant to convey his annoyance. "Of course you have no idea. I mean that little to you."

"What are you talking about?"

"The awards. The nominations are announced Thursday morning. It's only quite possibly the biggest thing to happen to me."

She tried to feel guilty for not remembering that he might or might not be nominated in a few days but failed. She had some bigger fish to fry just then.

"Sorry. But I'm unclear how I did something that impacts whether or not you get nominated for an acting award."

"Seriously? Mom and Dad flew out here to support me and celebrate with me if I am fortunate enough to be nominated and all mom could talk about for the last half hour is that you're *engaged*. This is the biggest moment of my career and you just couldn't deal with me getting some of the attention."

Some of the attention? Asher had been getting all of their attention since the second he came out of the womb.

"You think I got engaged to steal your thunder?"

"Why else would you drop this bomb on Mom right now?"

Hadley barked a laugh. Was he serious? How could someone possibly be more self-absorbed? "I didn't drop any bombs on Mom and I am certainly not trying to ruin your life. Heaven forbid Mom talk about me in front of you for more than one second. What will you ever do having to listen to her go on and on and on and on about me instead of asking you how you're doing? I mean, not that I know what that's like at all."

"Oh, don't be so dramatic." He was unbelievable. "I understand it's hard being my sister. I am a very tough act to follow. You don't have to go and do unexpected things to get attention. Mom and Dad love you. Please stop trying to make everything about you. I don't get to see them as often as you do and I'd like this week to be about me."

Hadley had to cover her mouth so she didn't let something slip that she'd regret. He had no idea what it was like to be her. "Is Mom there?"

"She's in the other room. She called Aunt Penny to tell her you were getting married. She plans on calling *everyone* and sharing the news. So much for the calls she was going to make on Thursday to tell them I was nominated. That's going to feel a little bit like an afterthought now, isn't it?"

Her mom was talking to Aunt Penny about *her*? She planned to call everyone? Her mom never called family about Hadley. It was always to share news about Asher. This was what it felt like to be bragged about. Hadley leaned back on the couch. Her mom was... excited for her. This never happened.

"Hadley? Are you still there?" Asher asked.

"I'm here. I'm sorry if this is making you feel like your possible nomination isn't as important as it is. I mean it's not the same as something as life-changing as getting married, but it's important." This felt too good. But even though this fake engagement was going to end sooner than later, she couldn't resist milking it for every bit of attention it was gaining her. "I'll call Mom and remind her why she's out there and encourage her to keep the focus where it should be."

Asher wasn't as pleased with this role reversal. "Thanks."

"I'll talk to you on Thursday! Good luck, big brother." Hadley hung up and let what just happened soak in for a minute. For the first time in her life, she had managed to outshine the sun. It was a glorious feeling.

She hadn't wanted to keep up the lie. Her plan had been to come clean, but what was one more little lie in the grand scheme of things? This was the first time one of the lies actually made her feel good. It wouldn't last forever, but it would be enough for now.

TYLER AND KATIE finished most of the chores on her list. The rest they'd have to tackle tomorrow. They had one more day before the buyer that Ben recommended showed up.

"I always pictured you here doing this kind of stuff," Katie said, taking a seat next to him on the weathered bench outside the tack room. She smelled like hay and sweat. It wasn't surprising that she turned down the other ladies' offer to go to the spa. That wasn't Katie's scene.

"Really?"

"For sure." She took a swig of water. "I know Chance wanted nothing to do with this life, but you always were eager to help my dad out and get your hands dirty. He always liked that about you."

Tyler remembered spending time with Lochlan, but the old man never said much. He usually complained about Chance and the attention he was showing Maura. It felt nice to know Lochlan had appreciated his help.

"Can I mow the field tomorrow? I really want to see that drum mower in action."

Katie smirked and wrinkled her freckled nose. "Can you get out of bed before nine? I know you got that pretty fiancée to snuggle with, but I'm sure you haven't been gone so long that you forgot that work on the ranch begins at sunup."

Tyler couldn't let his mind wander to what it would be like to cuddle Hadley. "I think I can manage that."

"Then you can mow." She finished her water and pulled out a handkerchief from her back pocket to wipe her face. Katie reminded him of her dad. They both had the same work ethic and similar mannerisms.

"How is your dad doing? I remember you said he was in Arizona, but I know he's been struggling a bit health-wise."

Katie gave him a sad smile. "He has his good days and bad days. His heart is bad shape. I'm working hard to help him make some positive life changes, but he's a stubborn old coot. Getting him to go away for some downtime was a huge accomplishment on my part."

"I'm sorry. I know it can't be easy when those parent/child roles get reversed. I suppose we're going through the same thing with Big E."

"Can I ask you something?"

That was always a loaded question. With so many secrets to keep, it was hard to know if he could answer honestly. "Maybe."

"What is it about this place that makes you want to sell it so bad?"

There were so many different answers to that question. Tyler's reasons were layered. "I can't stay and Ethan can't run this place by himself."

"Why can't you stay? I mean, I know you have a job and stuff in Portland, but people move and change jobs all the time. Something bigger is holding you back."

Tyler put his elbows on his knees and clasped his hands together. The lie was easier than the truth on this one. "I'm marrying Hadley. We have a life in Portland. She doesn't want to live here and wherever she goes, I go."

"You're in love with her. It's obvious. Anyone who sees you two together can tell."

Tyler wasn't sure if he should be proud of his acting skills or worried that he was more smitten than he even realized. "That's why we're getting married."

"She loves this place. I see that, too. She isn't afraid to get her hands dirty. Heck, she got a manicure this morning and was out in the field helping us with irrigation pipes this afternoon. Who else would do that?"

"You."

Katie chuckled. "Nah, I wouldn't have gotten the manicure in the first place."

"True. She's one of a kind," Tyler said, meaning it wholeheartedly.

"I bet if you asked her, she would consider staying here."

Tyler shook his head. Katie didn't know his fiancée wasn't real, so maybe he needed to be real. "It's not Hadley that's driving me away. It's me. Being here cuts a little too deep. There's too much pain buried out there in those fields."

"I know losing your mom and dad was hard—"

"It's not just that." Losing his parents was incredibly hard, but it was how he had lost them and the fact that he couldn't save them that was the greater issue. "I can't stay somewhere I never truly felt loved."

Katie squared her shoulders to him. "What are you talking about? You were loved. Your brothers would all lay down their lives for you. Your mom and dad loved you. Big E has always been a little rough around the edges, but he loves you boys in his way."

"It's nice that you think so, but I remember things a little differently than you do. My parents…" He couldn't talk about his parents. The emotion was too raw. "Big E never seemed to be happy about having to take care of us. His behavior over the years speaks volumes, plus, where is he right now? He took off and refuses to contact any of us when we need him to help us get this ranch up and running."

"The guest ranch looks up and running to me. You and Ethan are doing a great job. He's proud of you."

"Big E doesn't know what pride is. Never has." Tyler could list too many examples of Big E being the exact opposite of proud. He was impossible to please, which was why they all gave up trying.

"Don't give up on him. Maybe he'll surprise you."

Tyler had to hold back a bitter laugh. He stood up and stretched his arms above his head. He needed to go finish a conversation with Hadley, and digging up the resentments he felt toward his grandfather wasn't going to put him in the right frame of mind.

"I can't hold out hope that he's going to change. A leopard can't change his spots, Katie."

HADLEY IMAGINED THAT this feeling she was experiencing was what being on cloud nine felt like. She turned up the radio and swayed to the country song playing on the only station that came in out here in the middle of Montana.

"Someone's in a good mood. Did you get into the wine that I bought the other day?" Tyler leaned against the doorjamb with his arms folded across that chest. A smile played on his lips. Those lips.

She reached for him. "Dance with me. I'm celebrating being the favorite child for once in my life."

Tyler's brow furrowed, but he took her hand and swayed back and forth with her. "How exactly did you become the favorite?"

Hadley wrapped her arms around his neck. "I didn't know until today, but my mom has been dreaming about my wedding since the day she found out she was having a girl."

"Really?" He placed his hands on her hips.

"Finding out we're engaged has her more excited than the possibility of Asher being nominated for an Emmy." Saying it out loud made it that much more incredible.

"Your mom still thinks we're engaged?

I thought maybe you would set the record straight."

"I was going to… I planned to, but then my brother called with the news that I was ruining his life by being more important than him and I couldn't do it. I have never been more important than him. Ever. I decided lying for a little longer wouldn't hurt anyone, even Asher. His ego needs a reality check."

Maybe that was mean. She was trying to care, but Asher had spent a lifetime being mean to her. Didn't he deserve it?

"I didn't realize you and your brother were on such bad terms."

"I wouldn't call it bad terms. Asher only thinks about Asher. My parents only think about Asher. They all think I should only think about Asher. It's refreshing to be a blip on my mom's radar even if it'll only be for a few days."

Tyler stopped swaying. "You deserve to be more than a blip on someone's radar."

Hadley swallowed hard. He was staring at her with those eyes. She brought her hand to his cheek. It was as smooth as silk, just like she had imagined it would be last night.

"You scare me, Tyler Blackwell. I could fall

under your spell and then what? Would you break my heart?"

"Would you break mine?"

She could feel his heart beating as fast as hers. She would never break his heart if he trusted her with it.

"I won't break yours if you don't break mine."

The air between them felt electric. He breathed in and she breathed out. "Seems like a fair compromise," he said, sliding his hand up to her neck. His thumb brushed against her bottom lip. "I'm going to kiss you now."

Kissing Tyler was like Christmas morning. Every kiss was a new present under the tree. They were all different but exactly what she was hoping for.

He pulled back but tugged her closer against him. She felt safe and loved in a way she'd never experienced with anyone else. He began to sway back and forth to the music again.

"I'm falling for you. I'm falling hard," he admitted. "My family is falling for you. Heck, even Katie loves you."

"I love your family. I love Katie. Everyone here is amazing." It was easy to talk about his family and friends. It was terrifying to say what she felt for him. "I could fall for you, too. I just don't want to ruin everything."

His forehead creased with concern. "How would you ruin everything?"

"You're my boss, so I'm not sure how this plays out. Do we go back to Portland and you give me a promotion and become my boyfriend? How's that going to look to everyone at the office? What's Kellen going to say?"

"I don't have answers. I would hope that everyone at the office knows you're the hardest-working person there and that my feelings for you have nothing to do with why you'd get promoted."

"And what's your family going to think? What's my family going to think? They're all waiting for a wedding and I just want to know what it's like to hold your hand and do this—" she kissed his cheek so she could feel the softness of his skin on her lips "—whenever I want to."

The happiest smile broke across his face. "You're going to kiss me whenever you want to now?"

"I think I might." Her nerves made her giggle like a schoolgirl. "Unless that's a problem for you."

"No, I have no problem with that because I think I'm going to be kissing you whenever I want, as well."

"Sounds like there could be a lot of kissing in our future."

"I hope so," he murmured before gently placing one more on her lips.

Hadley let herself enjoy the kiss a couple of minutes longer before she pulled back. "You need a shower and I need some food. Kissing is nice but it's not going to fill my belly. Get ready and take me to dinner, Mr. Blackwell."

Tyler took off his hat and held it over his heart. He bowed his head. "Whatever you say, Miss Sullivan."

CHAPTER EIGHTEEN

WHO CARED WHAT the family thought? That was what Hadley and Tyler had decided over dinner the night they came clean about their feelings for each other. No one said they had to get married anytime in the near future. Maybe they wanted a long engagement. Even better, maybe Tyler would be okay with telling the truth and ending the engagement lie altogether.

"Please tell me you have an amazing plan to sabotage this meeting today." Ethan sidled up next to her as she watched the new guests feed the animals at the petting zoo. "And an even better plan to sabotage the meeting on Wednesday."

"I don't know if I can do this," Hadley confessed. She'd been thinking about it and now that Tyler admitted how he felt about her, there was no reason to keep up being a double agent. "I have to tell you something."

"Hadley, please. You promised me you

would give me time to work on him. I can't work on him if he sells the ranch out from under me."

"Ethan, I'm falling in love with your brother."

"Great!" His wide eyes and broad smile made him seem genuinely happy for her.

"And he is falling in love with me. There's no big lie for you to reveal. We're actually together."

Ethan laughed at the irony of the situation. "You're telling me that while lying about being in love you both really fell in love with each other?"

"I can't explain it. He's different here. Look at him." Tyler was standing by the horse barn with Conner. He planned to take the buyer around the property on horseback. He was all smiles. "He's never that happy at the office."

Ethan watched his brother for a minute and bounced on the balls of his feet. "That's why you have to keep helping me."

Why wasn't he listening to her? She didn't want to do this anymore. The lies weren't worth the risk of making Tyler miserable.

"I'm not in this for the promotion anymore. I'm in it for your brother."

"Perfect! He belongs here, Hadley. You both do, especially now that you're in love."

"Falling in love," she corrected. She didn't want him to misunderstand where they were in this relationship.

"Especially since you're both falling in love. Help me. Help me convince him to stay. All of us working together could make this ranch something amazing."

Hadley needed a second to process what he was offering. Stay in Montana? Permanently? That was an option that she had not bothered to consider because being together hadn't been a possibility until now. She didn't hate the idea.

"I don't know."

"But you'll think about it?"

"Staying has to be his choice."

"But you love this idea."

The more she thought about it, the more excited she got. She loved the ideas they had come up with already and had been disappointed that she wouldn't get to see them through.

"If he wanted to stay, I would consider staying with him." Ethan nearly hopped out of his shoes. "*But* if he wants to go back to Portland, then I want to go back to Portland, too. We're a package deal."

"I wouldn't have it any other way," Ethan said, giving her a side-hug. "But I need this week to help him realize that staying would make him happy. I can't have buyers roaming the ranch without some guarantee that you're going to help me make it a little less desirable to them."

"Howard Yonk is traveling here from Bozeman. He's interested in reverting this back to a working ranch. Tyler put together the selling points without me. I don't know what we have to offer that I need to downplay or what we don't that I need to make him aware of."

"The water rights," Ethan blurted. "If he wants this to be a working ranch, the fact that Double T has the water rights now makes it a less desirable sale, correct?"

"Correct. I was going to bring that up with the Mendes people, as well. Is there anything that puts cattle at risk around here? A reason someone wouldn't want to bring their livestock?"

"You could make something up about problems with brucellosis being transferred from wild animals to domestic cattle around these parts. There were concerns a while back with regards to the wild elk and bison by Yellowstone."

"Okay. That could work. Good thing you're a vet because I have no idea what brucellosis is."

"A rancher will know."

Hadley wasn't sure how she was going to work in all these negatives during a sales pitch, but she had a couple of hours to figure it out. Ethan better be right about Tyler needing a little encouragement to stay. If she was going to take this risk, she needed it to pay off for all of them.

HOWARD YONK DECIDED that he wanted to spend his golden years running a cattle ranch. He had grown up on a ranch outside Billings, but his family had sold it when his grandfather died.

"Mr. Yonk, it's good to meet you," Tyler said, greeting him outside the guest lodge. "Tyler Blackwell, we spoke on the phone."

Howard was at least six foot seven and had a mustache as thick as it was gray. His hands were the size of frying pans and his boots must have had to have been custom ordered they were so large. He completely enveloped Tyler's hand in his as they shook.

"Well, it's nice to meet you, Mr. Blackwell. Please call me Howard. I appreciate you being able to make time for me."

"I was happy to do it. Please call me Tyler. I'm glad it worked out while I was here to give the tour personally. I want to make sure you see all the facilities and get a feel for the land. It's truly a beautiful piece of property, situated here in the foothills of the mountains. It doesn't get any better than this."

Tyler had been rehearsing all morning. He had all the sales pitches down pat and all the important numbers memorized—acreage, number of horses for sale, age of the machinery, number of ranch hands, square footage of the structures. It helped that he had lived here when it was a working ranch, so he knew exactly how it would work.

"Would you like to come in the lodge and get a drink before we tour the facilities?"

"That sounds like a perfect way to start." Howard adjusted his black wool gambler hat with its silver conch accents. Put the man in a black vest over his white button-down shirt and he'd look like he stepped right out of a Wild West movie.

They took a seat at the bar and Tyler waved the bartender over. Hadley planned to discuss the possibility of expanding the bar with the Mendes family in a couple of days. Since Howard wasn't looking to maintain the guest lodge, there was no reason to mention it.

Hadley had gone on and on about how they could add some card tables and maybe even put in a small stage for some live music. She was full of ideas. He loved listening to her when she was so passionate about something.

The two men discussed Howard's trip down from Bozeman and Tyler got some background on the ranch Howard grew up on. It sounded quite a bit bigger than the Blackwell Ranch. His grandfather herded three times the number of cattle Big E did back in the day.

Hadley entered the room from the dining hall. She had on a blue sundress and the new cowboy boots she bought herself at Brewster's when Lydia came by to take her shopping yesterday. She was beautiful and falling for him. The thought made him grin from ear to ear.

"Howard, I'd like you to meet my fiancée. Hadley, this is Mr. Yonk."

Howard got to his feet and Hadley's eyes widened. "Mr. Yonk, so good to meet you."

"Please call me Howard." He took her hand and gave her knuckles a kiss. "How do I get to take the tour with her instead of you?" he asked Tyler.

"I get that a lot. And trust me, I'd rather go somewhere with her than anyone else."

Hadley put her arm around Ty's shoulder and kissed his cheek. "That almost makes me sound like I'm your favorite."

He hadn't thought about it like that, but she kind of was. Was this how it felt to favor something or someone?

They chatted a little longer so Hadley could wield her charm. Howard was completely under her spell by the time they were ready to head out to the horse barn.

Ethan was waiting outside the guest lodge. "I hate to interrupt your meeting, but I need you to help me with something. It will only take a couple minutes. I am so sorry."

"The work on a ranch is never done," Howard said.

Tyler was still annoyed even though his guest understood. "Could Conner help you? Or Katie?"

"They can't help me. I know it's a bad time, but I wouldn't be asking if I didn't need you."

His brother knew he had this appointment. He knew he had this appointment at this time. He had all morning to ask for his help, but he waited until the buyer was here. Tyler kept a smile plastered on his face.

"Hadley, can you take Howard over to the horse barn and I'll meet you guys over there?"

"Of course." She was a lifesaver. "Shall we?"

HADLEY HOOKED ARMS with Howard and led him in the direction of the barn. The man was a giant. She wasn't sure what horse Tyler planned to put him on. Perhaps the horseback riding would go badly and that would help discourage him from buying. She walked him by the small corral where the two mares and the foals were grazing.

"These are our newest members of the family."

"Have you named the foals yet?" Howard asked.

"Not yet. I think the boys are feeling the pressure. It's like naming a child. You don't want to mess it up because the baby will have that name forever."

"People forget that most things can change. People change their names all the time. Mistakes happen. They don't have to ruin everything forever, though."

Wise words from Mr. Yonk. They continued their walk to the barn. Hadley tried to calm her nerves. She was afraid Tyler would find out what she was doing and not understand. He couldn't understand until Ethan helped him see what the ranch really meant to him.

"What I love about this ranch is all the different lodging accommodations we have here. Besides the brand-new guest lodge, we have the four cabins on the northwest side and then there's the owner's house." Hadley knew he wasn't planning on running it as a guest ranch, but playing up the guest facilities might turn him off.

"Well, sounds like I could let everyone who would work here live right on the property if I wanted to."

"Oh, that's right, you're the one looking to revert it back to a full-time working ranch. We have another interested buyer who's looking to keep it as is."

"There's another buyer?"

"Shoot!" Hadley smacked herself on the forehead. "Please don't tell Tyler that I said that. I don't think I was supposed to mention that."

"Don't you worry. I didn't hear anything about other buyers," Howard said, patting her hand.

Conner had some of the horses exercising in the outdoor riding arena. They stopped there to watch.

"Do you ride often?" Hadley asked.

"Not as much as I did when I was young, but it's one of the things I am most looking forward to getting back to. I think it was Daniel Boone who said, 'All you need for happiness is a good gun, a good horse and a good wife.'"

"Sounds like something he would say," Hadley replied. She was a city girl and had no idea if that sounded like Daniel Boone or not. "Do you have all those things, Mr. Yonk?"

"Howard," he corrected her. "And I have a very good gun, a couple good horses and one very horrible ex-wife. She's part of the reason I'm looking for a ranch away from everything."

"I'm sorry to hear that."

"Hadley!" Grace came down the path from the guest lodge as they had planned.

"Excuse me one second. What was that about the work on a ranch is never done?" She laughed with Howard and went to talk to Grace.

"Did you hear what he did?" Grace tried to sound a bit hysterical.

"Who?"

"Ben. He blew it! The water rights belong to the Thompsons now. Judge Edwards ruled in their favor and now we're screwed."

"Shh!" Hadley glanced over her shoulder to make sure Howard heard every word but thought she didn't want him to. She pushed Grace a little farther away. "The gentleman over there is our potential buyer," she murmured.

"What? Why didn't you tell me?" Grace flailed her arms and had acting unhinged down pat.

"You didn't give me a chance," Hadley said while fighting the urge to laugh. If she lost it, Grace would crack up and everything would be ruined. This was ridiculous. She would not repeat this farce with the next buyer. "Get out of here and pray he didn't hear what you said."

Grace stomped away while Hadley tried to control her expression. She needed to look frazzled, not amused. This was serious. If she wanted Howard Yonk to walk away from this sale, she had to do her part.

"Sorry about that. There's always some kind of drama going on here. Plus my sister-in-law is under so much stress being pregnant and all."

Howard nodded, but was definitely mulling over everything he had heard.

"Tell me more about your family. Do you have any children?"

"Three girls who won't talk to me anymore thanks to that horrible ex-wife I mentioned before."

Howard's life was far from happy. "I'm sorry to hear that, too."

Tyler came jogging down the path a minute later. He seemed clearly displeased with whatever it was that Ethan used to buy them some time to put on their little show.

"So sorry for the delay, Howard. I hope Hadley has been good company at least."

"She's a doll, but I think I'm going to head back home without the tour."

Hadley was a bit shocked that it worked. He wasn't even going to look at the property.

Tyler was beside himself. "What? Howard, please. If we get out there on horseback and you see the land, you are going to fall in love, I promise."

"I might, but I doubt this is the property for me. You have a lot going on here and it's probably a little too guest and not enough working ranch for me. I won't waste your time when I am almost certain this isn't for me."

"But, sir."

"Mr. Yonk… I mean, Howard, please. I'm sure I'm not half the salesperson my fiancé is. If you let him show you around, he might be able to answer some of your questions better than I can, perhaps get you to change your mind," Hadley said, hoping she could cover her tracks well enough.

"You are a sweet young lady, Hadley. It was a pleasure talking to you. I'm just going to head back up to my truck and be on my way."

Tyler followed him down the path. He turned around, put his hands up and mouthed, "What happened?"

"Nothing, I swear," Hadley mouthed back.

Liar, liar, pants on fire. One buyer down. One to go.

CHAPTER NINETEEN

"SO WALK ME through it one more time. You're heading to the horse barn…" Tyler paced back and forth in front of the couch in the cabin. He didn't even care if he wore out the new carpet.

"We went down to the horse barn. I showed him the baby horses."

"You didn't call them baby horses, did you?"

"No. I called them the foals. Do you really think he decided not to buy the ranch because I didn't call baby horses by their proper name?"

Tyler raked a hand through his hair. This wasn't Hadley's fault, he kept telling himself. "No. Okay, so then what?"

"We kept walking. I asked him if he rides horses often. He said he hadn't ridden in a while. He quoted Daniel Boone. Something about guns and horses and wives help you find happiness. I asked him if he had those things and he told me he had a bad divorce, his daughters don't talk to him anymore and then he said he wasn't interested in buying the ranch anymore."

"So you reminded him about the miserable parts of his life and he left?"

"How is this my fault? I asked a perfectly innocent question. Are you telling me you weren't going to ask him if there was a Mrs. Yonk at any point during your conversation? You would have, don't even lie."

Tyler sat down on the couch next to her. He would have asked the man about his family eventually. She hadn't said anything he wouldn't have said. "I know it's not your fault, it's just so frustrating. I don't understand what triggered him."

"Maybe he's not as ready to buy as Rachel heard. He shows up here, it's hot, there's a lot of walking, he's a big guy, maybe he realized the life of a rancher is a hard one and he's not ready for it."

Hadley had spent the last half hour trying to calm Tyler down, but he took it so personally that Howard left without seeing the property. The Blackwell Ranch was more than the guest lodge. It was the land that made it special.

"I didn't even get to show him the best parts

of this place. He didn't get to see the pond or the wildflower fields."

Hadley threw her arm around him. "It didn't work out. It wasn't meant to be. Howard Yonk thinks a gun, a horse and a wife are the perfect recipe for happiness. That sounds more like the plot for a new series called *CSI Montana* if you ask me."

Tyler laughed, and she kissed his cheek because she could do that now whenever she wanted.

"He's not the right guy to take over this land," she added. "We have another potential buyer coming on Wednesday. Let's see how that goes."

She was right. Yonk was only the first one. They had the Mendes family coming in a couple of days and if that fell through, they'd find another and another and another until the right one showed up. Someone would buy it eventually.

Hadley curled up against him. "You know, you promised me that one of these days we would sit out on the front porch and watch the sunset. Can we do that tonight?"

He kissed the top of her head because he

could do that anytime he wanted now. "I would love to watch the sunset with you."

Tyler's phone rang. He unwound himself from Hadley and grabbed his phone off the desk. It was Kellen. He hadn't spoken to him or emailed him in days. He probably was worried that Tyler was dead.

"I thought I was on vacation. Business partners don't call when you're on vacation."

"I'm thrilled that you're having so much fun that you forgot all about me."

"I could never forget you." Tyler smiled at Hadley. He could never forget *her*. She lay back on the couch and kicked off those cowboy boots. She was so cute. He wanted to spoil her to let her know that she was special.

"I was wondering if you looked at the research that Eric did. I also forwarded you his analysis for Kingman this morning. He worked on it over the weekend and it's excellent."

"I looked at the research and it was decent." It was better than decent. It was thorough and well written. If the analysis was at the same level, he didn't have a leg to stand on to convince Kellen to demote him and give the job to Hadley.

This day was going from bad to worse. "I still propose we do both."

"Both what?"

"Both get jobs." He couldn't speak freely in front of Hadley. If she knew there was no promotion at the end of this, she would lose all trust in him.

"You mean give both Hadley and Eric the brand strategist title?"

"Yes."

"Listen, I reached out to Hadley and she agreed to talk to me about her career when she gets back. I don't think she'll be so opposed to being patient and setting some goals. Maybe in a year, we can move her up a notch."

"A year?" There was no chance she would agree to that. He could not let her down like this.

Her brow furrowed and she gave him a questioning look. He winked and smiled, hoping to ease her mind. He motioned that he'd be right back and ducked out onto the porch, where he could say what he needed to say.

"I already told her the job is hers," he admitted as he sat down on the bench where he was going to watch the sunset later.

Kellen didn't take the news well. "Excuse me?"

"Before I left. I told her the job was hers. I can't take it back. I didn't realize you would have such a problem with it. I didn't think Eric would turn things around so fast. I'll forgo my bonus and we can use that money to cover her raise."

"Are you kidding me? I thought this was a partnership. I thought we made decisions that affect the whole company together. Was I wrong?"

"I was wrong, so I'll take the hit on this one."

"Are you sleeping with her? Is that what this is about?"

"No!" He was falling in love with her, but he was definitely not sleeping with her. "It's not like that."

"It better not be. If I find out different, you and I are going to have a serious problem."

"Says the guy who hired his nephew." Kellen wasn't going to dictate whom Tyler could date or not date. He also wasn't going to let anyone believe Hadley hadn't earned her position in the company by being the most qualified person for the position.

"That's not the same thing and Eric is more than capable of doing the job."

"It's playing favorites and you know I hate that. It's giving someone special treatment because they are related to you. It's nepotism, plain and simple."

"You can accuse me of whatever you want. Regardless of my ties to Eric, I came to you for your approval to hire him. I didn't offer him the job *before* you said you were fine with it."

"I said I messed up. And that I would absorb the cost of that mistake. What more do you want from me?"

"I want a partner who wants to be a partner."

When they started 2K Marketing, Tyler thought he wanted to be a partner. Today, he wasn't so sure. Kellen wasn't the same person he went into business with. He had lost some of his edge and no longer pushed himself to be as creative as Tyler knew he could be. To be fair, Tyler wasn't the same person Kellen went into business with either.

"I'll talk to you on Monday when I get back," he said before hanging up.

Tyler and Hadley's relationship was not going to go over well. Kellen would assume things that weren't true. She deserved better than to have her integrity called into question.

This was his fault and he had no idea how to make it better.

Maybe she would be okay with keeping their relationship a secret. It might be interesting to go from pretending to be in love, to actually falling in love, to pretending not to be in love. Maybe she'd think that was ironic.

Or maybe she'd be so angry she'd quit her job and him. He had really messed things up.

HADLEY HATED BEING a liar. And hated even more that she was becoming so adept at it. It made her question everything she believed about herself and her values. If she could lie so easily, what did that say about her moral compass?

Tyler didn't suspect she had anything to do with chasing off Howard. He'd have no clue when she did the same to the Mendes family on Wednesday. Ethan kept texting her smiley faces and telling her she was awesome. She didn't feel awesome. She felt deceitful.

If she could get Tyler to admit that he wanted to stay, maybe it would all be worth it. The end would justify the means. He loved *and* hated this ranch. She needed to get him to dig deeper. To put some demons to rest.

The only way they were going to do that was if he was out there. She ran back to the bedroom to change.

"Go riding with me," she said, finding him sitting on the porch staring at the gazing pasture.

"You want to go riding? With me?"

"I want you to show me what you would have showed Mr. Yonk. I think you wanted to see it as much as you wanted him to see it." She held out her hand and pulled him to his feet. He tugged her against him and kissed her until she was breathless.

"Thank you," he whispered.

"For what?"

"For knowing exactly what I need."

They walked down to the barn hand in hand. They saddled up a couple of horses and headed out. Tyler told more stories about cattle wrangling as a kid, complete with runaway heifers and troublesome bulls. He showed her the tree where he had almost been killed by that angry moose. And the entrance to the forest where he shared his first kiss with a lucky little girl named Danielle. His demeanor changed as soon as they started to follow the creek to the dilapidated bridge.

Hadley could sense the sadness overtaking him. He got quiet, somber.

"Tell me about them," she said as the road came into view.

"I don't like talking about them."

"I know, but maybe if you do, it won't hurt so much. Holding things in is what usually causes all the pain."

"I wouldn't even know where to start."

Hadley dismounted her horse. Her heart pounded. She wanted to do something good. To do right by him after a day of lying. "I'm here with you, for you to lean on."

Tyler slid off his horse. She took him by the hand and they walked side by side with their horses in tow. The water danced over the rocks in the creek bed. The sound of birds chirping in the trees filled the air. The grass was long and green along the natural embankment.

"What was your dad like?" she prompted him.

"He looked a lot like Jon. Tall, skinny. But when I was a kid, I thought he was the most manly guy I knew. He had strong, calloused hands and these deep wrinkles around his eyes when he smiled. He was always clean-shaven. He said Mom didn't like beards. I thought it was because she didn't like how they looked, but now I think she probably didn't like kissing him if he had all that hair around his mouth. They used to kiss all the time. It was so embarrassing that they'd kiss in front of us when I was little."

"Was he a yeller or did he spank you guys when you got in trouble?"

"Neither. Dad was quiet. Unless he was with his friends and they were playing cards. They used to have these poker games and that was the only time I saw my dad smoke. He'd sit at the table with a cigarette in his mouth and the perfect poker face. My brothers and I used to imitate them with straws as the cigarettes and pennies as poker chips."

"And your mom, what was she like?"

"An excellent cook. That was one of the big things we missed when she was gone. Big E made us all take turns being in charge of dinner. Jon was the only one who mastered something more impressive than spaghetti noodles and sauce or hot dogs. She used to make these hand pies filled with peaches or apples, sometimes blueberries. She always smelled like cocoa butter. She used to have this lotion that she put on every morning and every night before bed. I remember I took the bottle after she died and put a little bit on my hands every day before I went to school so I could feel like she was still close. I was so sad when the bottle ran empty. I didn't have the courage to ask Big E if he'd buy me another bottle. Men didn't put on lotion. Chance cried every night for almost a week after it was gone. He didn't use it, but he liked that I smelled like her because we slept in the same room and when he closed his eyes, it was like she was there."

"Your memories are beautiful."

"Not all of them."

"Most of them, though. It sounds like they were good people. I'm sorry I won't get to meet them."

Tyler fell silent again. They made it to the road. He glanced in the direction of the bridge. "I could introduce you," he said.

Hadley was surprised that he'd offered. "I'd like that." She assumed he'd take her over to the water but he turned up the road, heading back to the north part of the ranch. They rode the horses toward the barn and Tyler explained where his parents were laid to rest.

"Up on that hill, behind the house, are their graves. I haven't been there since their funeral.

I don't know if any of us ever went back up there again."

Hadley was proud of him for facing down this fear. "Are you sure you want to go now?"

He shook his head no, but took her by the hand and started up the hill. The view from there was breathtaking. The mountains to the west, the plains to the east, the whole Blackwell Ranch to the south. It was like they were up here looking over everyone. There was only one headstone for the two of them. Husband and wife. Father and mother. Son and daughter.

Tyler squeezed Hadley's hand a little tighter. "Hadley, this is my mom and dad. Mom and Dad, this is Hadley."

"They must be so proud of the man you have become. Of the men you and your brothers have all become."

Tyler's eyes were damp with unshed tears. His chin quivered ever so slightly.

"I warned them that the water was rising too fast that night. I had been out in the storm. I got caught in it when I was out fooling around on the other side of the creek. We weren't supposed to go on that side. I never listened, though."

Tears rolled down his cheeks and he wiped

his running nose with the sleeve of his shirt. Hadley stayed quiet, giving him a chance to compose himself.

"When I got to the house, my dad was loading up the pickup. He said one of the wranglers said he'd lost a calf and he thought it had crossed the bridge. I told my dad there was no calf. I had just been there. I would have seen it. He wouldn't listen to me, though. I ran over to my mom and told her the creek was rising fast, that I had trouble getting across, but she wouldn't listen either. She told me we'd talk about disobeying her rules later. If it had been Jon that told my dad he didn't see a calf, he would have listened. He would have agreed to recheck the grazing pasture. If it had been Ben or Ethan or Chance who told my mom the water was rising, who begged her not to go, she would have stayed behind. She would have sent someone else to go with my dad if they had asked."

"You can't really believe that. Your parents made their decision based on several factors. They wouldn't have changed their mind if one of your brothers had said the same thing you did."

Tyler shook his head, the tears coming nonstop now. "They didn't care about me. They didn't listen to me. I was the one who was easy to dismiss. Easy to forget. Easy to ignore. It's my fault they died that night. If I had been Jon, Ben, Ethan or Chance, they would have listened. They wouldn't have tried to cross that bridge. They'd be above the ground instead of under it."

Hadley had no words that would take away this pain. She wrapped her arms around him and held him as tightly as she could. He had been a ten-year-old boy who allowed himself to carry the weight of his family's world for the next twenty years. No wonder he didn't want to be here. It wasn't that he felt guilty for not *doing* something. He blamed himself for not *being* something.

How could she begin to make him see himself the way she saw him?

CHAPTER TWENTY

TYLER WOKE UP on Tuesday in the bedroom. He didn't remember how he even got there. All he knew was that he was alone and alone was the last thing he wanted to be.

His whole body ached and it felt like someone had reached under his skin and smashed his insides. He was raw and exposed. One big bruise, tender and vulnerable.

He shuffled out to the sitting room, where Hadley was wrapped up like a burrito in the buffalo-check comforter that he'd been sleeping under for over a week.

His throat was dry and his cheeks felt crusty. Did he cry himself to sleep? Real manly. He opened the minifridge to get a water bottle. Hadley popped up at the sound of the door closing.

"Ty?"

"Sorry, I didn't mean to wake you up."

She unraveled herself from her blanket and

wrapped herself around him like a koala bear. "Are you okay?"

He shrugged. "I don't even remember coming back and taking over the bed."

"You were kind of a mess." She ran her fingertips up and down his arm.

"That's embarrassing."

"Don't say that."

He wouldn't say it again, but that didn't make him feel any different. He couldn't shut off the emotions because he wanted to. If he could, he would have done that yesterday.

"I'm sorry I got lost in those memories. Once we sell this ranch, I'll be able to put all that in the past where it belongs." At least that was his hope. Once this place was gone, he could move on.

Hadley stared up at him. "I wish you wouldn't run from this. I feel like you're so close to getting some closure."

Tyler had plenty of closure. He didn't need to rehash his parents' death any more than he had. He was done with that. "I'm good and closed."

"That's not what closure means."

"I'm kidding. I hear what you're saying and I will take it into consideration."

"I feel like that's your way of telling me you don't want to talk about this anymore."

"How about we do more cuddling and less talking."

He pulled her close again and pressed his cheek against the top of her head. All he needed right now was her. She made him feel safe. She was the only one he could trust with all this.

They snuggled on the couch and having her there lulled him right back to sleep. He slept so hard, he didn't even hear the knocking on the door until Hadley was answering it.

She slipped outside and closed the door behind her. Tyler got anxious and went to the door to see what was going on. He saw shadows through the curtains. She was on the front porch with someone.

"I don't know if he'll go for that," Hadley said.

"I have to try. Don't I?" Ethan was out there with her. Tyler was about to open the door, but stopped.

"If you think so. But part of me wonders if maybe Jon should do it. Not that he doesn't love you. He does. But he thinks of Jon like the big, big brother."

"I can talk to Jon. He would do it."

What was it that they thought they needed to do exactly? Tyler gripped the doorknob but didn't turn it yet.

"Are you ready for tomorrow?" Ethan asked.

"Ready as I'm ever going to be. I can't wait for all this to be over."

"I don't blame you. It's a lot."

"It's too much. I can't do it anymore. Tomorrow is the absolute end of it. Please don't ask me to do anything else."

"I won't. You won't have to worry about Tyler. I promise you that I am looking out for him."

"I better go back. He might wake up and wonder where I am."

Tyler let go of the door and sat back down on the couch before Hadley came inside. He heard her close the door and the sound of her padding across the carpeted sitting room.

"Who was that?" he asked, choosing not to pretend to be oblivious.

"It was Ethan. He wanted to see if we needed any more bath towels. I told him we were good until tomorrow."

The hair on the back of Tyler's neck stood on end. Why would she lie to him?

"Did he want anything else?"

"I think we might get together with Jon and Lydia tonight. He's going to get back to us."

"Did you tell him what happened yesterday?"

She tensed. He silently begged her not to lie again.

"I told him you were really disappointed about losing the buyer and that it was an emotionally draining day. I didn't tell him what happened on the hill."

What happened on the hill. She left out the part about his emotional breakdown? He wasn't buying it. She was lying again. He felt sick.

What could she not wait to be over? Why was Ethan promising to take care of him? She wouldn't have to worry about him. This was all too much. His mind began to race with all these thoughts. He tried to decipher their conversation. His heart began to break in two. Had she been talking about this relationship? Did she want out and she didn't want to hurt him? Did she go to Jon and Ethan so they would pick up the pieces when she told him it was over?

"Are you okay?" she asked.

"I'm fine." He scratched the back of his

head. "I should take a shower. I can't sleep the day away."

"Are you sure? No one would hold it against you if you took the day off."

"I'm sure," he said, standing up and heading for the bedroom. "I'm fine. You don't need to worry about me. I'm tougher than I look." He went into the bathroom and closed the door. He stared at himself in the mirror and saw why she was worried. Dark circles emphasized bloodshot eyes. His hair was a mess. The salt from his tears left white tracks down his cheeks.

She was such a good liar. He'd said it the whole time they were here. The fear that none of it was real overwhelmed him. She didn't want to break him. She promised not to break his heart. Would she keep her promise, or did she simply ask his brother to help him through it?

WORRY WAS HADLEY'S constant companion today. Tyler had been acting weird ever since he got out of the shower. Distant. Guarded. He must have felt bad about breaking down yesterday. She didn't want him to regret letting her in. At the same time, she felt woefully un-prepared to help.

He'd been inconsolable last night. It was so scary that she had texted Ethan when Tyler finally fell asleep, so someone else knew what was going on. The last thing she wanted was to become so close and then lose him to his guilt.

"I'll go see if Katie needs a hand. I want to make sure things are ready for the Mendes visit tomorrow," Tyler said, grabbing his hat off the table.

Hadley closed her laptop. "Let me change my shoes and I'll come with you."

"No, you don't have to."

"I want to."

"I don't need a babysitter—I'm fine."

"I wasn't coming to babysit. I was coming because I'd rather be with you fixing things than sitting here alone."

"Well, maybe I need a little space." He didn't bother to wait for her reply. He slipped out the door and was gone.

She texted Ethan to abort any attempts at a heart-to-heart chat today if they ran into each other.

After tomorrow, she would finally be done with double agent duties. Selling the ranch would take a back seat to convincing Tyler she was in love with him. Her plan was simple. She was going to offer to stay in Falcon Creek with him. It would be his choice, but she wanted him to know it was an option that he might not have considered because he thought all she cared about was being a brand strategist for 2K.

The job wasn't her goal anymore. Her new goal was to love Tyler until her dying breath. She would be willing to do that anywhere. Even here. Yesterday, it became crystal clear that he never hated the ranch. He didn't hate Falcon Creek. He loved this ranch. Every square inch of it. Tyler hated himself. He hated himself because he thought he wasn't enough for people.

Tyler was more than enough for Hadley. He could potentially be everything.

Her phone rang with an unknown number. She answered to find Jon on the line.

"I heard there was an incident yesterday."

"I guess you could call it that," she said. "It's important that you know he blames himself for not being able to stop your parents from going out in the storm the night they died."

"We all wish we could have stopped them from going out that night."

"He believes you all would have stopped them. That they didn't listen to him because he wasn't enough. Use your own adjective. Smart enough, responsible enough, important enough. He doesn't think he'll ever *be* enough for anyone. It made him very emotional. It was scary."

"I bet it was. Thank you for being there for him."

"I love your brother. He's definitely more than enough." It felt good to say that and mean it. It wasn't part of some trick.

"How can I help?"

Ethan's plan was to talk to him, but Hadley wondered if Jon wouldn't be a better choice. Tyler constantly compared Jon to their dad. He thought they looked alike. He thought his father favored Jon. If Tyler needed his father, Jon was the next best thing.

"He has a lot of respect for you. I'm sure he would listen to you if you talked to him about what happened."

"I'll call him and invite you guys over for dinner tonight. If you wouldn't mind helping

Lydia put the girls to bed, I'll try talking to him."

"I would so appreciate that. Thank you."

The door to the cabin swung open and Tyler stomped in. He glanced in her direction and took notice that she was on the phone. He grabbed his sunglasses off the desk.

Hadley hung up.

"Who was that?" he asked.

"My mom. She's still beyond excited about these impending wedding plans."

"Right, well, Katie's waiting for me."

"Bye," she said as he let the door slam shut behind him. There was a heavy black cloud hanging over them today. She couldn't wait for it to be blown away and the sun to shine again.

TYLER APPRECIATED THE sheer amount of physical labor needed on the ranch. Nothing relieved stress like pushing the body to its limits. And nothing pushed the limits like hay baling.

Since he mowed the field on Sunday, it was good and dried out by Tuesday. Tyler drove the baler and rake around and then spent the rest of the afternoon moving the hay bales into the hay barn. His arms were going to be so sore tomorrow, but he didn't care. The burn in his muscles was welcomed over the burning in his chest every time he thought about Hadley.

"You tired yet?" Katie asked. This was the third time she'd checked on him and he was beginning to wonder if she was in on the conspiracy to handle him with kid gloves.

He heaved another bale off the truck and into its row. "I'm never tired. Are you tired?"

"I'm exhausted," she admitted. She lifted off her hat and wiped her brow with her arm. "I've got to go give my dad a call. Looks like you'll be done by the time I get back. I'll see you tomorrow, then?"

"Is there anything else you need me to help with?" He wasn't real eager to return to the cabin and pretend that Hadley wanted to be with him.

"I've always got things I need help with, but didn't you say Jon and Lydia invited you over for dinner? If I was you, I'd go home and clean up so I'm not late for that. Lydia can cook."

Katie was sweet but she never seemed to pick up on what was really going on behind the scenes around here. Maybe it was because she was so focused on her job, she missed the little signs people threw out. The last place Tyler wanted to go to for dinner was Jon's. Ethan and Hadley had obviously set the whole thing up so Jon could prepare him for the impending breakup. Jon's text a little while ago about dinner seemed forced.

It was unlikely Tyler could get out of it, though. If he didn't go there, Jon would simply show up here and force him into the conversation anyways.

"I'll see you tomorrow," he said to Katie. Once he finished with the hay, he headed back to the cabin. He was itchy and all scratched up. A shower sounded mighty fine right about now.

Hadley wasn't on the phone with "her mom" this time. He was surprised that he had been so easily fooled by her earlier lies now that he was onto her. She wasn't as good as he had thought.

"You're back." She popped up and came over to greet him.

He held up his arms to stop her from hugging him. "I'm sweaty as all get out. I need a shower."

She didn't hide her disappointment. Her face fell and she stepped aside to let him get to the bedroom.

"What do you want to do about dinner?"

she asked as if she didn't know they were expected at Jon's.

"Jon invited us over, but I'm not that hungry." She wasn't the only one who could lie. "Can we talk about this after I get cleaned up?"

"Sure."

Tyler let the warm water soothe his sore muscles. It felt good to just stand under the stream and focus on the water massage. Once the water ran cold, he knew he had to get out and face Hadley and her feigned ignorance.

He got dressed and came out to get a bottle of water. Hadley stared at him but didn't say a word. He grabbed a water and headed back to the bedroom.

"Are you mad at me about something?" she asked from the doorway.

"Nope."

"Nope?" she repeated. "That sounds like a solid yep."

"Why would I be mad at you?" He wasn't angry, he was disappointed. He was trying to come to terms with where this was headed... or more importantly not headed.

"I don't know, that's why I'm asking."

Calling her out on lying meant possibly not finding out what her big plan was. He decided it was better to play it cool and see what she was up to.

"We really need to get ready for dinner. Jon and Lydia are expecting us."

Hadley had on one of his plaid button-down shirts over her white T-shirt. The sleeves were too long and she had them rolled up. She fidgeted with the cuffs.

"We're going?"

"Unless you don't want to."

"I feel like I should warn you that I might have mentioned to Ethan that I was worried about you and he might have told Jon."

The knot in his stomach tightened, but at least she was being honest. "So am I walking into an intervention tonight?"

She sat down on the bed next to him and reached up to cup his cheek with her hand. She brushed her fingertips across his temple. Her eyes welled with tears.

He braced himself for what she was thinking.

"I wasn't sure what to do last night. Or what to say. All I could do was hold you and reassure you I wasn't going anywhere." Big, fat tears rolled down her cheeks. He rubbed them away with his thumb. "I care about you,

Tyler. And I would do anything to take this pain away from you."

"It's not your responsibility to fix me. I'm not broken."

"I know you're not. But I'm falling in love with you and it hurts me to see you struggling with this."

He didn't hear her correctly. She couldn't have said there was still a chance. He could have sworn she'd been plotting with Ethan to leave him.

He kissed her because he could do that now whenever he wanted. "Did you say you're falling in love with me?"

"Falling, fallen. Take your pick," she whispered. "And I need you to take care of yourself and be open to whatever your brothers might say tonight."

She was tricky by throwing in her needs, as well. He cared too much about her to ignore how this was impacting her.

"I will listen to what they say. I promise."

Hopefully, his brothers wanted to talk about their parents' death as much as he did.

CHAPTER TWENTY-ONE

THE BUTTERFLIES IN Hadley's stomach needed some antianxiety medication. They were bouncing off the walls. He wasn't happy about this dinner, but he wasn't shut off anymore either.

Tyler parked in Jon's driveway but didn't get out of the car. "I'm not sure I want to do this," he said. His hands were shaking even though they were gripping the steering wheel.

"Your family loves you and they only want to support you," she reassured him.

He took a deep breath and opened his door. Jon's doorbell sent his dog into a barking fit. Jon answered the door with Gen on his hip. "Come on in. We've been waiting for you."

That probably wasn't what Tyler wanted to hear. He didn't move too fast, much to Gen's dismay.

"Come on, Uncle Tyler. Lydia made fried chicken. You're going to love it."

Ben and Ethan were both there. Rachel and Grace were not. It was clear that this was about talking to Tyler and not so much about a family dinner. Lydia was quick to get the food on the table and there was little dinner conversation. Hadley noticed Tyler's leg bouncing. She put her hand on his knee to calm him down.

"Hadley, the girls got new nail polish colors the other day. I thought maybe we could take them upstairs and give them fancy manicures. Are you up for that?" Lydia asked, knowing she wouldn't say no.

"Sounds fun."

Tyler set his fork down even though he wasn't finished. The invitation was a clear sign he would be alone with his brothers during this confrontation.

"These mashed potatoes are my new favorite food," Hadley offered up, hoping someone else would help squash the silence.

"Thanks. My secret is whipping cream. I love them but I can't make them every day if I want to fit into a wedding dress in a few months."

"Everything was delicious," Tyler said.

Lydia gave him a soft smile. "You two are welcome anytime. I hope you know that."

Tyler responded with a nod. Soon, everyone's plate was empty.

"We'll tidy up," Jon said, clearing the table. "Come on, boys. Let's get this done so the little girls can get their makeovers."

Hadley followed Gen and Abby to their room. She tried to stay present with them but her heart and mind were down in that kitchen with Tyler. Tyler was vulnerable. From what she had seen, the Blackwell men were good at giving each other a hard time rather than being supportive. Tyler needed them to find their compassionate side.

"He'll be fine. Those guys love each other something fierce. I know Jon is so protective of all of them," Lydia said while the girls went to wash their hands.

Hadley picked up one of the twin's stuffed rabbits. Its velvety soft ears were soothing. "Being here has shown me a side of Tyler I had no idea existed. He's got this tough exterior but inside there's this tender heart."

"It's a Blackwell thing. They have a hard time letting their guard down. They've been through a lot. Hopefully, Tyler will trust that no one is here to hurt him."

"CAN YOU GUYS just cut to the chase? Whatever you want to say to me, please just say it so we can be done," Tyler said, hoping to make this as painless as possible.

"I'll start," Ethan said. Jon and Ben busied themselves with scraping dishes and putting them in the dishwasher. "Hadley said you blame yourself for what happened to Mom and Dad."

"And you're here to tell me I'm not."

"Of course you're not," Ethan said. "But I know I can't simply say it and you're going to believe it."

"I was there. I know what happened." Tyler sat down at the kitchen island.

"What happened?" Jon challenged.

"I was out in the grazing pastures on the other side of the creek when the storm came in. I saw the water rising and barely made it across the bridge without getting knocked into the creek. There was no calf running loose over there. I was there. I know there wasn't."

"But there was a calf loose. We know it was out there," Ben said.

"It wasn't by the bridge and it wasn't on the other side of the creek, though, was it? I came home and I told Dad what I saw and he didn't listen to a word I said. He told me to go inside and dry off."

"Sounds like something Dad would say," Ethan said. "Maybe he said that because he cared about you and he didn't want you to catch a cold."

They didn't understand it went beyond this one interaction. "If Jon had been the one who was out there and told Dad not to bother with that part of the ranch, he would have listened."

"I was fifteen. You were ten. That's a big difference."

"The difference was he trusted you and he cared about what you thought and felt," Tyler explained.

"Dad had to make a judgment call. The wrangler told him he thought that's where the calf went. He had an adult telling him one thing and a ten-year-old telling him something else."

"I also begged Mom not to go. I told her it wasn't safe. She was more worried about me going in and preparing for our talk when she got back than listening to what I was saying."

"Because you weren't supposed to be over there," Jon said, sounding like his parent rather than his sibling. "Never mind the rain and safety issues, we were told not to go on that side of the creek, period. I know that when the girls don't do what I say, I tend to be focused on that versus whatever kind of baloney they are trying to distract me with so I won't punish them."

"I wasn't trying to distract her. I was trying to protect her!" He knew this would be frustrating. They weren't listening to what he was saying any more than their parents had listened to him that night.

"We understand that you weren't. What Jon is saying is that from the point of view of a parent, it may have seemed like you were," Ben said, handing Jon the used glasses. "It wasn't because she didn't care about you. You were in trouble and she was missing a calf. She was overwhelmed. It wouldn't have mattered which one of us got busted for being over there, she would have been mad at any of us."

Tyler shook his head. "If Chance or Ethan or even you had gone out there and told Mom you were scared and you wanted her to stay with you, she would have. She would have gotten a ranch hand to go with Dad."

"Well, unless we can have a séance or get one of those ghost whisperers to come and communicate with Mom, I'm not sure how you can convince us that's true, or how we can convince you it's not." Ben was too much like Big E to understand. "Mom and Dad made a bad judgment call that night and they paid the price. You're wasting a lot of time and emotional energy feeling like you could have done something about it."

"You guys act like I'm basing this feeling on this one event! I spent my whole life trying to get their attention and earn their respect and couldn't manage it. That night was the proof I needed that they didn't care about what I had to say. I wasn't enough to get them to choose me instead of that stupid calf."

"Your whole life?" Ben laughed. "You were ten. You barely had a life at that point."

Ethan gave him a warning look. "Don't do that."

"What?" Ben was annoyed. "He's remembering all of this from the viewpoint of a little kid. There's no way his perception is accurate given his age."

"He has a right to his feelings. And yes, he was ten and that's how he remembers it," Ethan said.

Tyler was done with this conversation. Hadley thought they would understand and they didn't. "I know how I felt at the time." He stood up and pushed the stool back in. "And I felt like that for a reason whether you believe that it was a good reason or not. Thanks for dinner, Jon, but Hadley and I need to go."

"Ty, stop," Ethan said, grabbing his arm. "Don't run away. We're trying to listen to what you're saying, but we need you to listen to what we're saying, as well. We were there. We grew up in the same house. Does it matter to you at all that we all agree Mom and Dad loved you? I would testify in any court of law that they loved you just as much as they loved me."

"Fine. They loved me. Thank you for helping me see the light. Hadley!" Tyler shouted, hoping she could hear him from wherever she was in the house. "Time to go!"

"They did love you, Ty. Stop beating yourself up and move on," Ben suggested.

"Put the blame where it belongs—on Mom and Dad. They are the ones who made the choice to go out and to cross that bridge," Jon added. "They are responsible for their own actions. Stop owning what's not yours to own."

"If you consider how the ranch really makes you feel, you'll realize you had so much more good happen here than bad," Ethan said. "That's what I've realized these last few months. Try focusing on the good."

Ben folded his arms across his chest. "He thrives on being miserable. And you know, Ty, it makes me a little mad that you don't appreciate all the things Mom and Dad did for you."

"Ben," Ethan pleaded to no avail.

Ben waved him off. "Mom and Dad were good parents. They sure did more for us than Big E ever did. We had food in our bellies, clothes on our back, they read bedtime stories and came to our Little League games. Mom and Dad loved all of us and he acts like they didn't show it when I know they did."

"Hadley!" Tyler had to get out of here *now*.

"I'm here. Are you ready?"

Tyler didn't answer. Instead he made a beeline for the front door.

"THANK YOU FOR DINNER," she called out, hoping Jon or Lydia could hear her.

Given the speed with which he was fleeing the house, the conversation was likely not as supportive as she had hoped it would be. She got in the car, ready to be what they had not.

"After the meeting with Mr. Mendes, I want

to go back to Portland and back to being me. I can't be here anymore. It's messing me up and I don't want to be messed up."

She put her hand over his on the gear shift. "Then we go back to Portland. I'll follow you anywhere."

"We'll leave Thursday. I'll buy the plane tickets tonight."

"Great. It's all going to be okay."

He was a ball of energy. His leg bounced like it did during dinner and he kept rolling his shoulders like they were stiff. "It will be as soon as we get out of here."

"Were any of them helpful?"

"Oh, well, let's see. Ben thinks I'm a spoiled brat who doesn't appreciate all the love and stuff my parents gave me while they were alive. I need to get over myself, according to Jon. Not everything is about me. And Ethan wants me to think about the good times."

"There were some good times. Weren't there?"

"That's not the point."

"I know. It's just I see you on the ranch and the way you smile when you're around the horses or talking to Katie. And I've watched you soak up the sun and breathe in the fresh air. There's a part of you that feels good when you're there."

"You know what makes me feel better than all that?"

"What?"

"You." He put his hand on her knee, giving her goose bumps. "I want to be with you and last time I checked, you live in Oregon."

Hadley's heart melted. She'd never felt like someone's number one choice before. But Ethan was pushing him to think about the good times because he believed that Tyler wanted to be in Montana deep down. Before she helped Ethan sabotage the second buyer tomorrow she needed to be sure.

"I do live there and I am all for going back to Portland, but I want you to know that I would support you one hundred percent if you wanted to consider siding with Ethan to keep the ranch in the family. If you want to stay here, I would stay with you."

"You would stay here? But Portland is your home. Your work, your friends are all there."

"I just want you to know it's an option. The ranch is a beautiful place with a ton of potential. So much so that I can't stop thinking about it. I'd stay with you if you wanted to stay. Or we can go back if that's what you decide. When you love someone, where they go, you go."

"Where you go, I go? I like the sound of that." He stared out at the road ahead of them. Hadley wished she could climb into his mind and see what he was thinking. "I want to go."

"Then, we go." She wouldn't argue with him. She was here because he had asked her to come and she would leave because what she wanted was to be near him.

When they got back to the cabin, Tyler opened his arms and she went to him. "I'm so sorry about everything."

This was the hug she'd been waiting all day for—the one that made her feel like he would also take care of her. He was stronger than she gave him credit for. He had a resiliency that had gotten him this far.

"I was most upset today because I thought I was going to lose you. And I was frustrated because I thought you told my brother before you told me."

"You aren't going to lose me. I love you."

"I love you, too." Those four words sent her heart into overdrive. He felt the same way.

There was nothing that could hurt them if they held on to that.

Everything was going to be fine. Tyler would go back to normal when they got home. Portland was home. Ethan would just have to deal with losing the ranch. It may have brought Tyler some joy, but there was too much misery to make it worth the risk.

CHAPTER TWENTY-TWO

MR. MENDES WAS expected any minute. Tyler checked his reflection in the side mirror of the F350 parked outside the lodge. Hadley had all of the marketing materials printed out and waiting for him. The flowers lining the steps of the lodge were freshly watered so they didn't look wilted in the afternoon sun.

After reading over Hadley's notes, it was clear that they had a very good shot of making this sale today. All Tyler had to do was keep it together.

"Okay, everything is set up inside. Here's the key to Room 210. It's vacant so he can see what a typical lodge room looks like." Hadley handed him a second key. "Here's the key to the Green Forest cabin. It's the bigger cabin with two bedrooms, but explain that the others only have one bedroom. Um, play up the growth potential. Lots of room to expand facilities."

"Got it. Room to grow."

"And smile. You're way cuter when you smile," she said with a wink.

Everything was fine. They were leaving for Billings tonight so they were close to the airport for their early-morning flight tomorrow. This weekend, he'd take her out for dinner somewhere downtown and show her his real home in the heart of the Pearl District. There, they could start their lives together without the interference of his brothers.

"I'm going to be inside at the bar. Introduce me if you want, but you don't have to. It's up to you."

"Showing off my beautiful fiancée seemed like the smart call."

"Maybe you should call me your girlfriend. I am so over the lies."

"I think that's the best idea you've had all day. I'll see you in there, girlfriend."

He fiddled with the keys she'd given him while he waited. The key fobs said 210 and Heavenly Pines. Wait, Hadley had clearly said he was supposed to take them to Green Forest. She must have handed him the key to their cabin by accident. He jogged up the steps and went inside to trade keys with her.

Ethan's hands were flailing as he spoke. Neither one of them noticed he was there.

"He's so close, Hadley. I know you think he's done with this place, but he's not. We need to do the same thing we did with Mr. Yonk. Please don't give up the plan to stop him from selling the ranch."

"I'm sorry, Ethan. I'm not going to sabotage this sale. The fake engagement is over. Tyler wants to go back to Portland. Nothing you say is going to change that."

"You're not going to sabotage *this* sale?" Tyler could feel the heat of his anger building in the center of his chest. Ethan knew they weren't engaged? Hadley had made promises to him to stop him from selling the ranch? The very weak foundation he and Hadley had been building completely crumbled to dust.

Hadley's eyes went wide. "Tyler."

"Am I hearing all this right? You did something to make Howard Yonk leave *and* you lied about it. And the plan today was to ruin this sale, as well?"

"Ty, she didn't—" Ethan started.

"Don't. Don't defend her. You knew we weren't engaged. How long?"

"Does it matter how long?"

"How long?" he practically screamed.

"I strongly suspected on Thursday and Grace and I confronted Hadley on Friday."

Tyler could only laugh and nod. Since Thursday. Practically the entire time they were here. This was unbelievable. Even more unbelievable than all the other lies Hadley had told over the last couple of days. At this point, he wasn't sure anyone had told him the truth the whole time they were in Montana.

He turned away from the two of them and focused on his breathing. He needed to get out of there. Ben came waltzing through the front doors, blocking Tyler's escape route.

"You don't get to be too self-righteous, Ty," Ethan said. "You're the one who came here and made Hadley lie to your entire family about an engagement that didn't exist."

"Whoa, what did I miss?" Ben said. "Did you just say he lied about his engagement?"

"Hadley was promised a promotion at work if she pretended to be his fiancée," Ethan blurted. "There, the truth is out. Go sell our family's ranch."

Lies. Hadley wasn't the only one guilty of lies. Tyler spun back around and made eye contact with Hadley. "There's no promotion," he confessed.

"What?" Ethan went toe-to-toe with him. "You promised her a promotion if she came here and pretended. All I did was ask her to keep pretending. Don't punish her because you're mad at me."

Hadley wiped the tears streaming down her face. Seeing her in pain extinguished some of his anger, but it was quickly replaced with a ton of guilt. She wasn't the only one who had to come clean.

"There was never a promotion. Kellen wouldn't agree to it. I've been fighting with him all week, but he wouldn't budge."

Hadley said nothing. She stared up at him in complete shock.

"You owe me ten dollars," Ben said to Ethan.

"Really? Right now?" Ethan shook his head in disgust. "That's what you have to say about all this?"

"What? We bet he wasn't engaged and I actually won."

Hadley sprinted away from the lodge. Tyler could only watch her go.

"Go after her!" Ethan gave Tyler a shove on the shoulder. "She did all this for you," Ethan continued. "She came here to help you save face. She agreed to help me to once again help you save face. She refused to help me because she wants nothing but to make you happy. She loves you, you knucklehead."

"Wait, they're not engaged, but they are in love?" Ben couldn't keep up.

Neither could Tyler. In the span of one minute, his entire life had imploded.

"Excuse me, I'm looking for Tyler Blackwell. I'm Martin Mendes. We have an appointment."

"I'm sorry, Mr. Mendes." He handed Ben the papers Hadley had put together. "I can't meet today, but my brother is very motivated to sell and I'm sure he'd love to walk you around."

Tyler couldn't spend the day acting like everything was all right when it was the exact opposite of that. There was no sign of her at Heavenly Pines, but then he remembered she had accidentally given him their key and held on to the Green Forest keys. He jogged over to that cabin and knocked on the door.

"Hadley, I know you're in there. Just let me in."

It took her a couple of seconds, but he heard the lock slide open. He pushed the door to find

Hadley on the chocolate-brown leather couch. She seemed so small and broken.

"I'm not even sure what to say," he said, choosing to stand rather than get too close to her.

"I think you said it all back there." She wiped her face with both hands. Her cheeks were red and splotchy.

"Why didn't you just tell me that Ethan knew? Why would you let me think he was still in the dark?"

"Does it matter? Because I sort of feel like none of this matters at all anymore."

"It matters to me. It matters because we were in this together and then you decided it was better to lie to me."

"We were in this together? Apparently, we were never in this together. You promised me a promotion if I pretended to be your fiancée. You couldn't get Kellen to agree and instead of telling me that it wasn't possible, you lied so I would keep pretending for you. I might have lied to you, but I did it so the rest of your family would still think you were happily engaged. I lied to protect you. You've been lying to me this entire time to protect yourself."

Her accusation cut like a knife. She wasn't

wrong and being called out on his selfishness was sobering.

"I fell in love with you and now you hate my guts for lying to you and I kind of hate your guts for lying to me. I was in a lose-lose scenario from the second I agreed to be your fake fiancée."

She hated him for lying. She wouldn't be able to look past it. He had come here ready to blame her for ruining everything when the truth was the detonator was in his hands.

Hadley wouldn't look at him. She stared down at her lap. "Do I even have a job when I get back to Portland or am I fired from that, as well?"

Her question gave him a tiny flicker of hope. Maybe if they went back to Portland and gave it some time—away from this ranch and away from his family—they could find a way to work this out.

"I have no plans to fire you and I don't hate your guts. I'm mad and I'm confused, but I could never hate you."

"It doesn't matter," she said again. "There's no coming back from this. I might be in love with you, but I don't trust you and you don't trust me, so there's literally nothing for us to talk about. It's over. We're over."

He wanted to tell her not to say that but couldn't. Without trust what did they have? These ten days together had been nothing but a waste of time. The reality of that was soul crushing. After all the misunderstandings and the little lies and the big lies, they couldn't recover.

"We still leave tonight for Billings," he said.

Hadley wouldn't make eye contact. "Let me know the cost of my room and I'll cover it."

"I can write it off as a business expense, so don't worry about it."

"This wasn't 2K business. I fell in love with you. I thought we had a future together. I will pay for my own room."

She was back to being herself. Challenging him at every turn. At least they still had that.

"Fine. Here's the key to our cabin. I'll let you go in and pack first. I'll be in the guest lodge. Text me when you're done and we can switch."

She sniffed. "Fine."

He grabbed the tissue box and set it in front of her. "I'll be waiting to hear from you."

She said nothing in reply. Instead, she pulled her knees up to her chest and hid her face.

His heart split in two as he heard her cry. Nothing would ever be fine again.

HADLEY MANAGED TO get everything stuffed into her suitcases except for the hat Tyler bought her that first trip to Brewster's. She loved it, but she wouldn't ever be able to wear it again without crying, so it was staying behind. Maybe one of the guests would make good use of it.

Her phone rang and Hadley was surprised to see it was Ethan.

"I am so sorry," he said. "I cannot begin to tell you how sorry I am. This is all my fault."

It was sweet of him to feel so guilty, but this was on her. She made the decision to lie and now it was coming back to bite her.

"Just because you asked me to lie doesn't mean I had to do it. I made the choice. I have to live with the consequences."

"I feel bad because I made you think that I would make you lose your promotion. I never would have done that. You are a marketing genius. My brother should make you his partner."

Tyler wasn't going to partner up with her professionally or personally. Working for Tyler wasn't going to be feasible anymore either. She would be looking for a new job as soon as she touched down in Portland. "Know anyone looking for someone in marketing?"

"I do actually."

She had been kidding. "I doubt you have a bunch of connections in Portland."

"Not in Portland. Here in Falcon Creek."

Hadley could only imagine what the marketing firm in Falcon Creek looked like. It was probably housed in the same building as the antiques shop. Around these parts, every business had multiple personalities.

"I'm not sure they can afford me. I'm a spoiled city girl, remember?"

"I know I can't afford you, but I still want you to come work for me."

Hadley must have heard him wrong. "For you?"

"You have had the most amazing ideas and vision for this ranch. If we were working together, this place could be fantastic."

"Tyler is voting to sell. You aren't going to be running it much longer."

"I believe I can convince Tyler to let me keep it if he can go back to Portland. I don't need him to help me run it if I have you."

"This is a wild plan."

"Wild but brilliant. I truly believe in us. You know what you're doing and the rest will work itself out."

"Can I think about it?"

"Sure. Take whatever time you need. I owe you that much."

Hadley hung up and blew her nose, hoping it would help her clear her fogged-up head. Could she stay here without Tyler? Going back to Portland with him was a terrible idea. Not even Kellen felt she was worthwhile enough to promote. 2K Marketing wasn't going to help her reach any of her long-term career goals.

Could she work with Tyler's family now that they all knew she was a liar? Ethan was the only one she'd be working for, and he was totally cool with it. She did love the ranch. Ethan would be easy to work for since he was generally a kind and caring person when he wasn't encouraging her to lie.

The pro and con list was leaning heavily in favor of moving to Montana. But they were *Tyler's* family. She felt strongly that she should at least give him a say. She wouldn't feel right about working for his family if he wasn't comfortable with it. She owed him that much.

She texted him that she was done packing,

but instead of leaving, she wheeled her bags out onto the front porch and waited for him on the bench. She watched him walk up the lane. Her heart began to beat wildly.

He stopped short of the front porch. "Sorry," he said, backing up. "I thought you said it was safe to come on over."

"I did. I needed to talk to you about something before you leave."

"Before *I* leave?" His wariness seemed to keep him on the ground level.

Hadley's throat suddenly felt very dry. She wished she had grabbed a water bottle. She tried to swallow down the lump in her throat as she walked over and leaned on the railing. "I can't work at 2K anymore."

He stared at her but said nothing. His chest rose and fell with heavy breaths.

"I'll write up an official letter of resignation and email it to you and Kellen, but I felt like I should tell you in person. I won't be giving any notice. My resignation is immediate."

"You can't do that. How are you going to support yourself?" He climbed halfway up the steps. "We can figure something out if this is what you want to do. Maybe you can work from home until you find something. I'll write you a letter of recommendation, make some calls if that would help."

"I don't need a letter or two weeks. I already have a job offer."

Tyler's brows pinched together. "How did you find a job in the last—" he looked at his watch "—twenty minutes?"

"Ethan asked me to come work for the ranch. He plans to ask you to vote to keep the ranch in the family with the condition that you do *not* have to stay and help him run it."

"Ethan? You're going to work for Ethan?"

"Maybe. I don't want to make it hard for you to visit your family or to come back here if you ever feel like doing that."

Tyler sat down on the porch steps. "You would choose Ethan over me?"

"I'm not choosing Ethan over you. I can't choose you. You don't want me."

He didn't deny it. Her chest ached at the thought of his not loving her anymore.

"You're going to leave Portland? Your friends, your life there?"

Her career was all she had going for her now and the ranch offered her the most potential for happiness. She didn't have a lot of options.

Ethan was offering her a chance to do something that she knew she'd be good at.

"I need to know if you would be okay with me being here. This is your family's land. If you want to call dibs, I will walk away and figure something else out."

He walked to the other end of the porch, keeping his distance. "Dibs? I told you I wanted to get out of here and as far away as possible. I'm leaving as soon as I pack my bags and I have no intentions of ever coming back."

"Then we wouldn't have to worry about seeing each other ever again. That could be helpful, huh?" The thought of it brewed up a new batch of tears.

"So much for where you go, I go. Is that what you want? To never see me again?"

She wanted to bury her face in the crook of his neck and inhale the sweet scent of his aftershave. She wanted to kiss him until they were both so dizzy from lack of oxygen. She wanted to marry him and promise to be with him forever. She wanted to erase every lie they had ever told one another.

But those things were impossible.

"I want you to be happy and I want to feel like I am valued and appreciated. Working for the Blackwell Guest Ranch could make me feel that way."

"Then who am I to say no? If this is where you want to work, this is where you should work. I'll tell Ethan that I'll vote to keep it as long as I can stay away. I'll also talk to Chance, who doesn't care what happens to this place as long as he doesn't have to do anything. Ethan will have the votes."

"Thanks."

He walked toward her but stopped a few feet away. The sun had tanned his skin over the last week. He was heartbreakingly handsome. "We never watched the sunset together," he said.

"Guess it wasn't meant to be." They weren't meant to be.

"Guess not." He pushed open the door to the cabin. "Goodbye, Hadley."

She wanted to be calm and cool, to say goodbye back. Instead, she was trying her best to strangle the sob that wanted to escape her throat. She picked up her bags and marched down the stairs, on her way to find a different Blackwell brother.

CHAPTER TWENTY-THREE

PORTLAND WAS A different place when Tyler returned from Montana. It was often a rainy and dreary city, but it was especially so this week. He didn't spend much time looking out the window, though. There was work to be done and a new associate strategist to hire.

"Can you go to the Kingman meeting with Eric this afternoon? I have a conflict and won't be able to make it," Kellen said, when they had their morning meeting.

"Sure."

"I'll have Veronica post Hadley's position on the website. The sooner we get that filled the better. The office has been a little lost while she was on that trip you sent her on and then she quit. I can't believe she quit without giving at least some notice. I'll be sure to say that to anyone calling for a reference."

No one would be calling for a reference. Tyler leaned back in his black leather office chair. The one that Hadley had picked out for him, calling it functional yet stylish. In fact, she had helped him choose most of the office furniture in this room because he trusted her taste more than anyone else's.

"I told you we were going to lose her if we didn't promote her." That was far from the reason she wasn't here anymore, but it made Tyler feel better to say it. It was the truth.

Kellen shrugged. "She'll be missed, but at least Eric's up to speed now and is ready to present to Kingman."

"Have him come in here so we can go over some talking points before the meeting."

"Are you okay?" Kellen asked on his way out. "You've been distant since you got back. Missing your vacation, aren't you? I don't know why you cut it short."

He was missing something. Some*one* was a bit more accurate. "I'm fine. Must be the Monday morning blues."

Kellen smiled and slipped out of Tyler's office to find Eric. Tyler reached for his notebook and a tiny pink slip of paper drifted to the floor. He picked it up and immediately recognized the handwriting.

*Call your brother Jon. Please. Pretty
please. Calling him back will rescue a
puppy from the pound and save a uni-
corn from an evil wizard. Please call.
You're the best boss ever,
Hadley*

The note made him want to laugh and cry.
How many of these had she written him in the
weeks leading up to their fateful trip to Falcon
Creek? She had no idea how he and his brothers
would change her life back then. How she would
forever change his.

"Okay, boss. I heard you wanted to meet
with me." Eric came in, holding a manila
folder. "We're going to go over the talking
points, right?"

"Right. I have to say, this is an excellent
brand analysis. You did a great job."

Eric's face warmed red. "Thanks."

Employees liked to be appreciated now and
then. It didn't hurt to give a little praise, let
them know when they had done a good job.
Tyler learned that from Hadley.

"What would you say is the main theme in
your analysis?"

Eric shifted anxiously in his chair. "I was

hoping to hear your thoughts on that. You're the boss, right? You know what the client is looking for better than anyone."

Tyler's brow furrowed. "That's not how it works, Eric. You did the analysis. You have all the answers there in your report. This is your show."

"Right. Right. Well, when you read the report, what stood out to you as the main theme? It's shaving, right?"

Tyler was more than confused. Baffled was more like it. "Eric, did you read your own report? It's excellent. Just summarize what you came up with. That's your main theme."

Eric opened his folder and shuffled through the papers inside. "I'm glad to hear you think the report was excellent. What were your favorite parts?"

A sinking feeling came over him. Tyler feared things were not as they seemed. "Eric, did you write these?"

"When you say these, what are you referring to specifically?"

"Specifically I would be referring to the market research and the brand analysis. Did you write them?"

"I reviewed them after I had one of my assistants pull some things together."

Tyler rubbed his temples, hoping to ward off the headache that was building. "One of your assistants? You don't have assistants, Eric. Who wrote these reports?"

"Hadley offered to put it together for me, and she's such a sweetheart, I couldn't tell her no, right?"

Tyler's jaw dropped. Of course it was Hadley. He stood up and opened his door. "Kellen!"

Everyone else in the office froze. No one said a word except for Eric.

"I had to tell Hadley what I wanted her to do. And then I had to proofread the reports. She's not a strong speller, but I caught all the errors, which is why it looks so good now."

"Kellen!"

His business partner came out of his office and weaved through the cubicles. "Why are you yelling?"

Tyler held the glass door open until Kellen was in the room. "Eric was telling me about how he had *Hadley* write these reports for him and that he can't present at the meeting today because he doesn't understand what they say.

This is your mess. You have to clean it up because I am not walking into that client meeting with Eric, who is no longer the brand strategist for our company."

Kellen's shock gave way to embarrassment. He took Eric to his office to discuss how they were going to handle this disaster. Tyler sat back down at his desk and scrubbed a hand over his face. Of course it had been Hadley. Those reports were perfect because she was perfect.

Hadley. Hadley. Hadley. It didn't matter where he was or what he was doing, she was everywhere.

Hadley would have loved the romantic comedy they played on the flight to PDX. What was Hadley's favorite drink at Black Rock Coffee? Hadley would have remembered it was Lee's birthday today and brought in a card for everyone to sign and a cake. Hadley had never sat on the love seat in his condo. Hadley smelled like wildflowers. Did Hadley watch the sunset over the Rockies without him?

It was supposed to be easier with her in a different state. Wasn't it? He wasn't supposed to think about her because he didn't have to see her every day, but her void was as strong as her presence.

On his way home from work, Tyler stopped by a pizza place and ordered a small gluten-free vegan pizza just to say he'd tried it. If Hadley liked it, maybe he would. He was wrong. There was a little too much Montana rancher in him to enjoy it. He ended up throwing half of it away. A half hour later, two very meaty sub sandwiches were delivered to his door.

He sat and ate at his kitchen island. His dining room table was covered with the mail he'd had on hold while he was gone. He hated to have the clutter, so once his belly was full, he began sorting through it. Ninety percent was junk mail and headed for the garbage or recycling.

The crown jewel of his held mail was a package. A brown-paper-wrapped box with his name and address written on it but no return address. It was postmarked from Texas. He knew only one person in Texas and that was his grandma Dorothy.

He opened it up not knowing what to expect. She sent the yearly obligatory birthday and Christmas cards but never a package before. It wasn't heavy and didn't make any interesting noises when he shook it. Maybe it was a box of money or, with his luck, something Grandma Dorothy crocheted in knitting class.

It wasn't either of those things. He pulled out a stack of letters. There must have been five bundles of old letters tied with twine. Why in the world was someone sending him their old mail? The letters were addressed to his grandmother. He had guessed correctly that the package was from her. The return address was hard to read because the tops of the envelopes were ripped raggedly across the top. He could make out Falcon Creek, MT, on the first few that he flipped through.

He said a quick prayer that these weren't love letters between his grandparents. That would be weird. He pulled out one of the letters from the first stack and tugged out the stationery inside. He recognized the handwriting immediately. He had two things from his parents in his possession. One was his dad's arrowheads and the other was a cookbook his mom had handwritten her recipes in. Tyler didn't cook any of them but sometimes he would page through it to remember family dinners.

For the next two hours, Tyler fell down the letter rabbit hole. His mom had written his grandmother almost weekly after Dorothy left. Each letter was filled with anecdotes about the boys and the ranch.

March 12, 1996—Ben and Ethan found the poison oak today in the forest. I've been making them wear mittens so they won't scratch at it. But you know them, they stole my hairbrush and were giving each other back scratches. At least they didn't ask Tyler and Chance to scratch it for them. I don't think I would survive if four of them had it!

April 3, 1996—Jon will never forgive me if he knew I was telling you this, but our little Romeo kissed his first girl today. He didn't tell me (of course not, he would never tell his MOM these things) but I overheard him telling his brothers. Ben bragged that he had already kissed two girls and Tyler claims he's never kissing anyone but me. He's so cute! I wish I could freeze him at this age, so innocent. He's going to be the one who has all the girls falling over themselves trying to get his attention. Those eyes!

July 20, 1996—It's been a rough week.
Ty got the stomach flu and was down for
the count for three days. Today was the
first day he managed to eat solid food and
it didn't come back up. My poor sweetie.
Oh, I'm not allowed to call him that anymore. He informed me that sweetie is
what boys call girls. Boys can't be sweet.
I am only allowed to call him Bud, Dude,
Ty or Tyler. I was also told a couple weeks
ago that I couldn't cuddle him anymore
because he's not a baby. But I guess when
you're sick, those rules don't apply. He's
been letting me rub his back and cuddle
whenever I want. I do love cuddling him
the most since he's so bound and determined to grow up faster than the rest of
them. Don't tell the others!

Letter after letter. Story after story. All five
boys were mentioned. All five drove their
mother frantic and broke her heart when they
were sad, sick or hurt. All five of them made
her smile and filled her heart to the point of
bursting. All five. Tyler was the best artist in
the family, her favorite to cuddle, the one who
was always pushing her away. He didn't re-

member doing that to her. Setting limits with her about what she could call him, how she could show him affection. He had been a challenge.

One thing was clear as he read her words. His mom loved him. She loved him as much as she loved Jon and Ben. Just as much as Ethan and Chance. They were all her favorites. She loved talking about horses with Jon and loved listening to Chance sing. She loved Ethan's curiosity. She couldn't get enough of Ben's wit. And she loved Tyler's eyes, his toothless grins, his hugs and kisses. She thought he was smart, too smart sometimes. She thought that about all of them at one time or another.

He wiped the tears from his eyes as he finished the last stack. He'd spent twenty years thinking he was nothing more than an afterthought. So many wasted years rewriting history to fit his ten-year-old misguided belief that he wasn't special. No one loved him any less. Sometimes he was a little standoffish. Sometimes he didn't see the bigger picture of what was going on in his mom's life.

Tyler had never considered how his personality impacted the way others related to him. It made him look back on his relationship with everyone differently, especially Hadley. He pushed her away with his words and his actions but was hurt when she withdrew. He demanded her loyalty, her honesty but didn't return it. He wanted to be her favorite person and refused to admit she was his.

Tyler didn't need a psychic or a séance to set him straight, but he had needed his mom. Grandma Dorothy gave him just that.

HADLEY AND ETHAN had two lists. One was the practical what-could-they-get-accomplished-before-the-end-of-the-summer-season list. And the other was the if-everything-worked-out-as-planned or the-sky-was-the-limit list.

"How long do you think it will take Tyler to get ahold of Chance?"

"No idea," Ethan said, opening his bag of potato chips. They were having a working lunch together in the guest lodge. "Chance sort of goes off the grid sometimes."

"So it's possible we won't know before summer ends?"

"I'll text Ty and see if he's heard back."

Talking about Tyler hadn't gotten any easier in the week that had gone by. She thought about him constantly. Ethan let her stay at the

Heavenly Pines while she made arrangements to sell her Portland condo. She was scheduled to go there this weekend and start packing.

The thought of being in Portland made her heart ache. What if they ran into each other out at dinner or at the grocery store? It was a silly worry since she'd never seen Tyler anywhere but at the office in all the years they'd worked together. She had no reason to go to 2K. Tyler had Veronica pack up her personal belongings and they were being shipped to Falcon Creek.

Still, she wondered what she would say or do if she ever saw him again. Smile on the outside and cry on the inside most likely. It took her a measly ten days to fall head over heels in love with Tyler Blackwell, but it would probably take a lifetime to get over him.

"Okay, regardless of Chance's vote, what is the next logical step for us?"

Even though they didn't have all the votes they needed, Ethan was moving forward as if he would be the eventual winner and the ranch would stay in the family. He had Hadley managing their social media accounts and booking large events. She was also in charge of their newest marketing campaign: weddings.

"Well, Jon and Lydia want to get married

this fall. I say we offer to have it here as sort of a test run for us. Then there's a bridal expo in Billings this January that we should try to get into," Hadley said. "The best part is that we could spare no expense on your wedding in December, use all the pictures from your wedding and Jon's for promotional purposes, and you could write the whole thing off as a business expense."

"You're a genius. Have I told you lately that you are a genius?" Ethan grinned as he took a bite of his sandwich.

Jon and Lydia had finally set a wedding date and would be the first of hopefully many weddings the ranch would host. Hadley was excited to help them but also feared that their wedding would be the first real possibility of seeing Tyler again. He had said he'd never be back, but surely he'd make an exception for his brother's wedding.

They finished eating and crossing items off their lists. Ethan got up to grab them some cookies from the buffet table.

One of the lobby receptionists came over. "Hadley Sullivan?"

"Yes."

The young woman was grinning from ear to

ear. She was quite possibly the happiest person Hadley had ever met. "You have a visitor."

A visitor? She didn't have any appointments today. She was meeting with some other wedding vendors later this week to talk about exclusivity agreements and had inquired with a contractor about setting something up to convert the barns by the creek into a spa. But there was nothing on her calendar for today.

"He's waiting for you. Out there." She pointed toward the lobby. The woman was shaking with excitement. Her giddiness was concerning.

"Okay, thanks." Hadley could only figure someone got their days and times mixed up. Ethan came back with the cookies just in time. She took her chocolate chip to go. "Someone's here. I'll talk to you later about the spa."

Ethan gave her a thumbs-up as he stuffed his cookie in his mouth. He was so long and lean but the man could eat.

Hadley headed for the lobby. She checked her phone for any emails she might have missed about a meeting. Pushing open the door, it took only a second to understand why the receptionist had been so beside herself.

Her visitor was dressed to kill in designer

jeans that fit like a glove and a black suit coat over a crisp white button-down. He lifted his black Stetson hat off his head like some kind of Southern gentleman when he saw her.

"Hadley," he said with a smile that would have made any other woman swoon.

"Asher."

CHAPTER TWENTY-FOUR

"WHAT ARE YOU doing here?" Hadley glanced around, wondering who else may have recognized him. The last thing she needed was her brother to cause some kind of scene.

"Surprise!" her mom shouted, popping out from behind him. Her mom might have been only five feet tall, but she had a personality that was ten times that size. That was when Hadley realized the whole family was there. Her dad smiled apologetically next to her mother.

She hadn't come clean with her parents yet. Asher got the news that he was nominated for the biggest award in television last Thursday, around the same time Tyler got on a plane and flew out of her life. It didn't seem like the best moment to tell them she wasn't getting married. Or had never truly been engaged. Instead, she told them she quit her job to work for the ranch full-time. She didn't imagine that would end up being an invitation for them to show up.

Heart hammering in her chest, Hadley held her arms up as if she might be able to corral them all somewhere out of sight. "What are you all doing here?"

"Well, we thought it was important for all of us to be together to celebrate the wonderful things happening in our family," her mom explained. "Asher offered to fly us out here to surprise you."

"That was so nice of you, Ash."

"It's nothing. Plus I wanted to check this place out since I got the news that I'll be filming that Western this winter."

"He got the part. Isn't that exciting?" their mom gushed.

"So great!" Hadley did her best to feign excitement. Of all the ways she imagined telling her parents the truth, in person, with Asher present was not one of them.

"Who do we need to talk to about getting a couple rooms for the weekend?" her dad asked.

"You want to stay here?"

"Where else would we stay?" Asher asked.

Hadley's brain had shut off. She couldn't handle this right now.

"I told you we should have called her and made sure it was okay to come out here," her dad said. "Maybe they're booked for the weekend."

"Are you booked for the weekend or do you have room for us? Where do you stay? Can we stay with you?" her mom asked.

"Is everything okay?" Ethan appeared at her side. He put his arm around Hadley's shoulders.

Everything was far from okay.

"Let me guess," Hadley's mom said, beaming like a proud mother of the bride. "You must be the Mr. Blackwell we've been waiting to meet. We're Hadley's parents, Jane and Jackson Sullivan."

Ethan didn't realize he wasn't the Mr. Blackwell they were hoping for. "Hadley's parents? Oh, man, nice to meet you!" He offered her father a hearty handshake and gave her mom a hug.

"And you probably already recognize our son, but this is Asher," her mom said.

Ethan had no clue who Asher was since he had no time to watch television. They shook hands anyways.

"Your daughter is absolutely the best. I cannot tell you how grateful we are that she's agreed to be part of the Blackwell Guest Ranch family."

Her dad's brows pinched together and Hadley's brain finally rebooted.

"This is Ethan. Ethan Blackwell. He's Tyler's brother and the one running the ranch right now."

"Oh!" her mom exclaimed. They all reshook hands and hugged as if he was someone new now.

"Where is this fiancé of yours?" Asher asked, scanning the room and giving a little head nod to one of the guests walking through the lobby who clearly recognized him. She snapped a picture with her phone.

Ethan looked to Hadley, knowing better than to touch that question. Hadley needed to get her family out of the lodge and somewhere a bit more private for the conversation they were about to have.

"Could we put my family up in the Green Forest cabin for the weekend?"

"I don't see why not," Ethan replied. "Let me go get the keys."

Hadley forced herself to smile. Hopefully they wouldn't have to stay the whole weekend. Once they learned the truth, they could go back to their lives and thinking Asher was the only golden child.

Once they got the keys, she drove with them around the ranch a bit before taking them to the cabin. Hadley shuddered when she walked in. The memory of Tyler ripping her heart out in this sitting room was still too fresh.

"This is our two-bedroom, two-bath cabin. It has wonderful views of the Rockies and one of the grazing pastures."

"It's lovely." Her mom ran her fingers across the coffee table, checking for dust.

There was a stone fireplace on one wall. Exposed wood beams ran across the vaulted ceilings. A painting of a Rocky Mountain sunset hung on the wall near the small café table and chairs. Her dad sat down on the leather couch.

"This is great, but when do we meet Tyler?" he asked. "The young man has some explaining to do."

Hadley tensed. They couldn't possibly know anything.

"Oh, Jackson. These days, they don't do things the way we did. She's almost thirty. We should be glad she's getting married, not complaining that he didn't ask for her hand."

Hadley would have taken offense had she

not been relieved. "I'm twenty-six, Mom. That's not over the hill, by the way."

She waved Hadley off. "Are we meeting him or what?"

There was a knock at the door, saving her from having to come clean. Probably Ethan. He had a thing about making sure all the guests had towels and those little soaps Sarah Ashley got for him.

She pulled open the door, grateful for his interruption.

"Hi." Dark hair, blue-sky eyes, shoulders strong enough to lift hay bales and lips she dreamed about every night.

"This must be the man of the hour!" Her mom squeezed in beside her. "Please tell me you are Tyler Blackwell because we already met one of the Blackwell boys and it wasn't him."

"You must be Hadley's mom," he said with that trademark Tyler smile. "I am Tyler Blackwell. It's a pleasure to finally meet you."

Hadley's heart was racing. Her mom pulled her back a step so Tyler could come in. Her mom was quick to make introductions.

"This is Hadley's dad, Jackson." The two men shook hands. Hadley's father was physically the opposite of Tyler in every way. Tyler was tall and lean with more hair on his head than Hadley's dad ever had. The outsides were different but Hadley knew that inside they were very much alike. Her father didn't wear his heart on his sleeve. He tended to keep his feelings to himself, but he loved his family and would do anything for them.

"And this is—"

"Asher Sullivan," Tyler finished for her mom. "It's great to meet you. Hadley and I watch your show every week. Well-deserved nomination. I hope you win."

Asher's chest puffed up with pride. "Thanks. Congratulations on your engagement. My sister is not easy to live with. I should know. But I hope you two will have a very happy life together."

Tyler's breath caught for a second, but he exhaled and smiled. "Thanks. I hope we do, too."

Those words were like daggers, shooting through Hadley's chest and leaving her unable to breathe. Why was he here? Why was he pretending to still be engaged? How could she survive having to say goodbye one more time?

"If you guys don't mind. I'm going to steal Hadley away for a couple minutes to take care of some ranch business. You three get settled in, unpack, whatever you need to do and we'll be back real soon to take you on a tour of the property. Maybe we'll get you on a horse, Jane?"

Hadley's mom giggled like a smitten teenager. "I don't know. I haven't ridden a horse in years."

"Well, if you're anything like your daughter, you'll pick it back up in no time." Tyler reached for Hadley's hand and led her outside.

She stared at their hands as he pulled her all the way to his car. He opened the passenger's side and waited for her to get in before closing it behind her.

A million questions ran through her head. She had a hard time choosing one to start with. Tyler got in and started it up.

"I'm sorry for taking over in there. I don't know what you were planning to tell them, but I needed to talk to you before you talked to them."

"What are you doing here?"

"I'm here because this is my favorite place in the world." His voice cracked with emotion.

"I'm confused," she said. "Is that sarcasm?"

"No." That didn't make any of this any

clearer. He continued, "I went back to Portland and I was sure I could go back to how things were, but nothing's right. The company isn't the same without you there. Everyone misses you."

"I miss them, too." She missed him the most, but telling him that wouldn't change anything.

"I found out you did the brand analysis on the Kingman account for Eric. I told Kellen he had to fire Eric or else. He didn't fight me. In fact, he wants to offer you the brand strategist job with a huge raise."

He was here about a job. Of course this was work-related. Tyler was all business all the time. He had no idea how much he was hurting her right now with this face-to-face offer that would have been a million times easier to turn down via email.

"I have a job. I don't want to work for 2K anymore."

"I was hoping you would say that," Tyler said with a breath of relief that twisted the knife in her chest.

He completely befuddled her. She knew he was hurt, but she didn't expect him to be cruel. "If you were worried I was going to be lured back by everyone else at the office, you can rest assured I will not. You have driven the message home that you don't want me in Portland. Thanks for coming all this way to make that clear."

He stopped the car in front of Heavenly Pines. "Hadley, you misunderstand."

She couldn't sit in the car with him for one more second. She bolted. Her anger colored everything red. She fought the stupid tears she didn't want to waste on him anymore.

"Hadley, I don't want you to come back to 2K because I'm not going back to 2K either. I told Kellen I'm done. Our partnership is being dissolved. He's agreed to buy me out."

"What? Why?" Tyler had everything he wanted. It didn't make any sense for him to throw it all away.

He took three long strides to close the distance between them. He gripped her face in his hands. "Because Portland isn't my home and I was worried that Kellen would tell you that I left 2K and offer you the job. I don't want you in Portland working for Kellen because I want to be here with you."

HADLEY GRABBED HIS wrists and pushed his hands away. The tears rolled down her face.

He hadn't meant to make her cry. Her blond hair was pinned up in the front with a few soft tendrils framing her face. She was so beautiful it hurt.

"Can we go inside? Talk a few things out?"

Hadley hesitated. Maybe he was coming on too strong, too fast. She wiped her cheek with the back of her hand. "Fine."

He needed to say all the right things when they got in there. This was his only shot at getting back what he had lost.

The log cabin they had called home for almost two weeks held so many pivotal memories given their short stay. This was where he'd said goodbye, thinking it was forever. It was also where she'd told him she loved him for the first time and where he told her the same thing.

"One week away from you has felt like a million years," he said once they were inside.

Hadley attempted to tidy up. She had papers and clothes scattered all over the sitting room. She snatched a bra off the couch and threw it back in the bedroom.

"Funny, because to me it feels like just yesterday you were telling me goodbye because we agreed that there was nothing left for us. No trust, no chance."

"Is that how you still feel? Because that's not how I feel. I wouldn't be here right now if I didn't think there was a chance for us." He put it out there. He wanted her back.

"I feel like you have this way of turning my world upside down over and over. Every time I think I catch my balance, you throw me for another loop."

Tyler sat down on the couch and patted the seat next to him. "Come, sit with me."

Hadley did as he asked. He didn't mean to make her feel so unsure all the time. He understood now that he did that to people. He would tell them to go away and then be mad when they listened. His fear of not being enough caused him to build an impenetrable wall around himself. But Hadley had gotten through.

"I'm sorry. For a lot of things. I'm sorry for lying to you about the promotion. That was selfish. Plain and simple."

"I'm sorry, too. The lies got out of control."

"I never should have asked you to lie. It was wrong and as long as I live I will make sure that no one in the Blackwell family ever asks you to do that again."

"I appreciate that." She fidgeted with her hands. "So you're back and this is your home."

"This is my home as long as you are here. I love you. I love that you call foals baby horses and that you think red licorice is part of a balanced diet. I love that you aren't afraid to get your hands dirty but you always wear lipstick. I love that you were obsessed with Harry Potter as a kid and your favorite food is mac and cheese. You are my favorite person in this entire world, Hadley. You are my home."

The tears were back in her eyes. "You…you don't have favorites."

"I didn't. Until now."

She took a couple of deep breaths. Tyler prayed that what he said was enough. That he was enough to win her back.

"On our very first night here, I told you that we have to trust each other if this is going to work."

Tyler swallowed hard. He could love her all he wanted but if she didn't trust him, she might not be able to love him back.

"Trust is essential."

"We both let each other down. We didn't trust each other to handle the truth. That's how the lies got so out of control."

"Exactly."

Hadley reached over and took him by the hand. "I'm trusting you with my truth because I think you just trusted me with yours. I love you, Tyler Blackwell. I love that you know the science behind skipping rocks. I love that you are a neat freak but never make me feel bad about being messy. I love that you get excited about things like hay balers. I love that you let me break rules as long as they have to do with kissing. You are my favorite person in the entire world and I am glad you're home. Don't ever leave me again."

Tyler's heart burst with joy and love. "I'm going to kiss you now," he warned.

"It's about time."

CHAPTER TWENTY-FIVE

HADLEY HEARD TYLER return from getting his bags out of the car. He'd been gone longer than she'd expected. Maybe he had everything from Portland with him.

"My family is probably wondering if we're ever coming back." Hadley stood in front of the bathroom mirror, reapplying her lipstick that had been thoroughly kissed off.

"There's something I want to ask you before we go," Tyler said from the living room.

She waited for him to ask his question, but he was quiet. She set down her makeup and stepped out of the bathroom. Tyler held out his hand. "Come here."

Hadley took his hand and let him lead her to the couch, asking her to sit.

"We've sort of done all this romance stuff backward. We were engaged before we even liked each other. I see you ditched the fake engagement ring."

She glanced down at her left hand and her bare ring finger. She couldn't stand to look at the ring when he left but also couldn't bear to get rid of it. She kept it hidden in a drawer in the bathroom. "I still have it if you want it back."

Tyler shook his head. "I say we throw that one in the creek. I have something a bit more real for you, if you'll wear it?" Tyler got down on one knee and Hadley's heart skipped a beat or two. He reached in his pocket and pulled out a tiny black ring box. He popped it open to reveal the gorgeous and very real diamond ring inside. "Hadley Sullivan, you are the love of my life. I would be honored to spend the rest of my life loving you. Will you be my real fiancée? Will you marry me?"

Hadley didn't have to think about it. She jumped off the sofa and tackled him to the floor. There wasn't anything she wanted more in this world than to be part of the Blackwell family. "Yes. A thousand times, yes."

Tyler gently rolled her over and kissed that newly applied lipstick off once again.

Hadley couldn't stop staring at the ring on her finger. It was a good thing her mother hadn't asked to see it until the real deal was in place. It felt a thousand times better to talk to her parents about her engagement and fiancé now that they were real.

"Are you sure you're ready to get to know the Sullivan family?"

Tyler twined his fingers with hers. "If you can survive the Blackwells, I should be able to get through a weekend with the Sullivans."

"Ah, you think because I only have one brother that it won't be so hard? You underestimate the power of Asher Sullivan, my friend."

Tyler's eyes went wide as the fear settled in. Hadley laughed and pulled him up the porch steps. Her family really wasn't that scary. She was actually excited to show them this amazing place where she planned to build a life with Tyler.

They took her family out on horseback and showed them all the sights, stopping at the pond to skip a few rocks. Her dad was pretty good. He managed to skip a rock nine times and was so close to making it all the way across. Tyler tried to teach her mom but she was about as hopeless as Hadley.

"You look really happy, sweetheart," her dad said as they stood by the horses, waiting for the rest of the group to finish with their rock skipping.

"I am, Dad. I'm really happy." Quite possibly the happiest she'd ever been.

"I have a feeling you weren't as happy when we first got here."

Hadley was surprised to hear him call her out. She didn't think her dad paid that much attention. "What makes you say that?"

"I'm not going to speculate about what's been going on the last few weeks, only because when your fiancé over there came to ask my blessing today, he assured me that he is one hundred and ten percent committed to making you the happiest person in the world. Said he couldn't explain, but you two were in need of a redo in the engagement department and wanted to do everything by the book this time."

Hadley placed her hand over her beating heart. Tyler asked permission to marry her. Everything was real this time.

"Sometimes you have to make a couple mistakes to figure out what you really want. I can promise you, Dad, that Tyler is what I want. This life with him on this ranch is definitely what I want."

"Then we'll just keep the fact that this is a redo to ourselves. No need to get your mother all worked up."

Hadley threw her arms around her dad. Their secret was safe with him. "Thank you."

"Do you have guests here year-round?" Asher asked, staring at his phone like he had been off and on the whole ride. He had a lot of research to do to learn how to play a real cowboy. In LA phones were used for constant ego stroking. On a ranch, phones were more for emergencies rather than checking your social media status.

"Summer is the main season but we're looking to expand into a year-round guest ranch. Hoping to be somewhere people come for weddings and corporate retreats."

"I told my producer I was visiting my sister, who's marrying a guy with a ranch in Montana, and he's been texting me about it ever since. Wants to know if he could send a location scout out here."

"A location scout? He wants to check this place out as the location for your movie?"

Asher flashed her his most charming smile. "You'd give us a deal, right? We're family after all."

"I'd have to talk to Tyler and Ethan, but I bet we could work something out." This was one time Hadley would happily mix her personal life with business. The media attention they could get would be priceless.

"You'd have to talk to me about what?" Tyler said, helping her mom up the rocky path to the horses.

"Asher was saying his producer wants to send a location scout out here to see if our ranch could serve as the setting for his new movie."

"Sounds like I need to get ahold of Chance."

Getting the last Blackwell brother's vote was imperative to making all of this happen. Without it, all the work Hadley and Ethan had been doing would be worthless.

SOME TWINS SWORE they could tell when the other was in pain or that they could read one another's minds. Tyler and Chance never claimed to have any psychic abilities. When Tyler broke his arm in seventh grade, Chance didn't have any sympathy for him let alone sympathy pains.

Still, Chance was the one Blackwell brother who Tyler never ignored. If he called, Tyler answered. If he texted, Tyler texted back. When he emailed pictures of Rosie, Tyler always replied back with a big thank-you. Unfortunately, Chance wasn't always as good at getting back to Tyler in return.

"How was your ride with the future in-laws?" Katie asked as she helped Tyler untack the horses.

"Good. I'm certain I made an excellent first impression."

"There never was a doubt that you would, was there?"

Tyler chuckled. "Given all the things that have happened the last couple weeks, I have learned not to take anything for granted."

"Yeah, you almost screwed things up big-time," she said, checking Goliath's hooves for stones.

"I learned my lesson. No more hiding my feelings or making up stories. Honesty is my new policy."

Katie got quiet. She ducked her head and averted her eyes. Hopefully, she'd forgive him for lying to her. It wasn't like he was trying to hurt anyone.

"I'm sorry for not being honest with you. Your friendship means a lot and I didn't want to deceive any of you. I just didn't want you to think I was a loser."

"No, I get it," she said, grabbing the currycomb from the grooming bucket. "Sometimes we have to keep things from people for the greater good."

"I don't know if I would call what I was doing for the greater good, but I appreciate your understanding. I wish my brother would understand that I need to talk to him."

"Which one?"

"Chance. I've called, texted, emailed. He won't respond. I need him to vote to keep the ranch but that's a little difficult when he won't communicate."

"Boy, I feel like that's a bit of karma coming for you, Ty. I seem to remember a time when Ben, Ethan and Jon were desperately trying to get ahold of you and all those calls went to voice mail."

Okay, that was true, but Chance would have gotten a call back had he been the one to reach out. It bugged Tyler that his twin wouldn't show him the same courtesy. "I'm going to have to go do this face-to-face if he keeps ignoring me."

"Sure would be nice if you could get him to

come home and bring Rosie with him. It would mean a lot to my dad to get to see his grand-daughter before he dies."

"I'll have to remember that when I make my case. I'm sorry for all you're going through, Katie. We're here for you. You know that, right?"

She finished brushing Goliath and turned to face Tyler. "I appreciate that, Ty. I really do. I wish Chance understood how important family was. I love looking at the pictures he sent me of Rosie, but you can't hug your computer screen."

"Chance feels very strongly about family. Lochlan was the one who made it clear that if Maura married him, they weren't his family anymore. Chance took that to heart. And when Maura was sick… Let's just say there are a lot of hard feelings."

"My dad isn't a perfect man. Not by a long shot. But he's not the only family Maura had."

Tyler could see the hurt in Katie's eyes. Chance lost his wife but Katie lost a sister. Neither one was any more or less tragic. "I'll try to remind him of that. I promise."

Once they finished with the horses, Tyler went back to the cabin to clean up. Hadley had taken her family into town to show them the exciting world of downtown Falcon Creek. He would meet them for dinner later.

After dinner and a stop for some ice cream at South Corner Drug and Sundries, Tyler and Hadley retreated to the Heavenly Pines. It was late, after nine. The sun had begun to sink behind the Rockies.

"I feel like there's so much to do and tomorrow is Friday. I don't know how I'm going to entertain my family and take care of all the things I promised Ethan I would get done before the weekend."

Tyler pulled Hadley over to the old bench on the front porch. "Isn't it time we stop thinking about work and watch the sunset together instead?"

"Who are you and what have you done with Tyler Blackwell? The man never stops thinking about business. He's all business all the time."

"Not this new and improved Tyler Blackwell. This Tyler makes time for what's really important, like his very real fiancée and her supersoft lips."

He kissed her slowly, taking his time to enjoy every moment of this second chance they had been given.

"Okay, I like this new Tyler a lot," Hadley said, pulling back for a breath. "He's a keeper."

She snuggled against him as the sky went from blue to the most vibrant shades of orange and purple. Nature at its finest. The quiet serenity of dusk settled in. This was how Tyler wanted to spend all his evenings going forward, with Hadley in his arms and the beauty of the ranch laid out before them.

Tyler was most definitely home.

EPILOGUE

"WHAT CAN I get you to drink, cowboy?"

Elias Blackwell removed his tan cattleman hat and set it on the bar in front of him. The bartender had more tattoos than a bird had feathers. He didn't mind a little ink, but this was ridiculous.

"Whiskey on the rocks."

"Coming right up."

Elias glanced over his shoulder at the empty stage in this hole-in-the-wall bar. Los Angeles wasn't exactly his favorite place to visit, and it was joints like this that made him realize why. Everyone standing around waiting for the show to start was on their phones and dressed like their clothes had been run through a shredder. Did anyone in LA own a pair of jeans that didn't have a hole in them? Even their cigarettes were electronic. This generation was interesting to say the least.

He had to remind himself he was here for a

reason and it didn't have anything to do with the people in the crowd but everything to do with the man who would be on stage in a few minutes.

"Here you go," the bartender said, setting the drink on the cocktail napkin with the words *Tuned Up* printed across it. "That'll be seven dollars. Do you want to pay now or start a tab?"

Goodness, he could get a whole bottle of whiskey for that price back home. Elias pulled out his wallet and threw down a ten-dollar bill. "I'll pay now. I can't afford to start a tab."

He set his hat back on his head, grabbed his drink and made his way through the crowd to find the perfect spot to watch the show. The lights dimmed and a young guy in black jeans—surprisingly not ripped—and a Tuned Up T-shirt got up on stage.

"I'm stoked to introduce this guy. He's been missing from the music scene for a couple years, but I'm happy to say he's making a comeback. Please welcome, Chance Blackwell."

The crowd erupted into applause and a few hoots and hollers. Elias was impressed with the reaction. They were excited to see the kid. Good for him.

It had been a long while since he'd seen his grandson. Ten long years to be exact. When he walked out on the stage it was clear that he was no longer a boy but a man. Mike's boys were all grown up, even the youngest.

They turned the lights down low as Chance began to strum his guitar. He acknowledged the crowd and then got lost in his song. It was as if he forgot everyone was there. The boy was talented.

Elias listened to three songs before he noticed the other Blackwell in the room. Tyler was working his way over to the side of the stage where the bar owner had stepped off. Most likely trying to find a way backstage. It was a good thing Tyler's source had been correct about Chance's whereabouts and even better that Elias's informant was able to pass that information on to him.

Tyler would hopefully convince Chance to go back to Montana. Chance was the last piece in this big ol' jigsaw puzzle. Thus far, everything else had worked the way Elias had hoped. No reason to think this wouldn't, as well.

Tyler glanced around the room. The last

thing Elias needed was for the plan to be spoiled because he got busted in the eleventh hour. It was time to go. He weaved through the crowd and out the front door.

Zoe had taught him how to use the app that alerted people to the fact that he needed a ride. People in their personal vehicles would just drive on over to wherever he was and pick him up. He didn't exactly get why someone would do that, but it was helpful when there were no taxis around.

Once he was back in his RV, there was only one last thing to do. He would drop this package off at the post office on his way out of the city tomorrow. His accomplice would know what to do with it as long as Tyler came through. It was about time the boy got this back and the whole family was where they belonged.

* * * * *

Turn the page for a sneak peek at The Rancher's Homecoming—*the stunning conclusion to the Return of the Blackwell Brothers miniseries—coming next month from acclaimed author Anna J. Stewart...*

CHANCE BLACKWELL MISSED a lot about performing.

He missed the way the room went silent as he sang words he'd painstakingly chosen. He missed the oddly intoxicating smell of beer, perfume and rejection. He missed the way the lights were dim enough for him to pretend he was alone, just him and his guitar.

What he didn't miss was walking off stage to find his longtime, long-suffering agent ready to pounce. Given the sour expression on Felix Fuller's face, there wasn't an "atta boy" in Chance's future.

"I thought you had new material." Felix's disappointment was clear and cut almost as deep as Chance expected. Only five years older than Chance's just turned thirty, Felix was as short as Chance was tall, pudgy where Chance was toned and as determined while Chance was…

Well, Chance didn't know exactly what he was anymore.

Chance sighed and gripped the guitar he'd received as a gift his first Christmas after leaving the Blackwell Family Ranch ten years before. His wife, Maura, had worked a second waitressing job on the sly to buy it from a local pawn shop that Christmas they spent in Nashville. He could still remember her sitting on the floor next to the anorexic tree he'd dragged out of the back of a tree lot, her freckled face alight with excitement as he unwrapped it. The instrument had been the greatest gift he'd ever received. Until Rosie was born at least.

"The new songs aren't ready," Chance lied. "And the crowd seems happy enough." Applause was applause, right?

"The crowd was being polite." Felix followed Chance down the narrow hallway. "You can't launch a comeback on old songs, Chance. Sentimentality will only get you so far. We need something new, something fresh. Something from the heart."

From the heart? Chance swallowed against the wave of grief-tinged nausea. If that's what was needed, no wonder his creative spark had been doused. "I need more time."

"You don't have more time." Felix nipped at his heels like an overanxious puppy. "Unless you don't have any interest in keeping a roof over Rosie's head. Or yours for that matter."

Chance's guts knotted. He could live in his car and be fine with it, but no way did he want anything less than complete stability for his daughter. "I can't write from a dry well, Felix." And that's exactly what he had. A dry, dusty well of inspiration. Ashes to ashes…

"Okay, okay, so let's look at the bright side." Felix's voice dropped as he gestured toward the frayed, dark green curtains. "They've missed you, Chance. Your fans, your audience, they want you back. Which means we've got to strike—"

"I told you before this gig, I'm only dipping my toe." Chance accepted the congratulatory slaps on the back and positive comments from patrons as he made his way to the makeshift dressing room that over the years had been occupied by far more talented and popular musicians than himself. Apparently they didn't care that he was singing songs from five years ago. "I'm not diving in all the way again. I'm not ready."

He knew what he should be drawing on, but

the idea of writing about Maura, about her illness, her death, scraped his heart raw whenever he plucked the first notes. The paralyzing grief over losing his wife had faded—for the most part. He'd come to terms with her being gone, but only because he didn't have a choice.

Rosie needed him. And when it came to his daughter, nothing else mattered.

Get 4 FREE REWARDS!

We'll send you 2 FREE Books plus 2 FREE Mystery Gifts.

Love Inspired® books feature contemporary inspirational romances with Christian characters facing the challenges of life and love.

FREE Value Over **$20**

YES! Please send me 2 FREE Love Inspired® Romance novels and my 2 FREE mystery gifts (gifts are worth about $10 retail). After receiving them, if I don't wish to receive any more books, I can return the shipping statement marked "cancel." If I don't cancel, I will receive 6 brand-new novels every month and be billed just $5.24 for the regular-print edition or $5.74 each for the larger-print edition in the U.S., or $5.74 each for the regular-print edition or $6.24 each for the larger-print edition in Canada. That's a savings of at least 13% off the cover price. It's quite a bargain! Shipping and handling is just 50¢ per book in the U.S. and 75¢ per book in Canada*. I understand that accepting the 2 free books and gifts places me under no obligation to buy anything. I can always return a shipment and cancel at any time. The free books and gifts are mine to keep no matter what I decide.

Choose one: ☐ **Love Inspired® Romance Regular-Print** (105/305 IDN GMY4)   ☐ **Love Inspired® Romance Larger-Print** (122/322 IDN GMY4)

Name (please print)

Address   Apt. #

City   State/Province   Zip/Postal Code

Mail to the **Reader Service:**
IN U.S.A.: P.O. Box 1341, Buffalo, NY 14240-8531
IN CANADA: P.O. Box 603, Fort Erie, Ontario L2A 5X3

Want to try two free books from another series? Call 1-800-873-8635 or visit www.ReaderService.com

---

*Terms and prices subject to change without notice. Prices do not include applicable taxes. Sales tax applicable in N.Y. Canadian residents will be charged applicable taxes. Offer not valid in Quebec. This offer is limited to one order per household. Books received may not be as shown. Not valid for current subscribers to Love Inspired Romance books. All orders subject to approval. Credit or debit balances in a customer's account(s) may be offset by any other outstanding balance owed by or to the customer. Please allow 4 to 6 weeks for delivery. Offer available while quantities last.

Your Privacy—The Reader Service is committed to protecting your privacy. Our Privacy Policy is available online at www.ReaderService.com or upon request from the Reader Service. We make a portion of our mailing list available to reputable third parties that offer products we believe may interest you. If you prefer that we not exchange your name with third parties, or if you wish to clarify or modify your communication preferences, please visit us at www.ReaderService.com/consumerchoice or write to us at Reader Service Preference Service, P.O. Box 9062, Buffalo, NY 14240-9062. Include your complete name and address.

LI18

Get 4 FREE REWARDS!

We'll send you 2 FREE Books plus 2 FREE Mystery Gifts.

Love Inspired® Suspense books feature Christian characters facing challenges to their faith... and lives.

FREE Value Over $20

YES! Please send me 2 FREE Love Inspired® Suspense novels and my 2 FREE mystery gifts (gifts are worth about $10 retail). After receiving them, if I don't wish to receive any more books, I can return the shipping statement marked "cancel." If I don't cancel, I will receive 4 brand-new novels every month and be billed just $5.24 each for the regular-print edition or $5.74 each for the larger-print edition in the U.S., or $5.74 each for the regular-print edition or $6.24 each for the larger-print edition in Canada. That's a savings of at least 13% off the cover price. It's quite a bargain! Shipping and handling is just 50¢ per book in the U.S. and 75¢ per book in Canada*. I understand that accepting the 2 free books and gifts places me under no obligation to buy anything. I can always return a shipment and cancel at any time. The free books and gifts are mine to keep no matter what I decide.

Choose one: ☐ **Love Inspired® Suspense Regular-Print** (153/353 IDN GMY5) ☐ **Love Inspired® Suspense Larger-Print** (107/307 IDN GMY5)

Name (please print)

Address   Apt. #

City   State/Province   Zip/Postal Code

Mail to the **Reader Service:**
IN U.S.A.: P.O. Box 1341, Buffalo, NY 14240-8531
IN CANADA: P.O. Box 603, Fort Erie, Ontario L2A 5X3

Want to try two free books from another series? Call 1-800-873-8635 or visit www.ReaderService.com.

HOME on the RANCH

YES! Please send me the **Home on the Ranch Collection** in Larger Print. This collection begins with 3 FREE books and 2 FREE gifts in the first shipment. Along with my 3 free books, I'll also get the next 4 books from the Home on the Ranch Collection, in LARGER PRINT, which I may either return and owe nothing, or keep for the low price of $5.24 U.S./ $5.89 CDN each plus $2.99 for shipping and handling per shipment*. If I decide to continue, about once a month for 8 months I will get 6 or 7 more books, but will only need to pay for 4. That means 2 or 3 books in every shipment will be FREE! If I decide to keep the entire collection, I'll have paid for only 32 books because 19 books are FREE! I understand that accepting the 3 free books and gifts places me under no obligation to buy anything. I can always return a shipment and cancel at any time. My free books and gifts are mine to keep no matter what I decide.

268 HCN 3760 468 HCN 3760

Name _____ (PLEASE PRINT)

Address _____ Apt. #

City _____ State/Prov. _____ Zip/Postal Code

Signature (if under 18, a parent or guardian must sign)

Mail to the **Reader Service:**

IN U.S.A.: P.O. Box 1341, Buffalo, New York 14240-8531
IN CANADA: P.O. Box 603, Fort Erie, Ontario L2A 5X3

* Terms and prices subject to change without notice. Prices do not include applicable taxes. Sales tax applicable in NY. Canadian residents will be charged applicable taxes. This offer is limited to one order per household. All orders subject to approval. Credit or debit balances in a customer's account(s) may be offset by any other outstanding balance owed by or to the customer. Please allow 3 to 4 weeks for delivery. Offer available while quantities last. Offer not available to Quebec residents.

Your Privacy—The Reader Service is committed to protecting your privacy. Our Privacy Policy is available online at www.ReaderService.com or upon request from the Reader Service.

We make a portion of our mailing list available to reputable third parties that offer products we believe may interest you. If you prefer that we not exchange your name with third parties, or if you wish to clarify or modify your communication preferences, please visit us at www.ReaderService.com/consumerschoice or write to us at Reader Service Preference Service, P.O. Box 9062, Buffalo, NY. 14240-9062. Include your complete name and address.

HRCBPA18R

Get 4 FREE REWARDS!

We'll send you 2 FREE Books plus 2 FREE Mystery Gifts.

FREE Value Over **$20**

Both the **Romance** and **Suspense** collections feature compelling novels written by many of today's best-selling authors.

YES! Please send me 2 FREE novels from the Essential Romance or Essential Suspense Collection and my 2 FREE gifts (gifts are worth about $10 retail). After receiving them, if I don't wish to receive any more books, I can return the shipping statement marked "cancel." If I don't cancel, I will receive 4 brand-new novels every month and be billed just $6.74 each in the U.S. or $7.24 each in Canada. That's a savings of at least 16% off the cover price. It's quite a bargain! Shipping and handling is just 50¢ per book in the U.S. and 75¢ per book in Canada*. I understand that accepting the 2 free books and gifts places me under no obligation to buy anything. I can always return a shipment and cancel at any time. The free books and gifts are mine to keep no matter what I decide.

Choose one: ☐ **Essential Romance**   ☐ **Essential Suspense**
                    (194/394 MDN GMY7)   (191/391 MDN GMY7)

Name (please print)

Address   Apt. #

City   State/Province   Zip/Postal Code

Mail to the **Reader Service**:
IN U.S.A.: P.O. Box 1341, Buffalo, NY 14240-8531
IN CANADA: P.O. Box 603, Fort Erie, Ontario L2A 5X3

Want to try two free books from another series? Call 1-800-873-8635 or visit www.ReaderService.com.

STRS18